THE MILLION DOLLAR
MYSTERY

THE PAPER SHE HAD PURLOINED WAS INDEED BLANK

THE MILLION DOLLAR MYSTERY

Novelized from the Scenario of
F. LONERGAN

BY

HAROLD MACGRATH

AUTHOR OF
THE MAN ON THE BOX,
THE GOOSE GIRL, HEARTS AND MASKS, ETC.

PROFUSELY ILLUSTRATED
WITH SCENES FROM THE PHOTO PLAY

GROSSET & DUNLAP
PUBLISHERS : NEW YORK

Published by arrangement with
The Bobbs-Merrill Company.

LIST OF ILLUSTRATIONS

v

LIST OF ILLUSTRATIONS

LIST OF ILLUSTRATIONS

LIST OF ILLUSTRATIONS

VIII

LIST OF ILLUSTRATIONS

THE MILLION DOLLAR
MYSTERY

The
Million Dollar Mystery

CHAPTER I

THERE are few things darker than a country road at night, particularly if one does not know the lay of the land. It is not difficult to traverse a known path; no matter how dark it is, one is able to find the way by the aid of a mental photograph taken in the daytime. But supposing you have never been over the road in the daytime, that you know nothing whatever of its topography, where it dips or rises, where it narrows or forks. You find yourself in the same unhappy state of mind as a blind man suddenly thrust into a strange house.

One black night, along a certain country road in the heart of New Jersey, in the days when the only good roads were city thoroughfares and country highways were routes to limbo, a carriage went forward cautiously. From time to time it careened like a blunt-nosed barge in a beam sea. The wheels and springs voiced their anguish continually; for it was a good carriage, unaccustomed to such ruts and hummocks.

"Faster, faster!" came a muffled voice from the interior.

1

"Sir, I dare not drive any faster," replied the coachman. "I can't see the horses' heads, sir, let alone the road. I've blown out the lamps, but I can't see the road any better for that."

"Let the horses have their heads; they'll find the way. It can't be much farther. You'll see lights."

The coachman swore in his teeth. All right. This man who was in such a hurry would probably send them all into the ditch. Save for the few stars above, he might have been driving Beelzebub's coach in the bottomless pit. Black velvet, everywhere black velvet. A wind was blowing, and yet the blackness was so thick that it gave the coachman the sensation of mild suffocation.

By and by, through the trees, he saw a flicker of light. It might or might not be the destination. He cracked his whip recklessly and the carriage lurched on two wheels. The man in the carriage balanced himself carefully, so that the bundle in his arms should not be unduly disturbed. His arms ached. He stuck his head out of the window.

"That's the place," he said. "And when you drive up make as little noise as you can."

"Yes, sir," called down the driver.

When the carriage drew up at its journey's end the man inside jumped out and hastened toward the gates. He scrutinized the sign on one of the posts. This was the place:

MISS FARLOW'S PRIVATE SCHOOL

The bundle in his arms stirred and he hurried up the path to the door of the house. He seized the ancient knocker and struck several times. He then placed the

MISS FARLOW'S PRIVATE SCHOOL

bundle on the steps and ran back to the waiting carriage, into which he stepped.

"Off with you!"

"That's a good word, sir. Maybe we can make your train."

"Do you think you could find this place again?"

"You couldn't get me on this pike again, sir, for a thousand; not me!"

The door slammed and the unknown sank back against the cushions. He took out his handkerchief and wiped the damp perspiration from his forehead. The big burden was off his mind. Whatever happened in the future, they would never be able to get him through his heart. So much for the folly of his youth.

It was a quarter after ten. Miss Susan Farlow had just returned to the reception room from her nightly tour of the upper halls to see if all her charges were in bed, where the rules of the school confined them after nine-thirty. It was at this moment that she heard the thunderous knocking at the door. The old maid felt her heart stop beating for a moment. Who could it be, at this time of night? Then the thought came swiftly that perhaps the parent of some one of her charges was ill and this was the summons. Stilling her fears, she went resolutely to the door and opened it.

"Who is it?" she called.

No one answered. She cupped her hand to her ear. She could hear the clatter of horses dimly.

"Well!" she exclaimed; rather angrily, too.

She was in the act of closing the door when the light from the hall discovered to her the bundle on the steps. She stooped and touched it.

"Good heavens, it's a child!"

She picked the bundle up. A whimper came from it, a tired little whimper of protest. She ran back to the reception room. A foundling! And on her doorstep! It was incredible. What in the world should she do? It would create a scandal and hurt the prestige of the school. Some one had mistaken her select private school for a farmhouse. It was frightful.

Then she unwrapped the child. It was about a year old, dimpled and golden haired. A thumb was in its rosebud mouth and its blue eyes looked up trustfully into her own.

"Why, you cherub!" cried the old maid, a strange turmoil in her heart. She caught the child to her breast, and then for the first time noticed the thick envelope pinned to the child's cloak. She put the baby into a chair and broke open the envelope.

"Name this child Florence Gray. I will send annually a liberal sum for her support and reclaim her on her eighteenth birthday. The other half of the inclosed bracelet will identify me. Treat the girl well, for I shall watch over her in secret."

Into the fixed routine of her humdrum life had come a mystery, a tantalizing, fascinating mystery. She had read of foundlings left on doorsteps—from paper-covered novels confiscated from her pupils—but that one should be placed upon her own respectable doorstep! Suddenly she smiled down at the child and the child smiled back. And there was nothing more to be done except to bow before the decrees of fate. Like all prim old maids, her heart was full of unrequited romance, and here was something she might spend its floods upon without let or hindrance. Already she was hoping that the man or woman who had left it might never come back.

The child grew. Regularly each year, upon a certain date, Miss Farlow received a registered letter with money. These letters came from all parts of the world; always the same sum, always the same line—"I am watching."

Thus seventeen years passed; and to Susan Farlow each year seemed shorter than the one before. For she loved the child with all her heart. She had not trained young girls all these years without becoming adept in the art of reading the true signs of breeding. There was no ordinary blood in Florence; the fact was emphasized by her exquisite face, her small hands and feet, her spirit and gentleness. And now, at any day, some one with a broken bracelet might come for her. As the days went on the heart of Susan Farlow grew heavy.

"Never mind, aunty," said Florence; "I shall always come back to see you."

She meant it, poor child; but how was she to know the terrors which lay beyond the horizon!

The house of Stanley Hargreave, in Riverdale, was the house of no ordinary rich man. Outside it was simple enough, but within you learned what kind of a man Hargreave was. There were rare Ispahans and Saruks on the floors and tapestries on the walls, and here and there a fine painting. The library itself represented a fortune. Money had been laid out lavishly but never wastefully. It was the home of a scholar, a dreamer, a wide traveler.

In the library stood the master of the house, idly fingering some papers which lay on the study table. He shrugged at some unpleasant thought, settled his overcoat about his shoulders, took up his hat, and walked from the

room, frowning slightly. The butler, who also acted in
the capacity of valet and was always within call when his
master was about, stepped swiftly to the hall door and
opened it.

"I may be out late, Jones," said Hargreave.

"Yes, sir."

Hargreave stared into his face keenly, as if trying to
pierce the grave face to learn what was going on behind it.

"How long have you been with me?"

"Fourteen years, sir."

"Some day I shall need you."

"My life has always been at your disposal, sir, since
that night you rescued me."

"Well, I haven't the least doubt that when I ask you
will give."

"Without question, sir. It was always so understood."

Hargreave's glance sought the mirror, then the smile-
less face of his man. He laughed, but the sound conveyed no sense of mirth; then he turned and went down
the steps slowly, like a man burdened with some thought
which was not altogether to his liking. He had sent an
order for his car, but had immediately countermanded it.
He would walk till he grew tired, hail a taxicab, and take
a run up and down Broadway. The wonderful illumina-
tion might prove diverting. For eighteen years nearly;
and now it was as natural for him to throw a glance over
his shoulder whenever he left the house as it was for
him to breathe. The average man would have grown
careless during all these years; but Hargreave was not
an average man; he was, rather, an extraordinary individual. It was his life in exchange for eternal vigilance,
and he knew and accepted the fact.

Half an hour later he got into a taxicab and directed

YOU MIGHT HAVE MARKED HIM FOR A SUCCESSFUL LAWYER

the man to drive down-town as far as Twenty-third Street and back to Columbus circle. The bewildering display of lights, however, in nowise served to lift the sense of oppression that had weighed upon him all day. South of Forty-second Street he dismissed the taxicab and stared undecidedly at the brilliant sign of a famous restaurant. He was neither hungry nor thirsty; but there would be· strange faces to study and music.

It was an odd whim. He had not entered a Broadway restaurant in all these years. He was unknown. He belonged to no clubs. Two months was the longest time he had ever remained in New York since the disposal of his old home in Madison Avenue and his resignation from his clubs. This once, then, he would break the law he had written down for himself. Boldly he entered the restaurant.

Some time before Hargreave surrendered to the restless spirit of rebellion, bitterly to repent for it later, there came into this restaurant a man and a woman. They were both evidently well known, for the head waiter was obsequious and hurried them over to the best table he had left and took the order himself.

The man possessed a keen, intelligent face. You might have marked him for a successful lawyer, for there was an earnestness about his expression which precluded a life of idleness. His age might have been anywhere between forty and fifty. The shoulders were broad and the hands which lay clasped upon the table were slim but muscular. Indeed, everything about him suggested hidden strength and vitality. His companion was small, handsome, and animated. Her frequent gestures and mutable eyebrows betrayed her foreign birth. Her age was a matter of importance to no one but herself.

They were at coffee when she said: "There's a young man coming toward us. He is looking at you."

The man turned. Instantly his face lighted up with a friendly smile of recognition.

"Who is it?" she asked.

"A chap worth knowing; a reporter just a little out of the ordinary. I'm going to introduce him. You' never can tell. We might need him some day. Ah, Norton, how are you?"

"Good evening, Mr. Braine." The reporter, catching sight of a pair of dazzling eyes, hesitated.

"The Countess Perigoff, Norton. You're in no hurry, are you?"

"Not now," smiled the reporter.

"Ah!" said the countess, interested. It was the old compliment, said in an unusual way. It pleased her.

The reporter sank into a chair. When inactive he was rather a dreamy-eyed sort of chap. He possessed that rare accomplishment of talking upon one subject and thinking upon another at the same time. So while he talked gaily with the young woman on varied themes, his thoughts were busy speculating upon her companion. He was quite certain that the name Braine was assumed, but he was also equally certain that the man carried an extraordinary brain under his thatch of salt and pepper hair. The man had written three or four brilliant monographs on poisons and the uses of radium, and it was through and by these that the reporter had managed to pick up his acquaintance. He lived well, but inconspicuously.

Suddenly the pupils of Braine's eyes narrowed; the eye became cold. Over the smoke of his cigarette he was looking into the wall mirror. A man had passed behind

THE PRINCESS PERIGOFF

him and sat down at the next table. Still gazing into the mirror, Braine saw Norton wave his hand; saw also the open wonder on the reporter's pleasant face.

"Who is your friend, Norton?" Braine asked indifferently, his head still unturned.

"Stanley Hargreave. Met him in Hongkong when I was sent over to handle a part of the revolution. War correspondence stuff. First time I ever ran across him on Broadway at night. We've since had some powwows over some rare books. Queer old cock; brave as a lion, but as quiet as a mouse."

"Bookish, eh? My kind. Bring him over." Underneath the table Braine maneuvered to touch the foot of the countess.

"I don't know," said the reporter dubiously. "He might say no, and that would embarrass the whole lot of us. He's a bit of a hermit. I'm surprised to see him here."

"Try," urged the countess. "I like to meet men who are hermits."

"I haven't the least doubt about that," the reporter laughed. "I'll try; but don't blame me if I'm rebuffed."

He left the table with evident reluctance and approached Hargreave. The two shook hands cordially, for the elder man was rather fond of this medley of information known as Jim Norton.

"Sit down, boy; sit down. You're just the kind of a man I've been wanting to talk to to-night."

"Wouldn't you rather talk to a pretty woman?"

"I'm an old man."

"Bah! That's a hypocritical bluff, and you know it. My friends at the next table have asked me to bring you over."

"I do not usually care to meet strangers."

"Make an exception this once," said the reporter, who had seen Braine's eyes change and was curious to know why the appearance of Hargreave in the mirror had brought about that metally gleam. Here were two unique men; he desired to see them face to face.

"This once. My fault; I ought not to be here; I feel out of place. What a life, though, you reporters lead! To meet kings and presidents and great financiers, socialists and anarchists, the whole scale of life, and to slap these people on the back as if they were every-day friends!"

"Now you're making fun of me. For one king there are always twenty thick brogans ready to kick me down the steps; don't forget that."

Hargreave laughed. "Come, then; let us get it over with."

The introductions were made. Norton felt rather chagrined. As far as he could see, the two men were total strangers. Well, it was all in the game. Nine out of ten opportunities for the big story were fake alarms; but he was always willing to risk the labor these nine entailed for the sake of the tenth.

At length Braine glanced at his watch, and the countess nodded. Adieux were said. Inside the taxicab Braine leaned back with a deep, audible sigh.

"What is it?" she asked.

"The luck of the devil's own," he said. "Child of the Steppes, for years I've flown about seas and continents, through valleys and over mountains—for what? For the sight of the face of that man we have just left. At first glance I wasn't sure; but the sound of his voice was enough. Olga, the next time you see that reporter, throw your arms around his neck and kiss him. What did I tell you? Without Norton's help I would not have been sure. I'm going to leave you at your apartment."

"The man of the Black Hundred?" she whispered.

"The man who deserted and defied the Black Hundred, who broke his vows, and never paid a kopeck for the privilege; the man who had been appointed for the supreme work and who ran away. In those days we needed men of his stamp, and to accomplish this end. . . ."

"There was a woman," she interrupted, with a touch of bitterness.

"Always the woman. And she was as clever and handsome as you are."

"Thanks. Sometimes . . ."

"Ah, yes!" ironically. "Sometimes you wish you could settle down, marry and have a family! Your domesticity would last about a month."

She made no retort because she recognized the truth of this statement.

"There's an emerald I know of," he said ruminatively. "It's quite possible that you may be wearing it within a few days."

"I am mad over them. There is something in the green stone that fascinates me. I can't resist it."

"That's because, somewhere in the far past, your ancestors were orientals. Here we are. I'll see you to-morrow. I must hurry. Good night."

She stood on the curb for a moment and watched the taxicab as it whirled around a corner. The man held her with a fascination more terrible than any jewel. She knew him to be a great and daring rogue, cunning, patient, fearless. Packed away in that mind of his there were a thousand accomplished deeds which had roused futilely the police of two continents. Braine! She could have laughed. The very name he had chosen was an insolence directed at society.

The subject of her thoughts soon arrived at his destination. A flight of stairs carried him into a dimly lighted hall, smelling evilly of escaping gas. He donned a black mask and struck the door with a series of light blows; two, then one, then three, and again one. The door opened and he slipped inside. Round a table sat several men, also masked. They were all tried and trusted rogues; but not one of them knew what Braine looked like. He alone remained unknown save to the man designated as the chief, who was only Braine's lieutenant. The mask was the insignia of the Black Hundred, an organization with all the ramifications of the Camorra without their abiding stupidity. From the assassination of a king, down to the robbery of a country post-office, nothing was too great or too small for their nets. Their god dwells in the hearts of all men and is called greed.

The ordinary business over, the chief dismissed the men, and he and Braine alone remained.

"Vroon, I have found him," said Braine.

"There are but few: which one?"

"Eighteen years ago, in St. Petersburg."

"I remember. The millionaire's son. Did he recognize you?"

"I don't know. Probably he did. But he always had good nerves. He is being followed at this moment. We shall strike quick; for if he recognized me he will act quick. He is cool and brave. You remember how he braved us that night in Russia. Jumped boldly through

THE BLACK HUNDRED

the window at the risk of breaking his neck. He landed safely; that is the only reason he eluded us. Millions—and they slipped through our fingers. If I could only find some route to his heart! The lure we held out to him is dead."

"Or in the fortress, which is the same thing. What are your plans?"

"I have in mind something like this."

And Hargreave was working out his plans, too; and he was just as much of a general as Braine. He sat at his library table, the maxillary muscles of his jaws working. So they had found him? Well, he had broken the law of his own making and he must suffer the consequences. Braine, who was Menshikoff in Russia, Schwartz in Germany, Mendoza in Spain, Cartucci in Italy, and Du Bois in France; so the rogue had found him out? Poor fool that he had been! High spirited, full of those youthful dreams of doing good in the world, he had joined what he had believed a great secret socialistic movement, to learn that he had been trapped by a band of brilliant thieves. Kidnapers and assassins for hire; the Black Hundred; fiends from Tophet! For nearly eighteen years he had eluded them, for he knew that directly or indirectly they would never cease to hunt for him; and an idle whim had toppled him into their clutches.

He wrote several letters feverishly. The last was addressed to Miss Susan Farlow and read: "Dear Madam: Send Florence Gray to New York, to arrive here Friday morning. My half of the bracelet will be identification. Inclosed find cash to square accounts." He would get together all his available funds, recover his child, and fly to the ends of the world. He would tire them out.

They would find that the peaceful dog was a bad animal to rouse. He rang for the faithful Jones.

"Jones, they have found me," he said simply.

"You will need me, then?"

"Quite possible. Please mail these and then we'll talk it over. No doubt some one is watching outside. Be careful."

"Very good, sir."

Hargreave bowed his head in his hands. Many times he had journeyed to the school and hung about the gates, straining his eyes toward the merry groups of young girls. Which among them was his, heart of his heart, blood of his blood? That she might never be drawn into this abominable tangle, he had resolutely torn her out of his life completely. The happiness of watching the child grow into girlhood he had denied himself. She at least would be safe. Only when she was safe in a far country would he dare tell her. He tried in vain to conjure up a picture of her; he always saw the mother whom he had loved and hated with all the ardor of his youth.

Many things happened the next day. There was a visit to the hangar of one William Orts, the aviator, famous for his daredevil exploits. There were two visitors, in fact, and the second visitor was knocked down for his pains. He had tried to bribe Orts.

There were several excited bankers, who protested against such large withdrawals without the usual formal announcement. But a check was a check, and they had to pay.

Hargreave covered a good deal of ground, but during all this time his right hand never left the automatic in his overcoat pocket, except at those moments when he

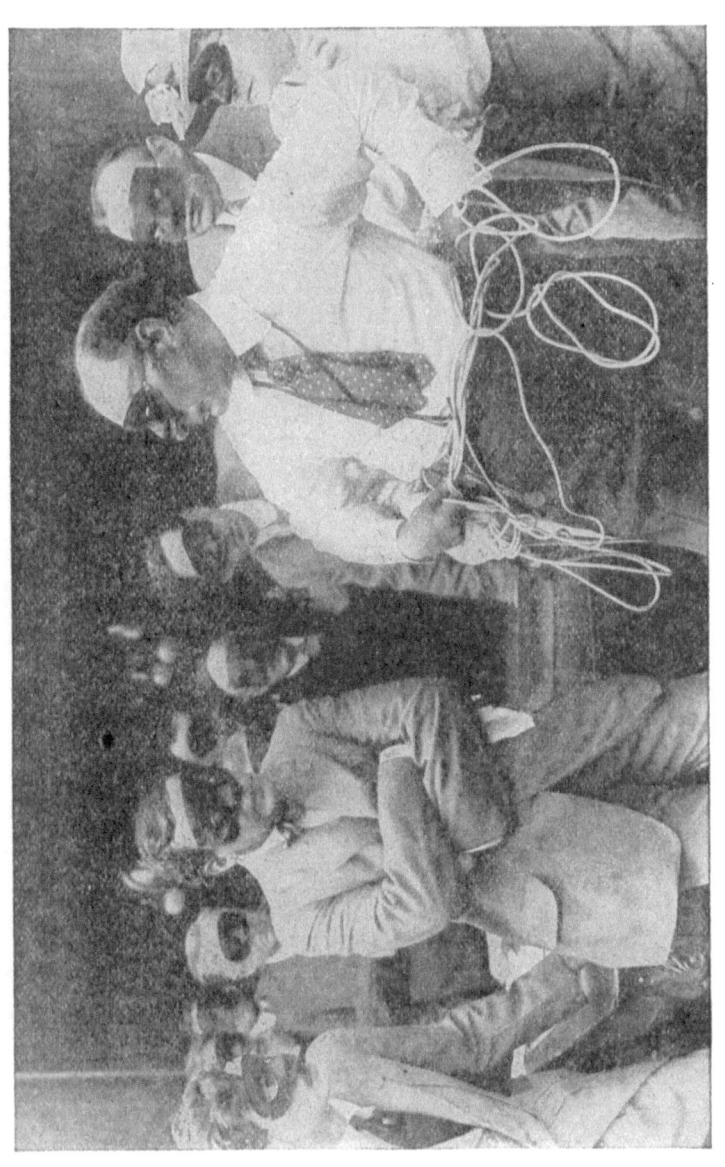

FIENDS FROM TOPHET

was obliged to sign his checks.   He would shoot and make inquiries afterward.

Far away a young girl and her companion got on the train which was to carry her to New York, the great dream city she was always longing to see.

And the spider wove his web.

Hargreave reached home at night.   He put the money in the safe and was telephoning when Jones entered and handed his master an unstamped note.

"Where did you get this?"

"At the door, sir.   I judge that the house is surrounded."

Hargreave read the note.   It stated briefly that all his movements during the day had been noted.   It was known that he had collected a million in paper money. If he surrendered this he would be allowed twenty-four hours before the real chase began.   Otherwise he should die before midnight.   Hargreave crushed the note in his hand.   They might kill him; there was a chance of their accomplishing that; but never should they touch his daughter's fortune.

"Jones, you go to the rear door and I'll take a look out of the front.   We have an hour.   I know the breed. They'll wait till midnight and then force their way in."

Hargreave saw a dozen shadows in the front yard.

"Men all about the back yard," whispered Jones down the hall.

The master eyed the man.

"Very well, sir," replied the latter, with understanding.   "I am ready."

The master went to the safe, emptied it of its contents, crossed the hall to the bedroom, and closed the door softly behind him, Jones having entered the same room through another door to befool any possible watcher. After a long while, perhaps an hour, the two men emerged from the room from the same doors they had entered. So whispered the watcher to his friends below.

"Hargreave is going up-stairs."

"Let him go. Let him take a look at us from the upper windows. He will understand that nothing but wings will save him."

Silence. By and by a watcher reported that he heard the scuttle of the roof rattle.

"Look!" another cried, startled.

A bluish glare came from the roof.

"He's shooting off a Roman candle!"

They never saw the man-made bird till it alighted upon the roof. They never thought of shooting at it until it had taken wing! Then they rushed the doors of the house. They made short work of Jones, whom they tied up like a Christmas fowl and plumped roughly into a chair. They broke open the safe, to find it empty. And while the rogues were rummaging about the room, venting their spite upon many a treasure they could neither appreciate nor understand, a man from the outside burst in.

"The old man is dead and the money is at the bottom of the ocean! We punctured her. She's gone!"

A thin, inscrutable smile stirred the lips of the man bound in the chair,

CHAPTER II

V ROON faced Hargreave's butler somberly. The one reason why Braine made this man his lieutenant was because Vroon always followed the letter of his instructions to the final period; he never sidestepped or added any frills or innovations of his own, and because of this very automatism he rarely blundered into a trap. If he failed it was for the simple fact that the master mind had overlooked some essential detail. The organization of the Black Hundred was almost totally unknown to either the public or the police. It is only when you fail that you are found out.

"The patrolman has been trussed up like you," began Vroon. "If they find him they will probably find you. But before that you will grow thirsty and hungry. Where did your master put that money?"

"He carried it with him."

"Why didn't you call for help?"

"The houses on either side are too far away. I might yell till doomsday without being heard. They will have heard the pistol shots; but Mr. Hargreave was always practising in the back yard."

"The people in those two houses have been called out of town. The servants are off for the night."

"Very interesting," replied Jones, staring at the rug.

"Your master is dead."

Jones' chin sank upon his breast. His heart was heavy, heavier than it had ever been before.

"Your master left a will?"

"Indeed, I could not say."

"We can say. He has still three or four millions in stocks and bonds. What he took to the bottom of the sea with him was his available cash."

"I know nothing about his finances. I was his butler and valet."

Vroon nodded. "Come, men; it is time we took ourselves off. Put things in order; close the safe. You poor jackals, I always have to watch you for outbreaks of vandalism. Off with you!"

He was the last to leave. He stared long and searchingly at Jones, who felt the burning gaze but refused to meet it lest the plotter see the fire in his. The door closed. For fully an hour Jones listened but did not stir. They were really gone. He pressed his feet to the floor and began to hitch the chair toward the table. Halfway across the intervening space he crumpled in the chair, almost completely exhausted. He let a quarter of an hour pass, then made the final attack upon the remaining distance. He succeeded in reaching the desk, but he could not have stirred an inch farther. The hair on his head was damp with sweat and his hands were clammy.

When he felt strength returning he lifted the telephone off the hook with his teeth.

"Central, central! Call the police to come to this number at once; Hargreave's house, Riverdale. Tell them to break in."

After what seemed an age of waiting to the exhausted

prisoner, with crashing and smashing of doors, the police appeared in the room.

"Where's your gag?" demanded the first officer to reach Jones' side.

"There wasn't any."

"Then why didn't you yell for help?"

"The thieves lured our neighbors away from town. The patrolman who walks this beat is bound and gagged and is probably reposing back of the billboard in the next block."

"Murphy, you watch this man while I make a call on the neighbors," said the officer who seemed to be in authority. When he returned he was frowning seriously. "We'd better telephone to the precinct to search for Dennison. There's nobody at home in either house and there's nobody back of the billboards. Untie the man." When this was done, the officer said: "Now, tell us what's happened; and don't forget any of the details."

Jones told a simple and convincing story; it was so simple and convincing that the police believed it without question.

"Well, if that ain't the limit! Did you hear any autos outside?"

"I don't recollect," said Jones, stretching his legs gratefully. "Why?"

"The auto bandits held up a bank messenger to-day and got away with twenty thousand. Whenever a man draws down a big sum they seem to know about it. And say, Murphy, call up and have the river police look out for a new-fangled airship. Your master may have been rescued," turning to Jones.

"If I were only sure of that, sir!"

When the police took themselves off Jones proceeded

to act upon those plans laid down by Hargreave early that night. When this was done he sought his bed and fell asleep, the sleep of the exhausted. When Hargreave picked up Jones to share his fortunes, he had put his trust in no ordinary man.

A dozen reporters trooped out to the Hargreave home, only to find it deserted. And while they were ringing bells and tapping windows, the man they sought was tramping up and down the platform of the railway station.

Through all this time Norton, the reporter, Hargreave's only friend, slept the sleep of the just and unjust. He rarely opened his eyes before noon.

Group after group of passengers Jones eyed eagerly. Often, just as he was in the act of approaching a couple of young women, some man would hurry up, and there would be kisses or handshakes. At length the crowd thinned, and then it was that he discovered a young girl perhaps eighteen, accompanied by a young woman in the early thirties. They had the appearance of eagerly awaiting some one. Jones stepped forward with a good deal of diffidence.

"You are waiting for some one?"

"Yes," said the elder woman, coldly.

"A broken bracelet?"

The distrust on both faces vanished instantly. The young girl's face brightened, her eyes sparkled with suppressed excitement.

"You are . . . my father?"

"No, miss," very gravely. "I am the butler."

"Let me see your part of the bracelet," said the young girl's guardian, a teacher who had been assigned to this delicate task by Miss Farlow, who could not bring herself to say good-by to Florence anywhere except at the school gates.

The halves were produced and examined.

"I believe we may trust him, Florence."

"Let us hurry to the taxicab. We must not stand here."

"My mother?"

"She is dead. I believe she died shortly after your birth. I have been with your father but fourteen years. I know but little of his life prior to that."

"Why did he leave me all these years without ever coming to see me? Why?"

"It is not for me, Miss Florence, to inquire into your father's act. But I do know that whatever he did was meant for the best. Your welfare was everything to him."

"It is all very strange," said the girl, bewilderedly. "Why didn't he come to meet me instead of you?"

Jones stared at his hands, miserably.

"Why?" she demanded. "I have thought of him, thought of him. He has hurt me with all this neglect. I expected to see him at the station, to throw my arms around his neck and . . . forgive him!" Tears swam in her eyes as she spoke.

"Everything will be explained to you when we reach the house. But always remember this, Miss Florence: You were everything in this wide world to your father. You will never know the misery and loneliness he suffered that you might not have one hour of unrest. What are your plans?" he asked abruptly of the teacher from Miss Farlow's.

"That depends," she answered, laying her hand protectingly over the girl's.

"You could leave Miss Farlow's on the moment?"

"Yes."

"Then you will stay and be Miss Florence's companion?"

"Gladly."

"What is my father's name?"

"Hargreave, Stanley Hargreave."

The girl's eyes widened in terror. Suddenly she burst into a wild frenzy of sobbing, her head against the shoulder of her erstwhile teacher.

Jones appeared visibly shocked. "What is it?"

"We read the story in the newspaper," said the elder woman, her own eyes filling with tears. "The poor child! To have all her castles-in-air tumble down like this! But what authority have you to engage me?" sensibly.

Jones produced a document, duly signed by Hargreave, and witnessed and sealed by a notary, in which it was set forth that Henry Jones, butler and valet to Stanley Hargreave, had full powers of attorney in the event of his (Hargreave's) disappearance; in the event of his death, till Florence became of legal age.

Said Jones as he put the document back in his pocket: "What is your name?"

"Susan Wane."

"Do you love this child?"

"With all my heart, the poor unhappy babe!"

"Thank you!"

Inside the home he conducted them through the various rooms, at the same time telling them what had taken place during the preceding night.

"They have not found his body?" asked Florence. "My poor, poor father!"

"No."

"Then he may be alive!"

"Please God that he may!" said the butler, with genuine piety, for he had loved the man who had gone forth into the night so bravely and so strangely. "This is your room. Your father spent many happy hours here preparing it for you."

Tears came into the girl's eyes again, and discreetly Jones left the two alone.

"What shall I do, Susan? Whatever shall I do?"

"Be brave as you always are. I will never leave you till you find your father."

Florence kissed her fervently. "What is your opinion of the butler?"

"I think we may both trust him absolutely."

Then Florence began exploring the house. Susan followed her closely. Florence peered behind the mirrors, the pictures, in the drawers of the desk, in the bookcases.

"What are you hunting for, child?"

"A photograph of father." But she found none. More, there were no photographs of any kind to be found in Stanley Hargreave's home.

When Norton awoke, he naturally went to the door for the morning papers which were always placed in a neat pile ·before the sill. He yawned, gathered up the bundle, was about to climb back into bed, when a head·line caught his dull eyes. Twenty-one minutes later, to be precise, he ran up the steps of the Hargreave home and rang the bell. He was admitted by the taciturn Jones, to whom the reporter had never paid any particular attention. Somehow Jones always managed to stand in shadows.

"I can add nothing to what has already appeared in the newspapers," replied Jones, as Norton opened his batteries of inquiries.

"Mr. Jones, I have known your master several years, as you will recollect. There never was a woman in this house, not even among the servants. There are two in the other room. Who are they? And what are they doing here?"

Jones shook his head.

"Well, I can easily find out."

Jones barred his path, and for the first time Norton gazed into the eyes of the man servant. They were as hard as gun metal.

"My dear Mr. Jones, you ought to know that sooner or later we reporters find out what we seek."

Jones appeared to reflect. "Mr. Norton, you claim to be a friend of Mr. Hargreave?"

"I do not claim. I am. More than that I do not believe he is dead. He was deep. He had some relentless enemies—I don't know where from or what kind—and he is pretending he's dead till this blows over and is forgotten."

"You are not going to say that in your newspaper?" Jones was visibly agitated.

"Not if I can prove it."

"If I tell you who those young ladies are, will you give me your word of honor not to write about them till I give my permission?"

Norton, having in mind the big story at the end of the mystery tangle, agreed.

"The elder is a teacher from a private school; the other is Stanley Hargreave's daughter."

"Good lord!" gasped the astonished reporter. "He

never mentioned the fact to me, and we've been together in some tight places."

"He never mentioned it to any one but me." Jones again seemed to reflect. At last he raised his glance to the reporter. "Are you willing to wait for a great story, the real story?"

"If there is one," answered Norton with his usual caution.

"On my word of honor, you shall have such a story as you never dreamed of, if you will promise not to divulge it till the appointed time."

"I agree."

"The peace and happiness of that child depends upon how you keep your word."

That was sufficient for Norton. "Your master knew me. He also knew that I am not a man who promises lightly. Now introduce me to the daughter."

With plain reluctance Jones went about the affair. Norton put a dozen perfunctory questions to the girl. What he was in search of was not news but the sound of her voice. In that quarter of an hour he felt his heart disturbed as it had never before been disturbed.

"Now, Mr. Norton," said Jones gloomily, "will you be so kind as to follow me?"

Norton was led to Jones' bedroom. The butler-valet closed the door and drew the window shade. Always seeking shadows. This did not impress the reporter at the time; he had no other thought but the story. Jones then sat down beside the reporter and talked in an undertone. When he had done he took Norton by the elbow and gently but forcibly led him down to the front door and ushered him forth. Norton jumped into his taxicab and returned to his rooms, which were at the top of the huge apartment hotel. He immediately called up his managing editor.

"Hello! This is Norton. Put Griffin on the Hargreave yarn. I'm off on another deal."

"But Hargreave was a friend of yours," protested the managing editor.

"I know it. But you know me well enough, Mr. Blair. I should not ask the transfer if it was not vitally important."

"Oh, very well."

"We shan't be scooped."

"If you can promise that, I don't care who works on the job. Will you be in the office to-night?"

"If nothing prevents me."

"Well, good-by."

Norton filled his pipe, drew his chair to the window, and stared at the great liner going down to sea.

"Lord, lord!" he murmured. Then he smiled and chuckled. Some bright morning he would have all New York by the ears, the police running round in circles, and the chiefs of the rival sheets tearing their hair. What a story! Four columns on the first page, and two whole pages Sunday. . . . And all of a sudden he ceased to smile and chuckle.

In the living room of the Countess Olga Perigoff's apartment the mistress lay reading on the divan. There was no cigarette between her well shaped lips, for she was not the accepted type of adventuress. In fact, she was not an adventuress; she was really the Countess Perigoff. Her maiden name had been Olga Pushkin; but more of that later.

When Braine came in he found her dreaming with half-closed eyes. He flourished an evening newspaper.

"Olga, even the best of us make mistakes. Here, just glance over this."

The Russian accepted the newspaper and read the heading indicated: "Aeronaut picked up far out at sea. Slips ashore from tramp steamer. Had five thousand in cash in his pockets."

"Hargreave escaped!"

"Not necessarily," she replied. "If it was Hargreave he would have had more than five thousand in his pockets. My friend, I believe it an attempt to fool you; or it is another man entirely." She clicked her teeth with the tops of her polished nails.

"There are two young women in the house. What the deuce can that mean?"

"Two young women? Oh! then everything's as simple as daylight. Katrina Pushkin, my cousin, had a child."

"Child? Hargreave had a child? What do you mean by keeping this fact from me?" he stormed.

"It was useless till this moment. He probably sent for her yesterday; but in his effort to escape had to turn her over to his butler. We shall soon learn whether Hargreave is dead or alive. We can use the child to bring him back."

The anger went out of his eyes. "You're a wonder, Olga."

"But you should have gone with Vroon last night. He does everything just as you tell him. When they reported that Hargreave had visited Ort's hangar you ought to have prepared against such a coup as flight through the air."

"I admit it. But a daughter! Well, I can bring him back," with a sinister laugh. "By the Lord Harry, I have him in my hands this time, that is, if this girl turns out to be his daughter. A million? Two, three, all he has in the world. I want you to pay a visit right away. Watch the butler, Jones. He'll lie, of course; but note how he treats the girl; and if you get the chance look around the walls for a secret panel. He might not have carried away the cash at all, only enough for his immediate needs, which would account for that five thousand on the man picked up at sea. If I could only get inside that house for an hour!"

"I believe I'll call at once. Leo, was Hargreave the man's real name?"

Braine laughed. "That is of no vital consequence. He will be Hargreave till the end of the chapter, dead or alive. You can tell me the news at dinner to-night."

So, later, when the butler accepted her card at the door, loath as he might be, there was nothing for him to do but admit her.

"Whom do you wish to see, madam?" stepping back into the shadow.

"Miss Hargreave. I'm an old friend of her mother's."

"There is no such person here."

"To whom, then, does this hat belong?" she asked quietly. She waved her hand indolently toward the hall rack.

Jones' lips tightened. "That belongs to Miss Gray, a kind of protégée of Mr. Hargreave's."

"Indeed! You have no objections to my seeing her? My maiden name was Olga Pushkin, cousin to Katrina, wife of Stanley Hargreave. I am, if you will weigh the matter carefully, a kind of aunt."

To Jones it was as if ice had suddenly come into contact with his heart's blood. But as he still stood in the shadow, she did not observe the pallor of his face.

"If you will state exactly why you wish to see her, madam."

"You seem to possess authority?"

"Yes, madam, absolute authority."

Jones produced his document and presented it to her.

"There is no flaw in that," she agreed readily. "I wish to see the child. I have told you why."

"Very well, madam." Why had they not telegraphed the child, even on the train, to return to Farlow's. He knew nothing of this woman, whether she was an enemy or a friend. He conducted his unwelcome guest into the library.

"How did you know that she was here?" suddenly.

But she was ready. "I did not. But the death of Mr. Hargreave brought me. And that youthful hat in the hall was a story all its own. Later I shall show you some papers of my own. You will have no cause to doubt them. They have not the legal power of yours, but they would find standing in any court."

Jones turned and went in search of Florence.

The countess lost no time in beginning her investigations, but she wasted her time. There was no secret panel in evidence.

"Who is she?" asked Florence as she looked at the card. "Did my father know countesses?"

"Yes," said Jones briefly. "Be very careful what you say to her. Admit nothing. She claims to be a cousin of your mother. Perhaps."

"My mother?" Without waiting for any further advice from Jones, whom Florence in her young years thought presuming upon his authority, she ran downstairs to the library. Her mother, to learn some facts about the mother of whom she knew nothing!

"You knew my mother?" she cried without ceremony.

Jones heard the countess say: "I did, my child; and heaven is witness that you are the exact picture of her at your age. And I knew your father."

Jones straightened, his hands shut tightly.

"Tell me about my father!"

The countess smiled. It was Katrina Pushkin come to life, the same impulsiveness. "I knew him but slightly. I was a mere child myself when he used to pinch my cheeks. I met him again the other night, but he did not recognize me; and I could not find it in my heart to awaken his memory in a public restaurant."

Presently Jones came in to announce that two detectives requested to see Florence. The two men entered, informing her that they had been instructed to investigate the disappearance of Stanley Hargreave.

"Who are you, miss?"

"I am his daughter."

"Ah!"

One of the detectives questioned Florence minutely, while the other wandered about the rooms, feeling the walls, using the magnifying glass, turning back the rugs. Even the girl's pretty room did not escape his scrutiny. By and by he returned to the library and beckoned to his companion. The two conferred for a moment. One chanced to look into the mirror. He saw the bright eyes of the countess gazing intelligently into his.

"I'm afraid we'll have to ask you to accompany us to the station, miss."

"Why?"

"Some technicalities. We must have some proof of your right to be in this house. So far as we have learned,

THE PEACEFUL BUTLER ENTERED INTO THE FIELD OF ACTION

Hargreave was unmarried. It will take but a few minutes."

"And I will accompany you," said the countess. "We'll
be back within half an hour. I'll tell them what I know."

Jones, in the hall, caught sight of the reporter coming
up the steps. Here was some one he could depend upon.

"Why, Mr. Norton!"

The reporter eyed the countess in amazement.

"You look surprised. Naturally. I am a cousin of
Miss Florence's mother. You might say that I am her
aunt. It's a small world, isn't it?" But if wishing could
poison, the reporter would have died that moment.

"Who are you and what are you doing here?" one of
the detectives demanded.

"I am going to ask that very question of you," said
Norton urbanely.

"We are from headquarters," replied one, showing his
badge.

"What headquarters? What are they asking you to
do?" he said to Florence.

"They say I must go to the police station with them."

"Not the least in the world," laughed the reporter.
"You two clear out of here as fast as your rascally legs
can carry you. I don't know what your game is, but I
do know every reputable detective in New York, and you
don't belong."

"Good heavens!" exclaimed the countess; "do you
mean to say that these men are not real detectives?"

"This girl goes to the police station, young man. So
much the worse for you if you meddle. Take yourself
off!"

"All in good time."

"Here, Jenner, you take charge of the girl. I'll handle this guy. He shall go to the station, too."

What followed would always be vividly remembered by Florence, fresh from the peace and happiness of her school life. Norton knocked his opponent down. He rose and for a moment the room seemed full of legs and arms and panting men. A foot tripped up Norton and he went down under the bogus detective. He never suspected that the tripping foot was not accidental. He was too busy.

The other man dragged Florence toward the hall, but there the peaceful butler entered into the field of action with a very unattractive automatic. The detective threw up his hands.

The struggle went on in the library. A trick of jiujutsu brought about the downfall of Norton's man, and Norton ran out into the hall to aid Jones. He searched the detective's pockets and secured the revolver. The result of all this was that the two bogus detectives soon found themselves in charge of two policemen, and they were marched off to the station.

"Your advent was most providential, Mr. Norton," said Jones in his usual colorless tones.

"I rather believe so. Why don't you pack up and clear out for a while?"

"I am stronger in this house than elsewhere," answered the butler enigmatically.

"Well, you know best," said the reporter.

The countess was breathing rapidly. No, on second thought she had no wish to throw her arms about the reporter's neck and kiss him.

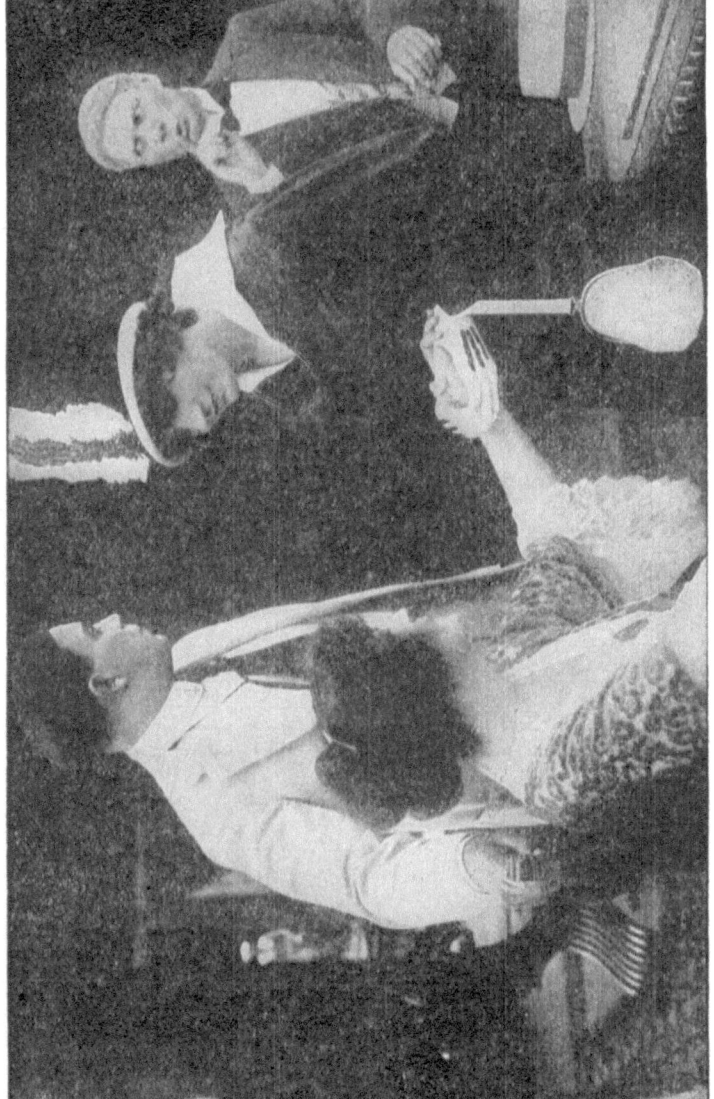

SHE HAD GAINED THE CONFIDENCE OF FLORENCE

CHAPTER III

THE countess did not remain long after the departure of the police with the bogus detectives. It had been a very difficult corner to wriggle out of, all because Braine had added to his plans after she had left the apartment. But for the advent of the meddling reporter the coup would have succeeded, herself apparently perfectly innocent of complicity. That must be the keynote of all her plans: to appear quite innocent and leave no trail behind her. She had gained the confidence of Florence and her companion. And she was rather certain that she had impressed this lazy-eyed reporter and the stolid butler. She had told nothing but the truth regarding her relationship. They would find that out. She was Katrina Pushkin's cousin. But blood with her counted as naught. She had room in her heart but for two things, Braine and money to spend on her caprices.

"How long has your highness known Mr. Braine?" asked the reporter idly, as he smoothed away all signs of his recent conflict.

"Oh, the better part of a year. Mr. Hargreave did not recognize me the other night. That was quite excusable, for when he last saw me I was not more than twelve. My child," she said to Florence, "build no hopes regarding your mother. She is doubtless dead. Upon some

33

trivial matter—I do not know what it was—she was confined to the fortress. That was seventeen years ago.
When you enter the fortress at St. Petersburg, you
cease to be."

"That is true enough."

"I did not recall myself to your father. I did not care
at that moment to shock him with the remembrance of
the past. Is not Mr. Braine a remarkable man?" All
this in her charming broken English.

"He is, indeed," affirmed Norton. "He's a superb
linguist, knows everybody and has traveled everywhere.
No matter what subject you bring up he seems well informed."

"Come often," urged Florence.

"I shall, my child. And any time you need me, call
for me. After all, I am nearly your aunt. You will find
life in the city far different from that which you have
been accustomed to."

She limped down to her limousine. In tripping up
Norton he had stepped upon her foot heavily.

"She is lovely!" cried Florence.

"Well, I must be on my way, also," said Norton. "I
am a worldly-wise man, Miss Florence. So is Jones here.
Never go any place without letting him know; not even
to the corner drug store. I am going to find your father.
Some one was rescued. I'm going to find out whether
it was the aviator or Mr. Hargreave."

Jones drew in a deep breath and his eyes closed for a
moment. At the door he spoke to the reporter.

"What do you think of that woman?"

"I believe that she told the truth. She is charming."

"She is. But for all her charm and truth I can not
help distrusting her. I have an idea. I shall call up your

THERE WAS A STORMY SCENE BETWEEN BRAINE AND THE PRINCESS

office at the end of each day. If a day comes without a
call, you will know that something is wrong."

"A very good idea." Norton shook hands with every
one and departed.

"What a brave, pleasant young man!" murmured
Susan.

"I like him, too; and I'd like him for a friend," said
the guileless girl.

"It is very good to have a friend like Mr. Norton,"
added Jones; and passed out into the kitchen. All the
help had been discharged and upon his shoulders lay the
burden of the cooking till such time when he could re-
instate the cook.

There was a stormy scene between Braine and the
countess that night.

"Are you in your dotage?" she asked vehemently.

"There, there; bring your voice down a bit. Where's
the girl?"

"In her home. Where did you suppose she would be,
after that botchwork of letting me go to do one thing
while you had in mind another? And an ordinary pair
of cutthroats, at that!"

"The thought came to me after you left. I knew you'd
recognize the men and understand. I see no reason why
it didn't work."

"It would have been all right if you had consulted a .
clairvoyant."

"What the deuce do you mean by that?" Braine demanded roughly.

"I mean that then you would have learned your friend
the reporter was to arrive upon the scene at its most
vital moment."

"What, Norton?"

"Yes. The trouble is with you, you have been so successful all these years that you have grown overconfident. I tell you that there is a desperately shrewd man somewhere back of all this. Mark me, I do not believe Hargreave is dead. He is in hiding. It may be near by. He may have dropped from the balloon before it left land. The man they picked up may be Orts, the aeronaut. The five thousand might have been his fee for rescuing Hargreave. Here is the greatest thing we've ever been up against; and you start in with every-day methods!"

"Little woman, don't let your tongue run away with you too far."

"I'm not the least bit afraid of you, Leo. You need me, and it has never been more apparent than at this moment."

"All right. I fell by the wayside this trip. Truthfully, I realized it five minutes after the men were gone. The only clever thing I did was to keep the mask on my face. They can't come back at me. But the thing looked so easy; and it would have worked but for Norton's appearance."

"You all but compromised me. That butler worries me a little." Her expression lost its anger and grew thoughtful. "He's always about, somewhere. Do you think Hargreave took him into his confidence?"

"Can't tell. He's been watched straight for forty hours. He hasn't mailed a letter or telephoned to any place but the grocery. There have been no telegrams. Some one in that house knows where the money is, and it's ten to one that it will be the girl."

"She looks enough like Katrina to be her ghost."

Braine went over to the window and stared up at the stars.

"You have made a good impression on the girl?" with his back still toward her.

"I had her in my arms."

"Olga, my hat is off to you," turning, now that his face was again in repose. "Your very frankness regarding your relationship will pull the wool over their eyes. Of course they'll make inquiries and they'll find out that you haven't lied. It's perfect. Not even that newspaper weasel will see anything wrong. Toward you they will eventually ease up and you can act without their even dreaming your part in the business. We must not be seen in public any more. This butler may know where I stand even though he can not prove it. Now, I'm going to tell you something. Perhaps you've long since guessed it. Katrina was mine till Hargreave—never mind what his name was then—till Hargreave came into the fold. So sure of her was I that I used her as a lure to bring him to us. She fell in love with him, but too late to warn him. I had the satisfaction of seeing him cast her aside, curse her, and leave her. In one thing she fooled us all. I never knew of the child till you told me."

He paused to light a cigarette.

"Hargreave was madly in love with her. He cursed her, but he came back to the house to forgive her, to find that she had been seized by the secret police and entombed in the fortress. I had my revenge. It was I who sent in the information, practically bogus. But in Russia they never question; they act and forget. So he had a daughter!"

He paced the floor, his hands behind his back; the woman watched him, oscillating between love and fear. He came to a halt abruptly and looked down at her.

"Don't worry. You have no rival. I'll leave the daughter to your tender mercies."

"The butler," she said, "has full power of attorney to act for Hargreave while absent, up to the day the girl becomes of legal age."

"I'll keep an eye on our friend Jones. From now on, day and night, there will be a cat at the knothole, and 'ware mouse! Could you make up anything like this girl?" suddenly.

"A fair likeness."

"Do it. Go to the ship which picked up the man at sea and quiz the captain. Either the aviator or Hargreave is alive. It is important to learn which at once. Be very careful; play the game only as you know how to play it. And if Hargreave is alive, we win. To-morrow morning, early. Tears of anguish, and all that. Sailors are easy when a woman weeps. No color, remember; just the yellow wig and the salient features. Now, by-by!"

"Aren't you going to kiss me, Leo?"

He caught her hands. "There is a species of Delilah about you, Olga. A kiss to-night from your lips would snip my locks; and I need a clear head. Whether we fail or win, when this game is played you shall be my wife." He kissed the hands and strode out into the hall.

The woman gazed down at her small white hands and smiled tenderly. (The tigress has her tender moments!) He meant it!

She went into her dressing-room and for an hour or more worked over her face and hair, till she was certain that if the captain of the ship described her to any one else he could not fail to give a fair description of Florence Hargreave.

NORTON REACHED THE CAPTAIN FIRST

But Norton reached the captain first. Other reporters
had besieged him, but they had succeeded in gathering the
vaguest kind of information. They had no description
of Hargreave, while Norton had. Before going down
to the boat, however, he had delved into the past of the
Countess Olga Perigoff. It cost him a pocketful of
money, but the end justified the means. The countess
had no past worth mentioning. By piecing this and that
together he became assured that she had told the simple
truth regarding the relationship to Florence's mother.
A cablegram had given him all the facts in her history;
there were no gaps or discrepancies. It read clear and
frank. Trust a Russian secret agent to know what he
was talking about.

So Norton's suspicions—and he had entertained some
—were completely lulled to sleep. And he wouldn't have
doubted her at all except for the fact that Braine had
been with her when he had introduced Hargreave. Hargreave had feared Braine; that much the reporter had
elicited from the butler. But there wasn't the slightest
evidence. Braine had been in New York for nearly six
years. The countess had arrived in the city but a year
ago. And Braine was a member of several fashionable
clubs, never touched cards, and seldom drank. He was
an expert chess player and a wonderful amateur billiard-
ist. Perhaps Jones, the taciturn and inscrutable, had
not told him all he knew regarding his master's past.
Well, well; he had in his time untangled worse snarls.
The office had turned him loose, a free lance, to handle
the case as he saw fit, to turn in the story when it was
complete.

But what a story it was going to be when he cleared
it up! The more mystifying it was, the greater the zest

and sport for him. Norton was like a gambler who played for big stakes, and only big stakes stirred his cravings.

The captain of the tramp steamer *Orient* told him the same tale he had told the other reporters: he had picked up a man at sea. The man had been brought aboard totally exhausted.

"Was there another body anywhere?"

"No."

"What became of him?"

"I sent a wireless and that seemed to bother him. It looked as though he did not want anybody to learn that he had been rescued. The moment the boat touched the pier he lost himself in the crowd. Fifty reporters came aboard, but he was gone. And I could but tell them just what I'm telling you."

"He had money."

"About five thousand."

"Please describe him."

The captain did so. It was the same description he had given to all the reporters. Norton looked over the rail at the big warehouse.

"Was it an ordinary balloon?"

"There you've got me. My Marconi man says the balloon part was like any other balloon; but the passenger car was a new business to him. It could be driven against the wind."

"Driven against the wind. Did you tell this to the other chaps?"

"Don't think I did. Just remembered it. Probably some new invention; and now it's at the bottom of the sea. Two men, as I understand, went off in this contraption. One is gone for good."

"For good," echoed the reporter gravely. "Gone for good, indeed, poor devil!"

Norton took out a roll of bills. "There's two hundred in this roll."

"Well?" said the captain, vastly astonished.

"It's yours if you will do me a small favor."

"If it doesn't get me mixed up with the police. I'm only captain of a tramp; and some of the harbor police have taken a dislike to me. What do you want me to do?"

"The police will not bother you. This man Hargreave had some enemies; they want either his life or his money; maybe both. It's a peculiar case, with Russia in the background. He might have laid the whole business before the police, but he chose to fight it out himself. And to tell the truth, I don't believe the police would have done any good."

"Heave her over; what do you want me to do for that handsome roll of money?"

"If any man or woman who is not a reporter comes to pump you tell them the man went ashore with a packet under his arm."

"Tie a knot in that."

"Say the man was gray-haired, clean-shaven, straight, with a scar high up on his forehead, generally covered up by his hair."

"That's battened down, my lad. Go on."

"Say that you saw him enter yonder warehouse, and later depart without his packet."

"Easy as dropping my mudhook."

"That's all." Norton gave the captain the money. "Good-by and many thanks."

"Don't mention it."

Norton left the slip and proceeded to the office of the warehouse. He approached the manager's desk.

"Hello, Grannis, old top!"

The man looked up from his work surlily. Then his face brightened.

"Norton? What's brought you here? Oh, yes; that balloon business. Sit down."

"What kind of a man is the captain of that old hooker in the slip?"

"Shifty in gun running, but otherwise as square as a die. Looks funny to see an old tub like that fixed up with wireless; but that has saved his neck a dozen times when he was running it into a noose. Not going to interview me, are you?"

"No. I'm going to ask you to do me a little favor."

"They always say that. But spin her out. If it doesn't cost me my job, it's yours."

"Well, there will be a person making inquiries about the mysterious aeronaut. All I want you to say is, that he left a packet with you, that you've put it in that safe till he calls to claim it."

Grannis nibbled the end of his pen. "Suppose some one should come and demand that I open the safe and deliver?"

"All you've got to do is to tell them to show the receipt signed by you."

The warehouse manager laughed. "Got a lot of sense in that ivory dome of yours. All right. But if anything happens you've got to come around and back me up. What's it about?"

"That I dare not tell you. This much, I'm laying a trap and I want some one I don't know to fall into it."

"On your way, James. But if you don't send me some

prize fight tickets next week for this, I'll never do you another favor."

In reply Norton took from his pocket two bits of pasteboard and laid them on the desk. "I knew you'd be wanting something like this."

"Ringside!" cried Grannis. "You reporters are lucky devils!"

"I'd go myself if there was any earthly chance of a real scrap. You make me laugh, Gran. You're always going, always hoping the next one will be a real one. But it's all bunk. The pugs are the biggest fakers on top of the sod. They've got us newspaper men done to a frazzle."

"I guess you're right. Well, count on me regarding that mysterious bundle in the safe."

"At three o'clock this afternoon I want you to call me up. If no one has called, why the game is up. But if some one does come around and make inquiries, don't fail to let me know."

"I'll be here till five. I'd better call you up then."

Then Norton returned home and idled about till afternoon. He went over to Riverdale. Five times he walked up and down in front of the Hargreave place, finally plucked up his courage and walked to the door. After all, he was a lucky mortal. He had a good excuse to visit this house every day in the week. And there was something tantalizing in the risk he took. Besides, he wanted to prove to himself whether it was a passing fancy or something deeper. That's the way with humans; we never see a sign "Fresh Paint" that we don't have to prove it.

He chatted with Florence for a while and found that, for all she might be guileless to the world, she was a good linguist, a fine musician, and talked with remarkable keenness about books and arts. But unless he roused her, the sadness of her position always lay written in her face. It was not difficult for him to conjure up her dreams in coming to the city and the blow which, like a bolt of lightning from a clear sky, had shattered them ruthlessly.

"You must come every day and tell me how you have progressed," she said.

"I'll obey that order gladly, whenever I can possibly do it. My visits will always be short."

"That is not necessary."

"No," said Norton in his heart, "but it is wise."

Always he found Jones waiting for him at the door, always in the shadow.

"Well?" the butler whispered.

"I have laid a neat trap. Whether this balloon was the one that left the top of this house I don't know. But if there were two men in it, one of them lies at the bottom of the sea."

"And the man who was found?" The butler's voice was tense.

"It was not Hargreave. I met Orts but once, and as he wore a beard then, the captain's description did not tally with your recollection."

"Thank God! But what is this trap?"

"I propose to find out by it who is back of all this, who Hargreave's real enemies are."

Norton returned to his rooms, there to await the call from Grannis. He was sorry, but if Jones would not take him into his fullest confidence, he must hold himself to blame for any blunder he (Norton) made. Of course, he could readily understand Jones' angle of vision. He knew nothing of the general run of reporters; he had heard of them by rumor and distrusted them. He was not aware of the fact that the average reporter carries more secrets in his head than a prime minister. It was, then, up to him to set about to allay this distrust and gain the man's complete confidence.

Meanwhile that same morning a pretty young woman boarded the *Orient* and asked to be led to the captain. Her eyes were red; she had evidently been weeping. When the captain, susceptible like all sailors, saw her his promises to Norton took wings.

"This is Captain Hagan?" she asked, balling the handkerchief she held in her hand.

"Yes, miss. What can I do for you?" He put his hands embarrassedly into his pockets—and felt the crisp bills. But for that magic touch he would have forgotten his lines. He squared his shoulders.

"I have every assurance that the man you picked up at sea is my father. I am Florence Hargreave. Tell me everything."

The captain's very blundering deceived her. "And then he hustled down the gangplank and headed for that warehouse. He had a package which he was as tender of as if it had been dynamite."

"Thank you!" impulsively.

"A man has to do his duty, miss. A sailor's always glad to rescue a man at sea," awkwardly.

When she finally went down the gangplank the sigh the captain heaved was almost as loud as the exhaust from the donkey engines which were working out the crates of lemons from the hold.

"Maybe she is his daughter; but two hundred is two hundred, and I'm a poor sailor man."

Then Grannis came in for his troubles. What was a chap to do when a pretty girl appealed to him?

"I am sorry, miss, but I can't give you that package. I gave the man a receipt and till it is presented to me the package must remain in yonder safe. You understand enough about the business to realize that. I did not solicit the job. It was thrust upon me. I'd give a hundred dol- lars if the blame thing was out of my safe. You say it is your fortune. That hasn't been proved. It may be gun- powder, dynamite. I'm sorry, but you will have to find your father and bring the receipt."

The young woman left the warehouse, dabbing her eyes with the sodden handkerchief.

"I wonder," mused Grannis, as he watched her from the window, "I wonder what the deuce that chap Norton is up to. The girl might have been the man's daughter. . . . Good lord, what an ass I am! There wasn't any man!" And so he reached over for the telephone.

Immediately upon receipt of the message the reporter set his machinery in motion. Some time before dawn he would know who the arch-conspirator was. He ques- tioned Grannis thoroughly, and Grannis' description tal- lied amazingly with that of Florence Hargreave. But a call over the wire proved to him conclusively that Flor- ence had not been out of the house that morning.

On the morrow the newspapers had scare heads about an attempt to rob the Duffy warehouse. It appeared that the police had been tipped beforehand and were on the grounds in time to gather in several notorious gunmen, who, under pressure of the third degree, vowed that they had been hired and paid by a man in a mask and had not the slightest idea what he wanted them to raid. Nothing further could be got out of the gunmen. That they, were lying the police had no doubt, but they were up against a stout wall and all they could do was to hold the men for the grand jury.

Norton was in a fine temper. After all his careful planning he had gained nothing—absolutely nothing. But wait; he had gained something—the bitter enmity of a cunning and desperate man, who had been forced to remain hidden under the pier till almost dawn.

CHAPTER IV

BRAINE crawled from his uncomfortable hiding place. His clothes were soiled and damp, his hat was gone. By a hair's breadth he had escaped the clever trap laid for him. Hargreave was alive, he had escaped; Braine was as certain of this fact as he was of his own breathing. He now knew how to account for the flickering light in the upper story of the warehouse. His ancient enemy had been watching him all the time. More than this, Hargreave and the meddling reporter were in collusion. In the flare of lights at the end of the gun-play he had caught the profile of the reporter. Here was a dangerous man, who must be watched with the utmost care.

He, Braine, had been lured to commit an overt act, and by the rarest good luck had escaped with nothing more serious than a cold chill and a galling disappointment.

He crawled along the top of the pier, listening, sending his dark-accustomed glance hither and thither. The sky in the east was growing paler and paler. In and out among the bales of wool, bags of coffee and lemon crates he slowly and cautiously wormed his way. A watchman patrolled the office side of the warehouse, and Braine found it possible to creep around the other way, thence into the street. After that he straightened up, sought a second-hand shop and purchased a soft hat, which he pulled down over his eyes.

48

He had half a dozen rooms which he always kept in readiness for such adventures as this. He rented them furnished in small hotels which never asked questions of their patrons. To one of these he went as fast as his weary legs could carry him. He always carried the key. Once in his room he donned fresh wearing apparel, linen, shoes, and shaved. Then he proceeded down-stairs, the second-hand hat shading his eyes and the upper part of his face.

At half past twelve Norton entered the Knickerbocker café-restaurant, and the first person he noticed was Braine, reading the morning's paper, propped up against the water carafe. Evidently he had just ordered, for there was nothing on his plate. Norton walked over and laid his hand upon Braine's shoulder. The man looked up with mild curiosity.

"Why, Norton, sit down, sit down! Have you had lunch? No? Join me."

"Thanks. Came in for my breakfast," said Norton, drawing out the chair. Braine was sitting with his back to the wall on the lounge-seat.

"I wonder if you newspaper men ever eat a real, true enough breakfast. I should think the hours you lead would kill you off. Anything new on the Hargreave story?"

"I'm not handling that," the reporter lied cheerfully. "Didn't want to. I knew him rather intimately. I've a horror of dead people, and don't want to be called upon to identify the body when they find it."

"Then you think they will find it?"

"I don't know. It's a strange mixup. I'm not on the story, mind you; but I was in the locality of Duffy's ware-house late last night and fell into a gunman rumpus."

"Yes, I read about that. What were they after?"

"You've got me there. No one seems to know. Some cock and bull story about there being something valuable. There was."

"What was it? The report in this paper does not say."

"Ten thousand bags of coffee."

Braine lay back in his chair and laughed.

"If you want my opinion," said Norton, "I believe the gunmen were out to shoot up another gang, and the police got wind of it."

"Don't you think it about time the police called a halt in this gunman matter?"

"Oh, so long as they pot each other the police look the other way. It saves a long trial and passage up the river. Besides, when they are nabbed some big politician manages to open the door for them. Great is the American voter."

"Take Mr. Norton's order, Luigi," said Braine.

"A German pancake, buttered toast and coffee," ordered the reporter.

"Man, eat something!"

"It's enough for me."

"And you'll go all the rest of the day on tobacco. I know something of you chaps. I don't see how you manage to do it."

"Food is the least of our troubles. By the way, may I ask you a few questions? Nothing for print, unless you've got a new book coming."

"Fire away."

"What do you know about the Countess Perigoff?"

"Let me see. H'm. Met her first about a year ago at a reception given to Nasimova. A very attractive woman. I see quite a lot of her. Why?"

"Well, she claims to be a sort of aunt to Hargreave's daughter."

"She said something to me about that the other night. You never know where you're at in this world, do you?"

The German pancake, the toast, the coffee disappeared, and the reporter passed his cigars.

"The president visits town to-day and I'm off to watch the show. I suppose I'll have to interview him about the tariff and all that rot. When you start on a new book let me know and I'll be your press agent."

"That's a bargain."

"Thanks for the breakfast."

Braine picked up his newspaper, smoked and read. He smoked, yes, but he only pretended to read. The young fool was clever, but no man is infallible. He had not the least suspicion; he saw only the newspaper story. Still, in some manner he might stumble upon the truth, and it would be just as well to tie the reporter's hands effectually.

The rancor of early morning had been subdued; anger and quick temper never paid in the long run, and no one appreciated this fact better than Braine. To put Norton out of the way temporarily was only a wise precaution; it was not a matter of spite or reprisal.

He paid the reckoning, left the restaurant, and dropped into one of his clubs for a game of billiards. He drew quite a gallery about the table. He won easily, racked his cue and sought the apartments of the countess.

What a piece of luck it was that Olga had really married that old dotard, Perigoff! He had left her a titled widow six months after her marriage. But she had had hardly a kopeck to call her own.

"Olga, Hargreave is alive. He was there last night.

But somehow he anticipated the raid and had the police in waiting. The question is, has he fooled us? Did he take that million or did he hide it? There is one thing left—to get that girl. No matter where Hargreave is hidden, the knowledge that she is in my hands will bring him out into the open."

"No more blind alleys."

"What's on your mind?"

"She has never seen her father. She confessed to me that she has not even seen a photograph of him."

There was a long pause.

"Do you understand me?" she asked.

"By the Lord Harry, I do! You've a head on you worth two of mine. The very simplicity of the idea will win out for us. Some one to pose as her father; a message handed to her in secret; dire misfortune if she whispers a word to any one; that her father's life hangs upon the secrecy; she must confide in no one, least of all Jones, the butler. It all depends upon how the letter gets to her. Bred in the country, she probably sleeps with her window open. A pebble attached to a note, tossed into the window. I'll trust this to no one; I'll do it myself. With the girl in our control the rest will be easy. If she really does not know where the money is Hargreave will tell us. Great head, little woman, great head. She does not know her father's handwriting?"

"She has never seen a scrap of it. Miss Farlow never showed her the registered letters. The original note left on the doorstep with Florence has been lost. Trust me to make all these inquiries."

"To-morrow night, then, immediately after dinner, a taxicab will await her just around the corner. Grange is the best man I can think of. He's an artist when it comes to playing the old-man parts."

"Not too old, remember. Hargreave isn't over forty-five."

"Another good point. I'm going to stretch out here on the divan and snooze for a while. Had a devil of a time last night."

"When shall I wake you?"

"At six. We'll have an early dinner sent in. I want to keep out of everybody's way. By-by!"

In less than three minutes he was sound asleep. The woman gazed down at him in wonder and envy. If only she could drop to sleep like that. Very softly she pressed her lips to his hair.

At eleven o'clock the following night the hall light in the Hargreave house was turned off and the whole interior became dark. A shadow crept through the lilac bushes without any more sound than a cat would have made. Florence's window was open as the arch-conspirator had expected it would be. With a small string and stone as a sling he sent the letter whirling skilfully through the air. It sailed into the girl's room. The man below heard no sound of the stone hitting anything and concluded that it had struck the bed.

He waited patiently. Presently a wavering light could be distinguished over the sill of the window. The girl was awake and had lit the candle. This knowledge was sufficient for his need. The tragic letter would do the rest, that is, if the girl came from the same pattern as her father and mother—strong-willed and adventurous.

He tiptoed back to the lilacs, when a noise sent him close to the ground. Half a dozen feet away he saw a shadow creeping along toward the front door. Presently the shadow stood up as if listening. He stooped again and ran lightly to the steps, up these to the door, which he hugged.

Who was this? wondered Braine. Patiently he waited, arranging his posture so that he could keep a lookout at the door. By and by the door opened cautiously. A man holding a candle appeared. Braine vaguely recognized Olga's description of the butler. The man on the veranda suddenly blew out the light.

Braine could hear the low murmur of voices, but nothing more. The conversation lasted scarcely a minute. The door closed and the man ran down the steps, across the lawn, with Braine close at his heels.

"Just a moment, Mr. Hargreave," he called ironically; "just a moment!"

The man he addressed as Hargreave turned with lightning rapidity and struck. The blow caught Braine above the ear, knocking him flat. When he regained his feet the rumble of a motor told him the rest of the story.

By the dim light of her bedroom candle Florence read the note which had found entrance so strangely and mysteriously into her room. Her father! He lived, he needed her! Alive, but in dread peril, and only she could save, him! She longed to fly to him at once, then and there. How could she wait till to-morrow night at eight? Immediately she began to plan how to circumvent the watchful Jones and the careful Susan. Her father! She slept no more that night.

"My Darling Daughter: I must see you. Come at

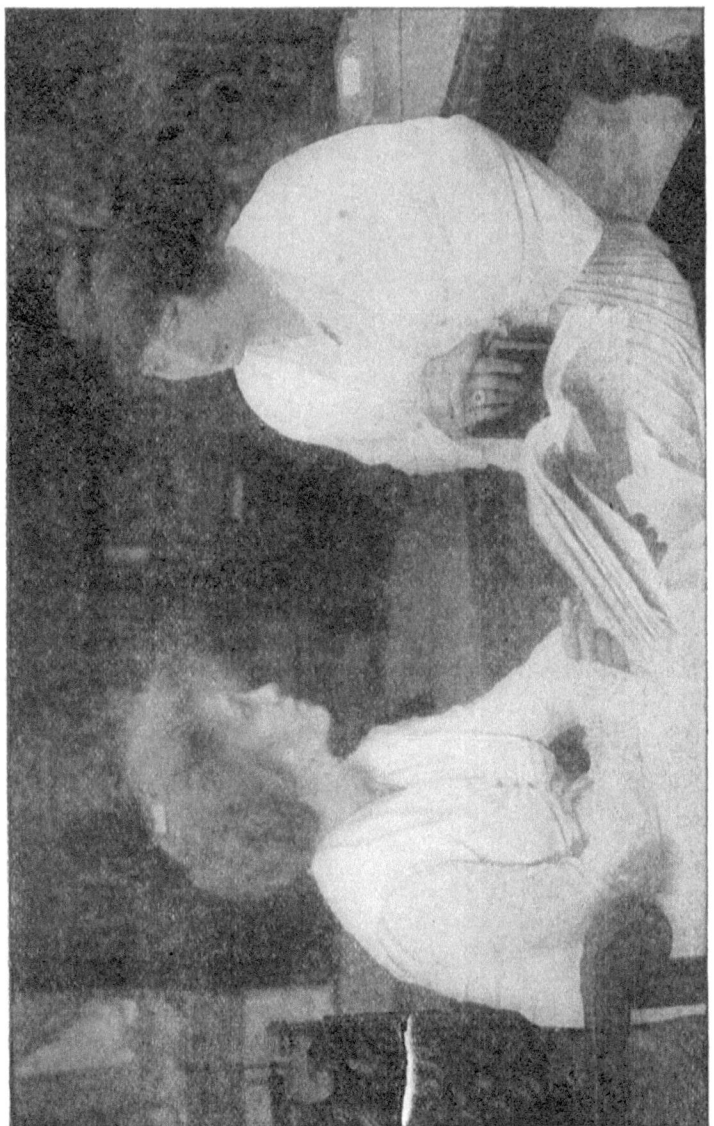

SHE READ WITH SUSAN . . . .

eight o'clock to-morrow night to 78 Grove Street, third
floor.   Confide in no one, or you seal my death warrant.
"Your unhappy

"FATHER."

What child would refuse to obey a summons like this?
A light tap on the door startled her.
"Is anything the matter?" asked the mild voice of
Jones.
"No. I got up to get a drink of water."
She heard his footsteps die away down the corridor.
She thrust the letter into the pocket of her dress, which
lay neatly folded on the chair at the foot of the bed, then
climbed back into the bed itself.   She must not tell even
Mr. Norton.
Was the child spinning a romance over the first young
man she had ever met?   In her heart of hearts the girl
did not know.
Her father!
It was all so terribly and tragically simple, to match a
woman's mind against that of a child.   Both Norton and
the sober Jones had explicitly warned her never to go anywhere, receive telephone calls or letters, without first consulting one or the other of them.   And now she had
planned to deceive them, with all the cunning of her sex.
The next morning at breakfast there was nothing unusual either in her appearance or manners.   Under the
shrewd scrutiny of Jones she was just her every-day self,
a fine bit of acting for one who had yet to see the stage.
But it is born in woman to act, as it is born in man to
fight, and Florence was no exception to the rule.
She was going to save her father.
She read with Susan, played the piano, sewed a little,

laughed, hummed and did a thousand and one things young girls do when they have the deception of their elders in view.

All day long Jones went about like an old hound with his nose to the wind. There was something in the air, but he could not tell what it was. Somehow or other, no matter which room Florence went into, there was Jones within earshot. And she dared not show the least impatience or restiveness. It was a large order for so young a girl, but she filled it.

She rather expected that the reporter would appear some time during the afternoon; and sure enough he did. He could no more resist the desire to see and talk to her than he could resist breathing. There was no use denying it; the world had suddenly turned at a new angle, presenting a new face, a roseate vision. It rather subdued his easy banter.

"What news?" she asked.

"None," rather despondingly. "I'm sorry. I had hoped by this time to get somewhere. But it happens that I can't get any farther than this house."

She did not ask him what he meant by that.

"Shall I play something for you?" she said.

"Please."

He drew a chair beside the piano and watched her fingers, white as the ivory keys, flutter up and down the board. She played Chopin for him, Mendelssohn, Grieg and Chaminade; and she played them in a surprisingly scholarly fashion. He had expected the usual schoolgirl choice and execution; *Titania*, the *Moonlight Sonata* (which not half a dozen great pianists have ever played correctly), *Monastery Bells*, and the like. He had prepared to make a martyr of himself; instead, he was distinctly and delightfully entertained.

"You don't," he said whimsically, when she finally stopped, "you don't, by any chance, know *The Maiden's Prayer?*"

She laughed. This piece was a standing joke at school. "I have never played it. It may, however, be in the cabinet. Would you like to hear it?" mischievously.

"Heaven forfend!" he murmured, raising his hands.

All the while the letter burned against her heart, and the smile on her face and the gaiety on her tongue were forced. "Confide in no one," she repeated mentally, "or you seal my death warrant."

"Why do you shake your head like that?" he asked.

"Did I shake my head?" Her heart fluttered wildly. "I was not conscious of it."

"Are you going to keep your promise?"

"What promise?"

"Never to leave this house without Jones or myself being with you."

"I couldn't if I wanted to. I'll wager Jones is out there in the hall this minute. I know; it is all for my sake. But it bothers me."

Jones was indeed in the hall, and when he sensed the petulance in her voice his shoulders sank despondently and he sighed deeply if silently.

At a quarter to eight Florence, being alone for a minute, set fire to a veil and stuffed it down the register.

"Jones," she called excitedly, "I smell something burning!"

Jones dashed into the room, sniffed, and dashed out again, heading for the cellar door. His first thought was naturally that the devils incarnate had set fire to the house. When he returned, having, of course, discovered no fire, he found Florence gone. He rushed into the hall. Her hat was missing. He made for the hall door with a speed which seemed incredible to the bewildered Susan's eyes. Out into the street, up and down which he looked. Far away he discovered a dwindling taxicab. The child was gone.

In the house Susan was answering the telephone, talking incoherently.

"Who is it?" Jones whispered, his lips white and dry.

"The countess. . . ." began Susan.

He took the receiver from her roughly.

"Hello, who is it?"

"This is Olga Perigoff. Is Florence there?"

"No, madam. She has just stepped out for a moment. Shall I tell her to call you when she returns?"

"Yes, please. I want her and Susan and Mr. Norton to come to tea to-morrow. Good-by."

Jones hung up the receiver, sank into a chair near by and buried his face in his hands.

"What is it?" cried Susan, terrified by the haggardness of his face.

"She's gone! My God, those wretches have got her! They've got her!"

Florence was whirled away at top speed. Her father! She was actually on the way to her father, whom she had always loved in dreams, yet never seen.

Number 78 Grove Street was not an attractive place, but when she arrived she was too highly keyed to take note of its sordidness. She was rather out of breath when she reached the door of the third flat. She knocked timidly. The door was instantly opened by a man who

"WHO IS IT?" WHISPERED JONES, HIS LIPS WHITE AND DRY

wore a black mask. She would have turned then and there and flown but for the swift picture she had of a well-dressed man at a table. He lay with his head upon his arms.

"Father!" she whispered.

The man raised his careworn face, so very well done that only the closest scrutiny would have betrayed the paste of the theater. He arose and staggered toward her with outstretched arms. But the moment they closed about her Florence experienced a peculiar shiver.

"My child!" murmured the broken man. "They caught me when I was about to come to you. I have given up the fight."

A sob choked him.

What was it? wondered the child, her heart burning with the misery of the thought that she was sad instead of glad. Over his shoulder she sent a glance about the room. There was a sofa, a table, some chairs and an enormous clock, the face of which was dented and the hands hopelessly tangled. Why, at such a moment, she should note such details disturbed her. Then she chanced to look into the cracked mirror. In it she saw several faces, all masked. These men were peering at her through the half-closed door behind her.

"You must return home and bring me the money," went on the wretch who dared to perpetrate such a mockery. "It is all that stands between me and death."

Then she knew! The insistent daily warnings came home to her. She understood now. She had deliberately walked into the spider's net. But instead of terror an extraordinary calm fell upon her.

"Very well, father, I will go and get it." Gently she released herself from those horrible arms.

"Wait, my child, till I see if they will let you go. They may wish to hold you as hostage."

When he was gone she tried the doors. They were locked. Then she crossed over to the window and looked out. A leap from there would kill her. She turned her gaze toward the lamp, wondering.

The false father returned, dejectedly.

"It is as I said. They insist upon sending some one. Write down the directions I gave to you. I am very weak!"

"Write down the directions yourself, father; you know them better than I." Since she saw no escape, she was determined to keep up the tragic farce no longer.

"I am not your father."

"So I see," she replied, still with the amazing calm.

Braine, in the other room, shook his head savagely. Father and daughter; the same steel in the nerves. Could they bend her? Would they break her? He did not wish to injure her bodily, but a million was always a million, and there was revenge which was worth more to him than the money itself. He listened, motioning to the others to be silent.

"Write the directions," commanded the scoundrel, who discarded the broken-man style.

"I know of no hidden money."

"Then your father dies this night." Grange put a whistle to his lips. "Sign, write!"

"I refuse!"

"Once more. The moment I blow this whistle the men in the other room will understand that your father is to die. Be wise. Money is nothing—life is everything."

"I refuse!" Even as she had known this vile creature

to be an impostor so she knew that he lied, that her father was still free.

Grange blew the whistle. Instantly the room became filled with masked men. But Florence was ready. She seized the lamp and hurled it to the floor, quite indifferent whether it exploded or went out. Happily for her, it was extinguished. At the same moment she cast the lamp she caught hold of a chair, remembering the direction of the window. She was superhumanly strong in this moment. The chair went true. A crash followed.

"She has thrown herself out of the window!" yelled a voice.

Some one groped for the lamp, lit it and turned in time to see Florence pass out of the room into that from which they had come. The door slammed. The surprised men heard the key click.

She was free. But she was no longer a child.

CHAPTER V

"GONE!"

Jones kept saying to himself that he must strive to be calm, to think, think. Despite all his warnings, the warnings of Norton, she had tricked them and run away. It was maddening. He wanted to rave, tear his hair, break things. He tramped the hall. It would be wasting time to send for the police. They would only putter about fruitlessly. The Black Hundred knew how to arrange these abductions.

How had they succeeded in doing it? No one had entered the house that day without his being present. There had been no telephone call he had not heard the gist of, nor any letters he had not first glanced over. How had they done it? Suddenly into his mind flashed the remembrance of the candle-light under Florence's door the night before. In a dozen bounds he was in her room, searching drawers, paper boxes, baskets. He found nothing. He returned in despair to Susan, who, during all this turmoil, had sat as if frozen in her chair.

"Speak!" he cried. "For God's sake, say something, think something! Those devils are likely to torture her, hurt her!" He leaned against the wall, his head on his arm.

When he turned again he was calm. He walked with

62

bent head toward the door, opened it and stood upon the
threshold for a space. Across the street a shadow stirred,
but Jones did not see it. His gaze was attracted by something which shone dimly white on the walk just beyond
the steps. He ran to it. A crumpled letter, unaddressed.
He carried it back to the house, smoothed it out and read
its contents. Florence in her haste had dropped the
letter.

He clutched at his hat, put it on and ran to Susan.

"Here!" he cried, holding out an automatic. "If any
one comes in that you don't know, shoot! Don't ask
questions, shoot!"

"I'm afraid!" She breathed with difficulty.

"Afraid?" he roared at her. He put the weapon in her
hand. It slipped and thudded to the floor. He stooped
for it and slammed it into her lap. "You love your life
and honor. You'll know how to shoot when the time
comes. Now, attend to me. If I'm not back here by ten
o'clock, turn this note over to the police. If you can't do
that, then God help us all!" And with that he ran from
the house.

Susan eyed the revolver with growing terror. For
what had she left the peace and quiet of Miss Farlow's;
assassination, robbery, thieves and kidnapers? She
wanted to shriek, but her throat was as dry as paper.
Gingerly she touched the pistol. The cold steel sent a
thrill of fear over her. He hadn't told her how to
shoot it!

Two blocks down the street, up an alley, was the garage
wherein Hargreave had been wont to keep his car. Toward this Jones ran with the speed of a track athlete.
There might be half a dozen taxicabs about, but he would
not run the risk of engaging any of them. The Black

Hundred was capable of anticipating his every movement.

The shadow across the street stood undecided. At
length he concluded to give Jones ten minutes in which to
return. If he did not return in that time, the watcher
would go up to the drug store and telephone for instructions.

But Jones did not come back.

"Where's Howard?" he demanded.

"Hello, Jones; what's up?"

"Howard, get that car out at once."

"Out she comes. Wait till I give her radiator a bucket
of water. Gee!" whispered Howard, whom Hargreave
often used as his chauffeur, "get on to his nibs! First
time I ever saw him awake. I wonder what's doing?
You never know what's back of those mummy-faced
head waiters. . . . All right, Jones!"

The chauffeur jumped into the car and Jones took the
seat beside him.

"Where to?"

"Number 78 . . ." and the rest of it trailed away,
smothered in the violent thunder of the big six's engines.

During the car's flight several policemen hailed it without success. Down this street, up that, round this corner,
fifty miles an hour; and all the while Jones shouted:
"Faster, faster!"

Within twelve minutes from the time it left the garage,
the car stopped opposite 78 Grove Street, and Jones got
out.

"Wait here, Howard. If several men come rushing
out, or I don't appear within ten minutes, fire your gun a
couple of times for the police. I don't want them if we
can manage without. They'd only bungle."

"All right, Mr. Jones," said the chauffeur. He had, in the past quarter of an hour, acquired a deep and lasting respect for the butler chap. He was a regular fellow, for all his brass buttons.

As Jones reached the curb, Florence came forth as if on invisible wings. Jones caught her by the arm. She flung him aside with a strength he had not dreamed existed in her slim body.

"Florence, I am Jones!"

She stopped, recognized him, and without a word ran across the street to the automobile and climbed into the tonneau. Jones followed immediately.

"Home!"

The car shot up the dimly lighted street, shone palely for a second under the corner lamp, and vanished.

"Ah, child, child!" groaned the man at her side, all the tenseness gone from his body. He was Jones again.

Still she did not speak, but stared ahead with unseeing eyes.

No further reproach fell from the butler's lips. It was enough that God had guided him to her at the appointed moment. He felt assured that never again would she be drawn into any trap. Poor child! What had they said to her, done to her? How, in God's name, had she escaped from them who never let anybody escape? Presently she would become normal, and then she would tell him.

"I found the lying note. You dropped it."

"Horrible, horrible!" she said almost inaudibly.

"What did they do to you?"

"He said he was my father. . . . He put his arms around me. . . . And I knew!"

"Knew what?"

"That he lied. I can't explain."

"Don't try!"

Suddenly she laid her head against the butler's shoulder and cried. It was terrible to hear youth weep in this fashion. Jones put his arm about her and tried to console her.

, "Horrible!" she murmured between the violent hic- jcoughs. "I was wrong, wrong! Forgive me!"

Unconsciously the arm sustaining her drew her closer.

"Never mind," he consoled. "Tell no one what has happened. Go about as usual. Don't let even Susan know. Whatever your poor father did was for your sake. He wanted you to be happy, without a care in the world."

"I promise." And gradually the sobs ceased. "But I feel so old, Jones, so very old. I threw over the lamp. I threw a chair through the window. They thought that it was I who had jumped out. That gave me the necessary time. I don't understand how I did it. I wasn't fright- ened at all till I gained the street."

They found Susan still seated in the chair, the auto- matic in her lap. She had not moved in all this time!   ·

Braine paced the apartment of the Countess Perigoff. From the living room to the boudoir and back, fully twenty times. From the divan Olga watched him nerv- ously. He was like a tiger, fresh in captivity. All at once he paused in front of her.

"Do you realize what that mere chit did?"

"I do."

"Planned to the minute. We had her; seven of us; doors locked, and all that. No weeping, no wailing; I could not understand then, but I do now. It's in the

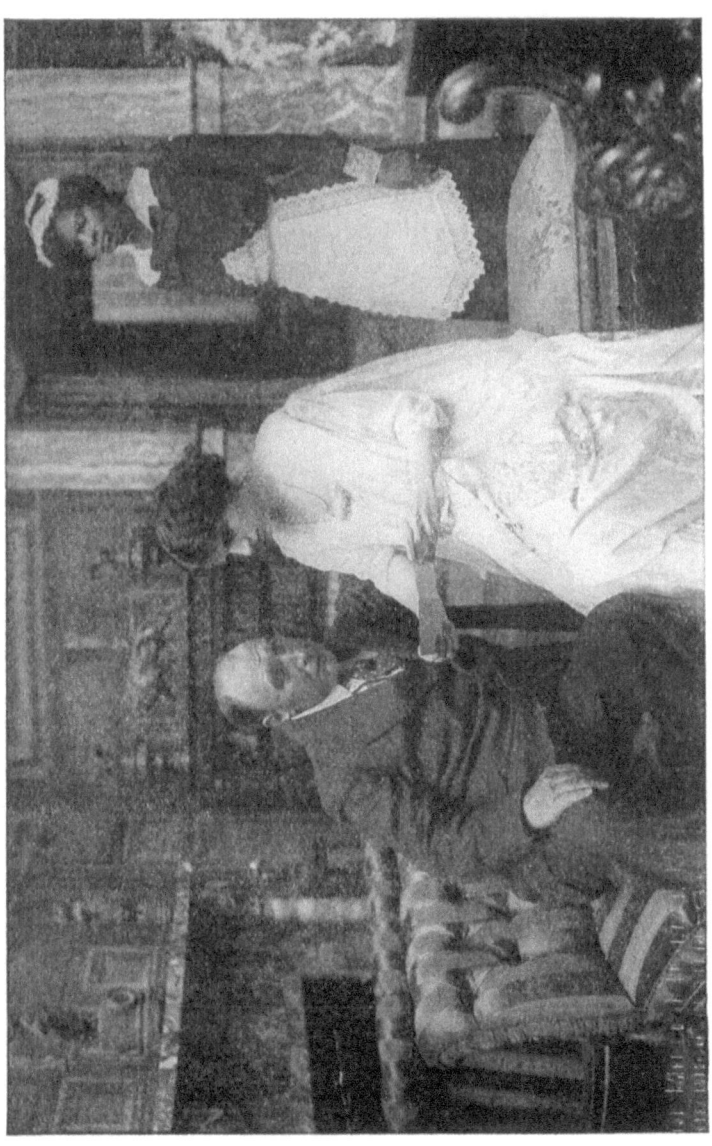

HE READ . . . FLORENCE . . . THE HIDING-PLACE IS DISCOVERED

blood. Hargreave was as peaceful as a St. Bernard dog till you cornered him, and then he was a lion. Oh, the devil! Slipped out of our fingers like an eel. And across the street, Jones in a racer! I never paid any particular attention to Jones, but from now on I shall. The girl may or may not know where the money is, but Jones does, Jones does! Two men shall watch. Felton on the street and Orloff from the windows of the deserted house. With opera glasses he will be able to take note of all that happens in the house during the day. He will be able to see the girl's room. And that's the important point. It was a good plan, little woman; and it would have been plain sailing if only we had remembered that the girl was Hargreave's daughter. Be very careful hereafter when you call on her. A night like this will have made her suspicious of every one. Our hope lies with you. Anything on your mind?"

"Yes. Why not insert a personal in the *Herald?*" She drew some writing paper toward her and scribbled a few words.

He read: "Florence—the hiding place is discovered. Remove it to a more secret spot at once. S. H."—He laughed and shook his head. "I'm afraid that will never do."

"If she reads it, Jones will. The man with the opera glasses may see something. There's a chance Jones might become worried."

"Well, we'll give it a chance."

It was midnight when he made his departure. As he stepped into the street, he glanced about cautiously. On the corner he saw a policeman swinging his night stick. Otherwise the street was deserted. Braine proceeded jauntily down the street.

And yet, from the darkened doors of the house across
the way, the figure of a man emerged and stood contem-
plating the windows of the Perigoff apartment. Suddenly
the lights went out. The watcher made no effort to follow Braine. The knowledge he was after did not necessi-
'tate any such procedure.

Of course, Florence read the "personal." She took the
newspaper at once to Jones, who smiled grimly.

"You see, I trust you."

"And so long as you continue to trust me no harm will
befall you. You were left in my care by your father. I
am to guard you at the expense of my life. Last night's
affair was a miracle. The next time you will not find it
so easy to escape."

Nor did she.

"There will be no next time," gravely. "But I am going to ask you a direct question. Is my father alive?"

The butler's brow puckered. "I have promised to say
nothing, one way or the other."

She laughed.

"Why do you laugh?"

"I laugh because if he were dead there would be no
earthly reason for your not saying so at once. But I hate
money, the name of it, the sound of it, the sight of it. It
is at the bottom of all wars and crimes. I despise it!"

"The root of all evil. Yet it performs many noble
deeds. But never mind the money. Let us give our
attention to this personal. Doubtless it originated in the
same mind which conceived the letter. Your father would
never have inserted such a personal. What! Give his
enemies a chance to learn his secret? No. On the other
hand, I want you to show this personal to all you meet
to-day, Susan, the reporter, to everybody. Talk about it.

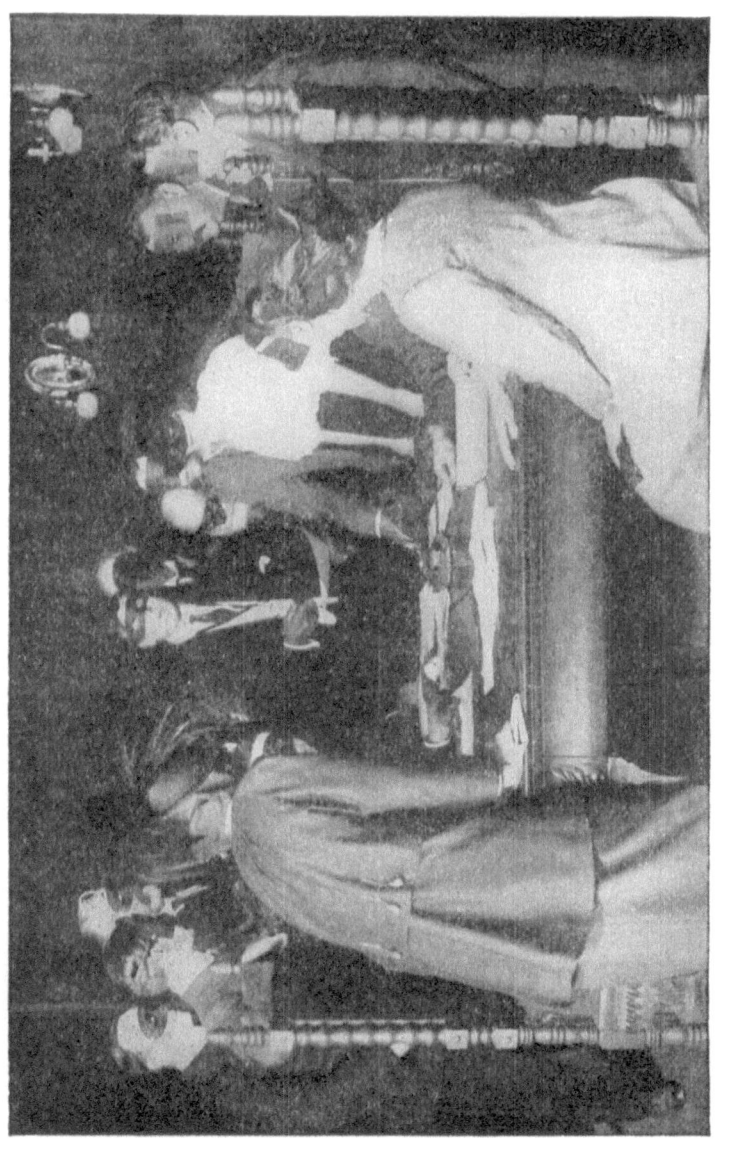

THAT NIGHT THERE WAS A MEETING OF THE ORGANIZATION

Say that you wonder what you shall do. Trust no one
with your real thoughts."

"Not even you, Mr. Jones," thought the girl as she
nodded.

"And tell them that you showed it to me and that I
appeared worried."

That night there was a meeting of the organization
called the Black Hundred. Braine asked if any one knew
what the Hargreave butler looked like.

"I had a glimpse of him the other night; but being un-
prepared, I might not recognize him again."

Vroon described Jones minutely. Braine could almost
see the portrait.

"Vroon, that memory of yours is worth a lot of
money," was his only comment.

"I hope it will be worth more soon."

"I believe I'll be able to recognize Mr. Jones if I see
him. Who is he and what is he?"

"He has been with Hargreave for fourteen years.
There was a homicidal case in which Jones was active.
Hargreave saved him. He is faithful and uncommuni-
cative. Money will not touch him. If he does know
where that million is, hot irons could not make him own
up to it. The only way is to watch him, follow him, wait
for the moment when he'll grow careless. No man is
always on his mettle; he lets up sooner or later."

"He is being watched, as you know."

Vroon nodded approvingly. "The captain of the tramp
steamer *Orient,* by the way, was seen with a roll of
money. He was in one of the water-front saloons, brag-
ging how he had hoodwinked some one."

"Did he say where he'd got the cash?" asked Braine.

"They tried to pump him on that, but he shut up. Well,

we have agreed that Felton shall watch from the street and Orloff from the window. Orloff will whistle if he sees Jones removing anything from any of the rooms. The rest will be left to Felton."

"And, Felton, my friend," said Braine softly—he always spoke softly when he was in a deadly humor— "Felton, you slept on duty the other night. Hargreave stole up, consulted Jones, and got away after knocking me down. The next failure will mean short shift. Be warned!"

"I saw only you, sir. So help me. I was not asleep. I saw you run down the street after the taxicab. I did not see any one else."

Braine shrugged. "Remember what I said."

Felton bowed respectfully and made his exit. He wished in his soul that he might some day catch the master mind free of his eternal mask. It was an iron hand which ruled them and there were friends of his (Felton's) who had mysteriously vanished after a brief period of rebellion. The boss was a swell; probably belonged to clubs and society which he adroitly pilfered. The organization always had money. Whenever there was a desperate job to be undertaken, Vroon simply poured out the money necessary to promote it. Whenever Braine and Vroon became engaged in earnest conversation they talked Slav. Braine was never called by name here; the 'boss, simply that.

Well, ten per cent. of a million was a hundred thousand. This would be equally divided between the second ten of the Black Hundred. Another ten per cent. would go to eighty members; the balance would be divided between Vroon and the boss. But his soul rebelled at being ordered about like so much dirt under another man's feet.

He would take his ten thousand and make the grand get-away.

The next afternoon the countess called upon Florence. Nothing was said about the adventure, and this fact created a vague unrest in the scheming woman's mind. She realized that she must play her cards more carefully than ever. Not the least distrust must be permitted to enter the child's head. Once that happened good-by to the wonderful emeralds. Was it that she really craved the stone? Was it not rather a venom acquired from the knowledge that this child's mother had won what she herself, with all her cleverness, was not sure of—Braine's love? Did he really care for her or was she only the cats-paw to pluck his hot chestnuts from the fire?

When Florence showed her the "personal," her vague doubts became instantly dissipated. The child would not have shown her the newspaper had there been any distrust on her part.

"My child, your father is alive, then?" animatedly.

"We don't know," sadly.

"Why, I should say that this proves it."

"On the contrary, it proves nothing of the sort, since I have yet to discover a treasure in this house. I have hunted in every nook, drawer; I've searched for panels, looked in trunks for false bottoms. Nothing, nothing! Ah, if I could only find it!"

"And what would you do with it?"

"Take it at once to some bank and offer the whole of it for the safe return of my father, every penny of it. I don't know what to do, which way to turn," tears gathering in her eyes and they were genuine tears, too. "There are millions in stocks and bonds and I can not touch a penny of it because the legal documents have not been found. I can't even prove that I am his daughter, except for half an old bracelet, and my father's lawyers say that that would not hold in any court."

"You were born in St. Petersburg, my dear. Have the embassy there look up the birth registers."

"That would not put me into possession. Nothing but the return of my father will avail me. And there's a horrible thought always of my not being his real daughter."

"There's no doubt in my mind. I have only to recall Katrina's face to know whose child you are. But what will you live on?" Here was a far greater mixup than she had calculated upon. Supposing after all it was only a resemblance, that the child was not Hargreave's, a substitute just to blind the Black Hundred? To keep them away from the true daughter? Her mind grew bewildered over such possibilities. The single and only way to settle all doubts was to make this child a prisoner. If she was Hargreave's true daughter he would come out of his hiding.

She heard Florence answering her question: "There is a sum of ten or twelve thousand in the Riverdale bank, under the control of my father's butler. After that is gone, I don't know what will happen to us, Susan and me."

"The door of Miss Farlow's will always be open to you, Florence," replied Susan, with love in her eyes.

This interesting conversation was interrupted by the advent of Norton. He was always dropping in during the late afternoon hours. Florence liked him for two reasons. One was that Jones trusted him to a certain extent and the other was that . . . that she liked him. She finished this sentence in her heart defiantly.

To-day he brought her a box of beautiful roses, and at the sight of them the countess smiled faintly. Set the wind in that quarter? She could have laughed. Here was her revenge against this meddler who took no particular notice of her while Florence was in the room. She would encourage him, poor grubbing newspaper writer, with his beggarly pittance! What chance had he of marrying this girl with millions within reach of her hand?

The peculiar thing about this was that Norton was entertaining the same thought at the same time: what earthly chance had he?

In the second-story window of the house over the way there was a worried man. But when his glasses brought in range the true contents of the box he laughed sardonically. "This watching is getting my goat. I smell a rat every time I see a shadow." He wiped the lenses of his opera glasses and proceeded to roll a cigarette.

When the countess and Norton went away Jones stole quietly up to Florence's room and threw up the curtain. Two round points of light flashed from the watcher's window, but the saturnine smile on Jones' lips was not observed. He went to the door, opened it cautiously, a hand to his ear. Then he closed the door, turned back the rug and removed a section of the flooring. Out of this cavity he raised a box. There was lettering on the lid; in fact, the name of its owner, Stanley Hargreave. Jones replaced the flooring, tucked the box under his arm and made his exit.

The man lounging in the shadow heard a faint whistle. It was the signal agreed upon. The man Felton ran across the street and boldly rang the bell. It was only then that Florence missed the ever present butler. She hesitated, then sent Susan to the door.

"I must see Mr. Jones upon vitally important business."

"He has gone out," said Susan, and very sensibly closed the door before Felton's foot succeeded in getting inside.

It was time to act. He ran around to the rear. The ladder convinced him that Jones had tricked him. He was wild with rage. He was over the wall in an instant. Away down the back street his eye discovered his man in full flight. He gave chase. As he came to the first corner he was nearly knocked over by a man coming the other way.

"Who are you bumping into?" growled Felton.

"Not so fast, Felton!"

"Who the devil are you?"

The stranger made a sign which Felton instantly recognized.

"Quick! What has happened?"

"Jones has the million and is making his getaway. See him hiking toward the water front?"

The two men began to run.

There followed a thrilling chase. Jones engaged a motorboat and it was speeding seaward when the two pursuers arrived. They were not laggard. There was another boat and they made for it.

"A hundred if you overtake that boat," said Felton's strange companion.

Felton eyed him thoughtfully. There was something familiar about that voice.

Great plumes of water shot up into the air. It did not prove a short race by any means. It took half an hour for the pursuer to overhaul the pursued.

"Is that Jones?"

JONES ENGAGED A MOTOR BOAT

"Yes." Felton fired his revolver into the air in hopes of terrifying Jones' engineer; but there was five hundred dangling before that individual's eyes.

"Let them get a little nearer," shouted the butler.

The engineer let down the speed a notch. The other boat crept up within twenty yards. Jones sought a perfect range. He would have to find this spot again.

"Surrender!" yelled Felton.

In reply Jones raised the precious box and deliberately dropped it into the sea. Then he turned his automatic upon his pursuers and succeeded in setting their boat afire.

All this within the space of an hour. During dinner that night (there was now a cook) Jones walked about the dining-table, rubbing his hands together from time to time.

"Jones," said Florence, "why do you rub your hands like that?"

"Was I rubbing my hands, Miss Florence?" he asked innocently.

CHAPTER VI

"DID you get the range?" asked the countess, when late that night Braine recounted his adventure.

"Range!" he snarled. "My girl, haven't I just told you that I had to fight for my life? My boat was in flames. We had to swim for it till we were picked up by a Long Island barge tug. I don't know what became of the motorman. He must have headed straight for shore. And I'm glad he did. Otherwise he'd be howling for the price of another boat. Olga, for the first time I've had to let one of the boys have a look at my face. Doesn't know the name; but one of these days he'll stumble across it, and the result will be blackmail, unless I push him off into the dark. It was accidental."

The countess leaned forward, her hands tightly clinched.

"But the box!"

Braine made a gesture of despair.

"Leo, are you using any drug these days?"

"Don't make fun of me, Olga," impatiently. "Did you ever see me drink more than a pint of wine or smoke more than two cigars in an evening? Poor fools! What! Let my brain go into the wastebasket for the sake of an hour or so of exhilaration? No, and never will I! I'm keen about the gray matter I've got, and by the Lord Harry, I'm going to keep it. There's only one dope

76

"LEO, ARE YOU USING ANY DRUGS THESE DAYS?"

fiend in the Hundred, and he's one of the best decoys we have; so we let him have his coke whenever he really needs it. But this man Felton has seen my face. Some day he'll see it again, ask questions, and then . . ."

"Then what?"

"A burial at sea," he laughed. The laughter died swifty as it came. "Threw it into eight hundred feet of water, on a bar where the sands are always shifting. He'll never find it, even if he took the range. He could not have got a decent one. The sun was dropping and the shadows were long. He threw the chest into the water and then began pegging away at us, cool as you please, and fired our tank."

"It looks to me as if he had wasted his time."

"That depends. Between you and me and the gatepost, I've a sneaking idea that this man Jones, whom nobody has given any particular attention, is a deep, clever man. He may have been honestly attempting to find a new hiding place; the advertisement in the newspaper may have drawn him. He may have thrown the box over in pure rage at seeing himself checkmated. Again, the whole thing may have been worked up for our benefit, a blind. But if that's the case, Jones has us on the hip, for we can't tell. But we can do what in all probability he expects we'll cease to do—watch him just as shrewdly as before."

Olga caught his hand and drew him down beside her. "I wasn't going to bother you to-night, but it may mean something vital."

"What?" alertly.

For reply she rose and walked over to the light button. She pressed it and the apartment became dark.

"Come over to the window, quick!" She dragged him

across the room. "Over the way, the house with the marble frontage."

A man emerged, lit a cigarette, and walked leisurely down the street.

"No!" she cried, as Braine turned to make for the door doubtless with the intention of finding out who the man was. "Every night after you leave he appears."

"Does he follow me?"

"No. And that's what bothered me at first. I believed he was watching some apartment above. But regularly when I turn out the lights he comes forth. So there's no doubt he watches you enter and takes note of your departure."

"But doesn't follow me. That's odd. What the devil is his idea?"

"I'd give a good deal to learn."

The shadow and the glowing cigarette disappeared around the corner, and the lights in the apartment were turned on again.

"He's gone. You really think he's watching me?"

"He is watching this apartment, I know that much."

And even at that moment the watcher was watching from his vantage behind the corner.

"Suspicious!" he murmured, tossing the cigarette into the gutter. "They're watching me for a change. I'll drop out. I know what I know. It's a great world. It's fine to be alive and kicking on top of it." He went on without haste and took the subway train for down-town.

"Is there any way I could get near him?" asked Braine.

"To-morrow night you might leave by the janitor's entrance. I'll keep the lights on till you're outside. Then

I'll turn them off and you can follow and learn who he is."

"It's mighty important."

"Don't scowl. At your age a wrinkle is apt to remain if you once get it started."

He laughed. "Wrinkles!" She could talk of wrinkles!

"They are more important than you think. Every morning I rub out the wrinkle I go to bed with."

"I wish you could rub out the general stupidity which is wrinkling my brain. I've made three moves and failed in each. What's come over me?"

"Perhaps you've had too many successes. The wheel of chance is always turning around."

"May I smoke?"

"Thanks. At least it proves you still have some consideration for me. You would smoke whether it was agreeable or not. But I like the odor of a good cigar. And it always helps you to think."

Braine lighted his cigar and began his customary pacing. At length he paused.

"Suppose we have a real old-fashioned coaching party out to the old mansion we know about?"

"And what shall we do there?"

"Make the mansion an enchanted castle where sometimes people who enter can't get out. Do you think you could get her to go?"

"I can try."

"Olga, I must have that girl; and I must have her soon. Sometimes I find myself mightily puzzled over the whole thing. If Hargreave is alive, why doesn't he turn up now that it's practically known that his daughter presides over his household? I might understand it if

I didn't know that Hargreave is really afraid of nothing. Where is the man with the five thousand, picked up at sea? What was the reason for Jones carrying that box out in broad daylight? Who is the chap watching across the street? Sometimes I believe in my soul—if I have one!—that Hargreave is playing with us, playing! Well," flinging the half consumed cigar into the grate, "the Black Hundred always goes forward, win or lose, and never forgets."

"We are a fine pair!" said the woman bitterly.

"We are exactly what fate intended us to be. They wrote you down in the book as a beautiful body with a crooked mind. They wrote me down as the devil, doomed to roam the earth's top till I'm killed."

"Killed?"

"Why, yes. I'm not the kind of chap who dies in bed, surrounded by the weeping members of the family, doctor, nurse, and priest. I'm a scoundrel; but it has this saving grace, I enjoy being the scoundrel. Now, I'm going up to the club. There's nothing like a game of billiards or chess to smooth that wrinkle which seems to worry you."

In the great newspaper office there was a mighty racket. Midnight always means pandemonium in the city room of a metropolitan daily. Copy boys were rushing to and fro, messengers and printers with sticky galleys in their hands; reporters were banging away at their typewriters, and intermingling you could hear the ceaseless clickety-click from the telegraph room.

The managing editor came out of his office and approached the desk of the night city editor.

"Editorial page gone down?"

"Twenty minutes ago," said the night city editor.

"I wanted a stick on that Panama rumpus."

"Too late."

"Where's Jim Norton?"

"At the chamber of commerce banquet. The major is going to throw a bomb into the enemy's camp."

"Nothing on the Hargreave stuff?"

"No. Guess I'd better put that in the cubbyhole. He's dead."

"No will found yet?"

"Not a piece as big as a postage stamp."

"That will leave the girl in a tough place. No will, no birth certificate; and, worst of all, no photograph of the old man himself. I don't see why Jim sidestepped this affair. He is the only man in town who knew anything about Hargreave."

"He hasn't given it up; but he wants to cover it on his own, turn the yarn over when he's got it, no false alarms."

"Ah! So that's the game?"

"Yes; and Jim is the sort every paper needs. When the time comes the story turns up, if there is one. Here he is now. Looks like an actor in the fourth act of a drama. Good-looking chap, though."

Norton came in through the outer gates. He was in evening clothes, top hat. A dead cigarette dangled between his lips.

"How much do you want?" asked the night city editor.

"Column and a half."

"Off with your glad rags!"

"Anything good?" asked the managing editor.

"The lid has been jammed on tight. No wine in any restaurant after one o'clock. There'll be a roundup of every gunman in town."

"Good work! Go to it."

It was one o'clock when Norton turned in his last sheet of copy and started for home. Just outside the entrance to the building a man with a slouch hat drawn down over his eyes stepped forward.

"Mr. Norton?"

"Yes." Norton stepped back suspiciously.

The other chuckled, raised and lowered his hat swiftly.

"Good lord!" murmured the reporter.

"Will you take a ride with me in a taxi?"

"All the way to Syracuse, if you say so. Well, I'll be tinker d—d!"

"No names, please!"

What took place in that taxicab was never generally known. But at ten o'clock the next morning Norton surprised the elevator boy by going out. Norton proceeded down-town to the national bank, where he deposited $5,000 in bills of large denominations. The teller had some difficulty in counting them. They stuck together and retained the sodden appearance of money recently submerged in water.

Florence was delighted at the idea of a coaching party. Often during her schoolgirl days she had seen the fashionable coaches go careening along the road, with the sharp, clear note of the bugle rising above the thunder of hoofs and rattling of wheels. Jones was not enthusiastic; neither was he a killjoy.

"But you are to go along, too," said Florence.

"I, Miss Florence?"

"The countess invited you especially. You will **go with a hamper.**"

"Ah, in my capacity as butler; very good, Miss Florence." To her he gave no sign of his secret great satisfaction.

The hour arrived, and the gay party bowled away. They wound in and out of the streets toward the country to the crack of the whip and the blare of the horn. Florence's enjoyment would have been perfect had it not been for the absence of Norton. Why hadn't he been invited? She did not ask because she did not care to disclose to the countess her interest in the reporter. They were nearing the limits of the city, when the coach was forced to take a sharp turn to avoid an automobile in trouble. The man puttering at the engine raised his head. It was Norton, and Florence waved her hand vigorously.

"A coaching party," he murmured; "and your Uncle James was not invited! Oh, very well!" He laughed, and suddenly grew serious. It would not hurt to find out where that coach was going.

He set to work savagely, located the trouble, righted it, and set off for the Hargreave home. He found Susan and bombarded her with questions which to Susan came with the rapidity of rain upon the roof.

"So Jones went along?"

"In his capacity of butler only."

Norton smiled. "Well, I'll take a jaunt out there myself. You are sure of the location?"

"Yes."

"Well, good-by. I'll go as a waiter, since they wouldn't invite me. I'm one of the best little waiters you ever heard of; and all things come to him who waits."

What a pleasant, affable young man he was! thought Susan as she watched him jump into the car and go flying up the street.

Jones was a good deal surprised when Norton turned up at the old Chilton manor.

"What made you come here dressed like this?" the butler demanded.

"I'm a suspicious duffer; maybe that's the reason."

"Do you know anything?"

"Well, no; I can't say that I do. But, hang it, I just had to come out here."

"Maybe it's just as well you did," said Jones moodily.

"I know this place. The housekeeper used to be my nurse, and if she is still on the job she may be of service to us. You don't think they'll question or recognize me?"

"Hardly. I'll put in a word for you. I'll say I sent for you, not knowing if we had enough servants to take care of the luncheon."

"And now I'll go and hunt up Meg."

Sure enough, his old nurse was still in charge of the house; and when her "baby" disclosed his identity she all but fell upon his neck.

"But what are you doing here, dressed up as a waiter?"

"It's a little secret, Meg. I wasn't invited, and the truth is I'm very desperately in love with the young lady in whose honor this coaching party is being given. And . . . maybe she's in danger."

"Danger? What about?"

"The Lord only knows. But show me about the house. I've not been here in so long I've forgotten the run of it. I remember one room with the secret panel and another with a painting that turned. Have they changed them?"

"No; it is just the same here as it used to be. Come along and I'll show you."

Norton inspected the rooms carefully, stowing away

in his mind every detail. He might be worrying about nothing; but so many strange things had happened that it was better to be on the side of caution than on the side of carelessness. He left the house and ran across Jones carrying a basket of wine.

"Here, Norton; take this to the party. I want to reconnoiter."

"All right, m'lud! Say, Jones, how much do you think I'd earn at this job?" comically.

"Get along with you, Mr. Norton. It may be the time to laugh, and then it may not."

"I'm going back into the house and hide behind a secret panel. I've got my revolver. You go to the stables and take a try at my car; see if she works smoothly. We may have to do some hiking. Where is the countess in this?"

"Leave that to me, Mr. Norton," said the butler with his grim smile. "Be off; they are moving back toward the house."

So Norton carried the basket around to the lawn, where it was taken from his hands by the regular servant. He sighed as he saw Florence, laughing and chatting with a man who was a stranger and whom he heard addressed as count. Some friend of the countess, no doubt. Where was all this tangle going to end? He wished he knew. And what a yarn he was going to write some day! It would read like one of Gaboriau's tales. He turned away to wander idly about the grounds, when beyond a clump of cedars he saw three or four men conversing slowly. He got as near as possible, for when three or four men put their heads together and whisper animatedly, it usually means a poker game or something worse. He caught a phrase or two as they came down the wind, and then he knew that the vague suspicion

that had brought him out here had been set in motion by
fate. He heard "Florence" and "the old drawing room;"
and that was enough.

He scurried about for Jones. It was pure luck that
he had had old Meg show him through the house, otherwise he would have forgotten all about the secret panel
in the wall and the painting. Jones shrugged resignedly.
Were these men of the countess' party? Norton couldn't
say.

Norton made his hiding place in safety; and by and
by he could hear the guests moving about in the room.
Then all sounds ceased for a while. A door closed
sharply.

"No; here you must stay, young lady," said a man's
voice.

"What do you mean, sir?" demanded the beloved voice.

"It means that no one will return to this room and that
you will not be missed until it is too late."

The sound of voices stopped abruptly, and something
like scuffling ensued. Later Norton heard the back of
a chair strike the panel and some one sat heavily upon
it. He waited perhaps five minutes; then he gently slid
back the panel. Florence sat bound and gagged under
his very eyes. It was but the work of a moment to lib-
erate her.

"It is I, Jim. Do not speak or make the least noise.
Follow me."

Greatly astonished, Florence obeyed; and the panel
slipped back into place. The room behind the secret
panel had barred windows. To Florence it appeared to
be a real prison.

"How did you get here?" she asked breathlessly.

THE SECRET PANEL

"Something told me to follow you. And something is always going to tell me to follow you, Florence."

She pressed his hand. It was to her as if one of those book heroes had stepped out of a book; only book heroes always had tremendous fortunes and did not have to work for a living. Oddly enough, she was not afraid.

"Who was the man?" he asked.

"The Count Norfeldt. Some one has imposed upon the countess."

"Do you think so?" with a strange look in his eyes.

"What do you mean?"

"Nothing just now. The idea is to get out of here just as quickly as we can. See this painting?" He touched a spot in the wall and the painting slowly swung out like a door. "Come; we make our escape to the side lawn from here."

At the stable they were confronted with the knowledge that Norton's car was out of commission; Jones could do nothing with it. Then Norton suggested that he make an effort to commandeer the limousine of the countess; but there were men about, so the limousine was out of the question.

"Horses!" whispered Jones. "There are several saddle horses, already saddled. How about these people, the owners?"

"Oh, they are beyond reproach. They have doubtless been imposed upon. But let us get aboard first. There will be time to talk later. I'll have to do some explaining, taking these nags off like this. We won't have to ride out in front where the picnickers are. There's a lane back of the stable, and a slight détour brings us back into the main road."

The three mounted and clattered away. To Florence it had the air of a prank. She was beginning to have such confidence in these two inventive men that she felt as if she was never going to be afraid any more.

When the Countess Olga saw the three horses it was 'an effort not to fly into a rage. But secretly she warned her people, who presently gave chase in the limousine, while she prattled and jested and laughed with her company, who were quite unaware that a drama was being enacted right under their very noses. The countess, while she acted superbly, tore her handkerchief into shreds. There was something sinister in the way all their plans fell through at the very moment of consummation; and that night she determined to ask Braine to withdraw from this warfare, which gradually decimated their numbers without getting anywhere toward the goal.

Jones shouted that the limousine was tearing down the road. Something must be done to stop it. He suggested that he drop behind, leave his horse, and take a chance at potting a tire from the shrubbery at the roadside.

"Keep going. Don't stop, Norton, till you are back in town. I'll manage to take good care of myself."

CHAPTER VII

WHEN all three finally met at the Hargreave home Florence suddenly took Jones by the shoulders and kissed him lightly on the cheek. Jones started back, pale and disturbed.

Norton laughed. He did not feel the slightest twinge of jealousy, but he was eaten up with envy, as the old wives say.

"You are wondering if I suspect the Countess Perigoff?" said Jones.

"I am." This man Jones was developing into a very remarkable character. The reporter found himself side glancing at the thin, keen face of this resourceful butler. The lobe of the man's left ear came within range. Norton reached for a cigarette, but his hands shook as he lit it. There was a peculiar little scar in the center of the lobe.

"Well," said Jones, "I can find no evidence that she has been concerned in any of these affairs."

"You are suspicious?"

"Of everybody," looking boldly into the reporter's eyes.

"Of me?" smiling.

"Even of myself sometimes."

Conversation dropped entirely after this declaration.

"You're a taciturn sort of chap."

"Am I?"

"You are. But an agreement is an agreement, and while I'd like to print this story, I'll not. We newspaper men seldom break our word."

Jones held out his hand.

"Sometimes I wish I'd started life right," said the reporter gloomily. "A newspaper man is generally improvident. He never looks ahead for to-morrow. What with my special articles to the magazines, I earn between four and five thousand the year; and I've never been able to save a cent."

"Perhaps you've never really tried," replied Jones, with a glance at his companion. It was a good face, strong in outline; a little careworn, perhaps, but free from any indications of dissipation. "If I had begun life as you did, I'd have made real and solid use of the great men I met. I'd have made financiers help me to invest my earnings, or savings, little as they might be. And to-day I'd be living on the income."

"You never can tell. Perhaps a woman might have made you think of those things; but if you had remained unattached up to thirty-one, as I have, the thought of saving might never have entered your head. A man in my present condition, financially, has no right to think of matrimony."

"It might be the saving of you if you met and married the right woman."

"But the right woman might be heiress to millions. And a poor devil like me could not marry a girl with money and hang on to his self-respect."

"True. But there are always exceptions to all rules in life, except those regarding health. A healthy man is a normal man, and a normal man has no right to re-

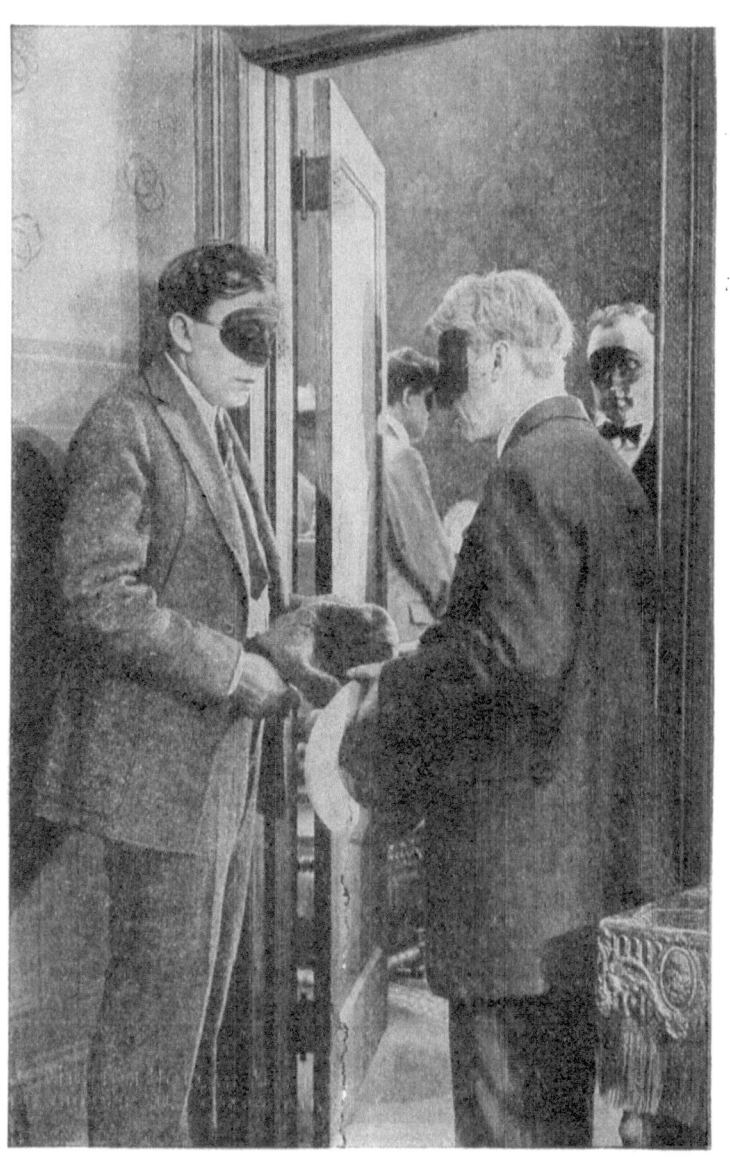

FOUR MEN WERE TOLD OFF

main single. You proved yourself a man this afternoon, considering that you did not know I occupied the wheel seat. Come to think it over, you really saved the day. You gave me the opportunity of steering straight for the police station. Well, good-by."

"Queer duck!" mused the reporter as, after telephoning, he headed for his office. Queer duck, indeed! What a game it was going to be! And this man Jones was playing it like a master. It did not matter that some one else laid down the rules; it was the way in which they were interpreted.

Braine heard of the failure. The Black Hundred was finding its stock far below par value. Four valuable men locked up in the Tombs awaiting trial, to say nothing of the seven gunmen gathered in at the old warehouse. Braine began to suspect that his failures were less due to chance than to calculation, that at last he had encountered a mind which anticipated his every move. He would have recognized this fact earlier had it not been that revenge had temporarily blinded him. The spirit of revenge ever makes for mental clarity.

There was a meeting that night of the Black Hundred. Four men were told off, and they drew their chairs up to Vroon's table for instructions. Braine sat at Vroon's elbow. These four men composed the most dangerous quartet in New York City. They were as daring as they were desperate. They were the men who held up bank messengers and got away with thousands. They had learned to swoop down upon their victims as the hawk swoops down upon the heron. The newspapers referred to them as the "auto bandits," and the men took a deal of pride in the furore they had created.

Vroon went over the Hargreave case minutely; he left

no detail unexplained. Bluntly and frankly, the daughter of Stanley Hargreave must be caught and turned over to the care of the Black Hundred. It must be quick action. Four valuable members were in the Tombs. They might or might not weaken under pressure. For the first time in its American career the organization stood facing actual peril; and its one possible chance of salvation lay in the fact that no one's face was known to his neighbor. He, Vroon, and the boss alone knew who and what each man was. But the plans, the ramifications of the organization might become public property; and that would mean an end to an exceedingly profitable business.

The daughter of Hargreave rode horseback early every morning. She sought the country road. She was invariably attended by the riding master of a school near by.

"You four will make your own plans."

"If she should be injured?"

"Avoid it if possible."

"We have a free hand?"

"Absolutely."

"We risk a bad fall from her horse if it's a spirited one."

"Pretend a breakdown in the road," interpolated Braine. "As they approach, draw and order them to dismount. That method will prevent any accident."

"We'll plan it somehow. It looks easy."

"Nothing is easy where that girl is concerned. A thousand eyes seem to be watching her slightest move."

"We shan't leave anything to chance. How many days will you give us?"

"Seven. A failure, mind you, will prove unhealthy to all concerned," with a menace which made the four stir uneasily.

The telephone rang. Braine reached for the receiver.

"A man just entered the Hargreave house at the rear. Come at once," was the message.

"Is your car outside?" Braine asked.

"We are never without it."

"Then let us be off. No one will stop us for speeding on a side street."

Fourteen minutes by the clock brought the car to a stand at the curb a few houses below the Hargreave home. The men got out. The watcher ran up.

"He is still inside," he whispered.

"Good! Spread out. If any one leaves that house, catch him. If he runs too fast, shoot. We can beat the police."

The man obeyed, and the watcher ran back to his post. He was desperately hoping the affair would terminate to-night. He was growing weary of this eternal vigilance; and it was only his fear of the man known as the boss that kept him at his post. He wanted a night to carouse in, to be with the boys.

The man for whom they were lying in wait was seen presently to creep cautiously round the side of the house. He hugged a corner and paused. They could see the dim outline of his body. The light in the street back of the grounds almost made a silhouette of him. By and by, as if assured that the coast was clear, he stole down to the street.

"Halt!"

Instantly the prowler took to his heels. Two shots rang out. The man was seen to stop, stagger, and then go on desperately.

"He's hit!"

By the time the men reached the corner they heard the

rumble of a motor. One dashed back to the car they had left standing at the curb. He made quick work of the job, but he was not quick enough. Still, they gave chase. They saw the car turn toward the city. But, unfortunately for the success of the chase, several automobiles passed, going into town and leaving it. Checkmate.

Braine was keen enough to-night.

"He is hit; whether badly or not remains to be seen. We can find that out. Drive to the nearest drug store and get a list of hospitals. It's a ten to one shot that we land him somewhere among the hospitals."

But they searched the hospitals in vain. None of them had that night received a shooting case, nor had they heard one reported. The man had been unmistakably hit. He would not have dared risk the loss of time for a bit of play-acting. Evidently he had kept his head and sought his lodgings. To call up doctors would be utter folly; for it would take a week for a thorough combing. This was the second time the man had got away.

"Perhaps I'm to blame," admitted Braine. "I should have advised Miles to stalk him and pot him if he got the chance. There's a master mind working somewhere back of all this, and it's time I woke up to the fact. But you," turning to the auto bandits, "you men have your instructions. More than that, you have been given a free rein. See that you make good, or by the Lord Harry! I'll break the four of you like pipestems."

"We haven't had a failure yet," spoke up one of the men, more courageous than his companions.

"You are not holding up a bank messenger this trip. Remember that. Drive me as far as Columbus Circle.

Leave me on the side street, between the lights, so I can take off this mask."

Later Braine sauntered into Pabst's and ordered a light supper. This night's work, more than anything else, brought home to him the fact that his luck was changing. For years he had proceeded with his shady occupations without encountering any memorable failure. He moved in the high world, quite unsuspected. He had written books, given lectures, been made a lion of, all the while laughing in his sleeve at the gullibility of human nature. But within the last two weeks he had received serious checks. From now on he must move with the utmost caution. Some one was playing his own game, waging warfare unseen. A battle of wits? So be it; but Braine intended to play with rough wits, and he wasn't going to care which way the sword cut.

He hated Stanley Hargreave with all the hatred of his soul; the hatred of a man balked in love. And the man was alive, defying him; alive somewhere in this city this very night, with a bullet under his skin.

"Is everything satisfactory, sir?" he heard the head waiter say.

"Satisfactory?" Braine repeated blankly.

"Yes, sir. You struck the table as though displeased."

"Oh!" Then Braine laughed relievedly. "If I struck the table, it was done unconsciously. I was thinking."

"Beg pardon, sir. Anything else, sir?"

"No. Bring me the check."

"Your master gives riding lessons?"

The groom who had led the horse back from Hargreave's eyed his questioner rather superciliously.

"Yes." The groom fondled the animal's legs.

"How much is it?"

"Twenty dollars for a ticket of five rides. The master is the fashion up here. He doesn't cater to any but the best families."

"Pretty steep. Who was that young lady riding this morning with your master?"

"That's the girl all the newspapers have been talking about," answered the groom importantly.

"Actress?"

"Actress! I should say not. That young woman is the daughter of Stanley Hargreave, the millionaire who was lost at sea. And it won't be long before she puts her finger in a pie of four or five millions. If you want any rides, you'll have to talk it over with the boss. He may or may not take any more rides. You'd probably have to ride in the afternoon, anyhow, as every nag is out in the morning."

"Where's the most popular road?"

"Toward the park; but Miss Hargreave always goes along the riverside road. She doesn't like strangers about."

"Oh, I see. Well, I'll drop in this afternoon and see your master. They say that riding is good for a torpid liver. Have a cigar?"

"Thanks."

The groom proceeded into the stables and the affable stranger took himself off.

A free rein; they could work it to suit themselves. There wasn't the least obstacle in the way. On the face of it, it appeared to be the simplest job they had yet undertaken. To get rid of the riding master in some natural way after he and the girl had started. It was like falling off a log.

"Susan," said Florence, as she came into breakfast after her exhilarating ride, "did you hear pistol shots last night?"

"I heard some noise, but I was so sleepy I didn't try to figure out what it was."

"Did you, Jones?"

"Yes, Miss Florence. The shots came from the street. A policeman came running up later and said he saw two automobiles on the run. But evidently there wasn't anybody hurt. One has to be careful at night nowadays. There are pretty bad men abroad. Did you enjoy the ride?"

"Very much. But there were some spots of blood on the walk near the corner."

"Blood?" Jones caught the back of a chair to steady himself.

"Yes. So some one was hurt. Oh, let's leave this place!" impulsively. "Let us go back to Miss Farlow's. You could find a place in the village, Jones. But if I stay here much longer in this state of unrest I shall lose faith in everything and everybody. Whoever my father's enemies are, they do not lack persistence. They have made two attempts against my liberty, and sooner or later they will succeed. I keep looking over my shoulder all the time. If I hear a noise I jump."

"Miss Florence, if I thought it wise, you should be packed off to Miss Farlow's this minute. But not an hour of the day or night passes without this house being watched. I seldom see anybody about. I can only sense the presence of a watcher. At Miss Farlow's you would be far more like a prisoner than here. I could not accompany you. I am forbidden to desert this house."

"My father's orders?"

Jones signified neither one way nor the other. He merely gazed stolidly at the rug.

"That blood!" She sprang from her chair, horrified. "It was his! He was here last night and they shot him! Oh!"

"There, there, Miss Florence! The man was only slightly wounded. He's where they never will look for him." Then Jones continued, as with an effort: "Trust me, Miss Florence. It would not pay to run away. The whole affair would be repeated elsewhere. We might go to the other end of the world, but it would not serve us in the least. It is not a question of escape, but of who shall vanquish the other. There is nothing to do but remain here and fight, fight, fight. We have put four of them in the Tombs, to say nothing of the gunmen. That is what we must do—put them in a safe place, one by one, till we reach the master. Then only may we breathe in safety. But if they watch, so do we. There is never a moment when help is not within reach, no matter where you go. So long as you do not deceive me, no real harm shall befall you. Don't cry. Be your father's daughter, as I am his servant."

"I am very unhappy!" And Florence threw her arms around Susan and laid her head upon her friend's shoulder.

"Poor child!" Susan, however, recognized the wisdom of Jones' statements. They were safest here.

The morning rides continued. To the girl, who loved the open, it was glorious fun. Those mad gallops along the roads, the smell of earth and sea, the tingle in the blood, were the second best moments of the day. The first? She invariably blushed when she considered what these first best moments were. He was a brave young man, good to look at, witty, and always cheerful. Why shouldn't she like him? Even Jones liked him—Jones, who didn't seem to like anybody. It did not matter whether he was wise or not; a worldly point of view was farthest from her youthful thoughts. It was her own affair; her own heart.

Five days later, as she and the riding master were cantering along the road, enjoying every bit of it, they heard the beat of hoofs behind. They drew up and turned. A rider was approaching them at a run. It was the head groom. The man stopped his horse in a cloud of dust.

"Sir, the stables are on fire."

"Fire?"

All the riding master's savings were invested in the stables. The fact that he had solemnly promised never to leave Florence alone, and that he had accepted a generous bonus slipped from his mind at the thought of fire, a terrible word to any horseman. He wheeled and started off at breakneck speed, his head groom clattering behind him.

Florence naturally wondered which of two courses to pursue: follow them, when she would be perfectly helpless to aid them, or continue the ride and save at least one horse from the terror of seeing flames. She chose the latter. But she did not ride with the earlier zest. She felt depressed. She loved horses, and the thought of them dying in those wooden stables was horrifying.

The fire, however, proved to be incipient. But it was plainly incendiary. Some one had set fire to the stables with a purpose in view. Norton recognized this fact almost as soon as the firemen. He had come this morning with the idea of surprising Florence. He was going out on horseback to join her.

His spine grew suddenly cold. A trap! She had been left alone on the road! He ran over to the garage, secured a car, and went humming out toward the river road. A trap, and only by the sheerest luck had he turned up in time.

Meantime Florence was walking her mount slowly. For once the scenery passed unobserved. She was deeply engrossed with thoughts, some of which were happy and some of which were sad. If only her father could be with her she would be the happiest girl alive.

She was brought out of her revery by the sight of a man staggering along the road ahead of her. Finally he plunged upon his face in the road. Like the tender-hearted girl she was, she stopped, dismounted, and ran to the fallen man to give him aid. She suddenly found her wrists clasped in two hands like iron. The man rose to his feet, smiling evilly. She struggled wildly but futilely.

"Better be sensible," he said. "I am stronger than you are. And I don't wish to hurt you. Walk on ahead of me. It will be utterly useless to scream or cry out. You can see for yourself that we are in a deserted part of the road. If you will promise to act sensibly I shan't lay a hand on you. Do you see that hut yonder, near the fork in the road? We'll stop there. Now, march!"

She dropped her handkerchief, later her bracelet, and finally her crop, in hope that these slight clues might bring her help. She knew that Jones would hear of the fire, and, finding that she had not returned with the riding master, would immediately start out in pursuit.

"BETTER BE SENSIBLE," HE SAID

She was beginning to grow very fond of Jones, who never spoke unless spoken to, who was always at hand, faithful and loyal.

From afar came the low rumble of a motor. She wondered if her captor heard it. He did, but his ears tricked him into believing that it came from another direction. Eventually they arrived at the hut, and Florence was forced to enter. The man locked the door and waited outside for the automobile which he was expecting. He was rather dumfounded when he saw that it was coming from the city, not going toward it.

It was Norton. The riderless horse told him enough; the handkerchief and bracelet and crop led him straight for the hut.

The man before the hut realized by this time that he had made a mistake. He attempted to re-enter the hut and prepare to defend it till his companions hove in sight. But Florence, recognizing Norton, held the door with all her strength. The man snarled and turned toward Norton, only to receive a smashing blow on the jaw.

Norton flung open the door. "Into the car, Florence! There's another car coming up the road. Hurry!"

It was not a long chase. The car of the auto bandits, looking like an ordinary taxicab, was a high-powered machine, and it gained swiftly on Norton's four-cylinder. The reporter waited grimly.

"Keep your head down!" he warned Florence. "I'm going to take a pot at their tires when they get within range. If I miss I'm afraid we'll have trouble. Under no circumstances attempt to leave this car. Here they come!"

He suddenly leaned back and fired. It was only

chance.   The manner in which the cars were lurching made a poor target for a marksman even of the first order.   Chance directed Norton's first bullet into the right forward tire, which exploded.   Going at sixty-odd miles an hour, they could not stop the car in time to avoid fatality.   The car careened wildly and plunged down the embankment into the river.

Florence covered her eyes with her hands, and, quite unconscious of what he was doing, Norton put his arms around her.

CHAPTER VIII

AFTER the affair of the auto bandits—three of whom were killed—a lull followed. If you're a sailor you know what kind of a lull I mean—blue-black clouds down the southwest horizon, the water crinkly, the booms wabbling. Suddenly a series of "accidents" began to happen to Norton. At first he did not give the matter much thought. The safe which fell almost at his feet and crashed through the sidewalk merely induced him to believe he was lucky. At another time an automobile came furiously around a corner while he was crossing the street, and only amazing agility saved him from bodily hurt. The car was out of sight when he thought to recall the number.

Then came the jolt in the subway. Only a desperate grab by one of the guards saved him from being crushed to death. Even then he thought nothing. But when a new box of cigarettes arrived and he tried one and found it strangely perfumed, and, upon further analysis, found it to contain a Javanese narcotic, a slow but sure death, he became wide awake enough. They were after him. He began to walk carefully, to keep in public places as often as he possibly could.

He was not really afraid of death, but he did abhor the thought of its coming up from behind. Except for the cigarettes they were all "accidents;" he could not

103

have proved anything before a jury of his intimate friends.

He never entered an elevator without scrupulous care. He never passed under coverings over the sidewalks where construction was going on. Still, careful as he was, death confronted him once more. It was his habit to have his coffee and rolls—he rarely ate anything more for his breakfast—set down outside his door every morning. The coffee, being in a silver thermos bottle, kept its heat for hours. When he took the stopper out and poured forth a cup it looked oddly black, discolored. It is quite probable that had there been no series of "accidents" he would have drunk a cup—and died in mortal agony. It contained bichloride of mercury.

Very quietly he set about to make inquiries. This was really becoming serious. In the kitchens down-stairs nothing could be learned. The maid had set the thermos bottle before the door at ten-thirty. Norton had opened the door at one-thirty—three hours after. The outlook was not the cheerfulest. He knew perfectly well why all these things "happened;" he had interfered with the plans of the scoundrels who were making every possible move to kidnap Florence Hargreave.

One afternoon he paid Florence a visit. Of course he told her nothing. They had become secretly engaged the day after he had rescued her from the auto bandits. They were secretly engaged because Florence wanted it so. For once Jones suspected nothing. Why should he? He had troubles enough. As a matter of fact, Norton was afraid of him in the same sense as a boy is afraid of a policeman.

But on this day, when the time came, he accosted the butler and drew him into the pantry.

THEY HAD BECOME SECRETLY ENGAGED

"Jones, they are after me now."

"You?   Explain."

Norton briefly recounted the deliberate attempts against his life.

"You see, I'm not liar enough to say that I'm not worried. I am, devilishly worried. I'm not worth any ransom. I'm in the way, and they seem determined to put me out of it."

"To any other man I would say travel. But to you I say when you leave your rooms don't go where you first thought you would—that is, some usual haunt. They'll be everywhere, near your restaurants, your clubs, your office. You're a methodical young man; become erratic. Keep away from here for at least three days, but always call me up by telephone some time during the day. Never under any circumstance, unless I send for you, come here at night. Only one man now watches the house during the day, but five are prowling around after dark. They might have instructions to shoot you on sight. I can't spare you just at present, Mr. Norton. You've been a godsend; and if it seems that sometimes I did not trust you fully it was because I did not care to drag you in too deep."

Deep? Norton thought of Florence and smiled inwardly. Could anybody be in deeper than he was? Once it was on the tip of his tongue to confess his love for Florence, but the gravity of Jones' countenance was an obstacle to such move; it did not invite it.

To be sure, Jones had no real authority to say what Florence should or should not do with her heart. Still, from all points of view, it was better to keep the affair under the rose till there came a more propitious hour in which to make the disclosure.

Love, in the midst of all these alarms! Sharp, desperate rogues on one side, millions on the other, and yet love could enter the scene serenely, like an actor who had missed his cue and come on too soon.

Oddly enough, there was no real love-making such as you often read about. A pressure of the hand, a glance from the eye, there was seldom anything more. Only once—that memorable day on the river road—had he kissed her. No word of love had been spoken on either side. In that wild moment all conventionalities had disappeared like smoke in the wind. There had been neither past nor future, only the present in which they knew that they loved. With her he was happy, for he had no time to plan over the future. Away from her he saw the inevitable barriers providing against the marriage between a poor young man and a very rich young woman. A man who has any respect for himself wants always to be on equal terms with his wife. It's the way this peculiar organization called society has written down its rules. Doubtless a relic of the stone age, when Ab went out with his club to seek a wife and drag her by the hair to his den, there to care for her and to guard her with his life's blood. It is one of the few primitive sensations that remain to us, this wanting the female dependent upon the male. Perhaps this accounts for man's lack of interest on the suffragette question.

Only Susan suspected the true state of affairs, being a woman. Having had no real romance herself, she delighted in having a second-hand one, as you might say. She intercepted many a glance and pretended not to see the stolen hand pressures. The wedding was already full drawn in her mind's eye. These two young people should be married at Susan Farlow's when the roses

ITH HER HE WAS HAPPY, FOR HE HAD NO TIME TO PLAN OVER THE FUTURE

were climbing up the sides of the house and the young robins were boldly trying their fuzzy wings. It struck her as rather strange, but she could not conjure up (at this wedding) more than two men besides the minister, the bridegroom and the butler.

By forsaking his accustomed haunts, under the advice of Jones, the hidden warfare ceased temporarily. You can't very well kill a man when you don't know where to find him. He ate his breakfasts haphazardly, now here, now there. He received most of his assignments by telephone and wrote his stories and articles in his club, in the writing rooms of hotels, and invariably despatched them to the office by messenger. The managing editor wanted to know what all this meant; but Norton declined to tell him.

It irked him to be forced to rearrange his daily life— his habits. It was a revolution against his ease, for he loved ease when he was not at work. He had the sensation of having been suddenly robbed of his home, of having been cast out into the streets. And on top of all this he had to go and fall in love!

There was no longer a shadow opposite the apartments of the Countess Perigoff. Braine came and went nightly without discovering any one. This rather worried him. It gave him the impression that the shadow had found out what he had been seeking and no longer needed to watch the coming and going of either himself or the Countess Perigoff.

"Olga, it looks as if we were at the end of our rope," he said discouragedly. "We have failed in our attempts so far. The devil watches over that girl."

"Or God," replied the countess gloomily. In nearly every instance their success has been due to chance.

"Somehow I'm convinced that we began wrong. We should have let Hargreave escape quietly, followed him, and made him fast when the right opportunity came. After a month or so his vigilance would have relaxed; he would have arrived at the belief that he had eluded us."

"Indeed!" ironically. "He wasn't vigilant all these years in which he did elude us. How about the child he never sought but guarded? Vigilance! He never was anything else all these seventeen years. The truth is, success has developed a coarseness in our methods. And now it is too late for finesse. We have tried every device we can think of; and there they are—the girl free, Norton unharmed, and the father as secure in his retreat as though he wore an invisible cloak. My head aches. I have ceased to be inventive."

"The two are in love with each other."

"Are you sure of that?"

"I have my eyes. But I begin to wonder."

"About what?"

"Whether or not Jones suspects me and is giving me rope to hang myself with. Not once have the police been called in and told what has really happened. They are totally at sea. And what has become of the man over the way?"

"By the Lord Harry!" exclaimed Braine, clapping his hands. "I believe I've solved that. We shot a man coming out of Hargreave's. Since then there's been no one across the way. One and the same man!"

"But that knowledge doesn't get us anywhere."

"No. You say they are in love?"

"Secretly. I don't believe the butler has an inkling of it. It is possible, however, that Susan has caught the

THEY WERE TO BE MARRIED

trend of affairs. But, being rather romantic, she will in nowise interfere."

Braine smoked in silence. Presently a smile twisted his lips.

"You have thought of something?" she asked.

"You might try it," he said. "They have accepted your friendship; whether with ulterior purpose remains to be learned. She has been to your apartments two or three times to tea and always got home safely."

"No," she said determinedly. "Nothing shall happen here. I will not take the risk."

"Wait till I'm through. Break up the romance in such a way that the girl will bar Norton from the house. That's what we've been aiming at; to get rid of that meddling reporter. We've tried poisons. Try your kind."

"What do you mean?"

"Lies."

"Ah! I understand. You want me to win him away from her. It can not be done."

"Pshaw! You have a bag full of tricks. You can easily manage to put him into an equivocal position out of which he can not possibly squirm so far as the girl is concerned. A little melodrama, arranged for the benefit of Florence. Fall into Norton's arms at the right moment, or something like that."

"I suppose I could. But if I failed . . ."

"You're too damnably clever to fail in your own particular work. Something has got to be done to keep those two apart. I've often thought of raiding the house and boldly carrying off the whole family, Susan and all. But a wholesale affair like that would be too noisy. Think it over, Olga; we have gone too far to back down now.

There's always Russia ; and while I'm the boss over here they never cease to watch me. They'll make me answer for a failure like this."

She eyed him speculatively. "You have money."

"Oh, the money doesn't matter. It's the game. It's the game of playing fast and loose with society, of pilfering it with one hand and making it kow-tow with the other. It's the sport of the thing. What was your thought ?"

"We could go away together, to South America."

"And tire of each other within a month," he retorted shrewdly. "No ; we are in the same boat. We could not live but for this never-ending excitement. And, more than that, we never could get far enough away from the long árm of the First Ten. We'll have to stick it out here. Can't you see ?"

"Yes, I can see."

But in her heart she knew that she would have lived in a hut with this man till the end of her days. She abhorred the life, though she never, by the slightest word, let him become aware of it. There was always that abiding fear that at the first sign of weakness he would desert her. And she was wise in her deductions. Braine was loyal to her because she held his interest. Once that failed, he would be off and away.

The next afternoon the countess, having matured her plans against the happiness of the young girl who trusted her, drew up before the Hargreave place and alighted. Her welcome was the same as ever, and this strengthened her confidence.

The countess was always gesticulating. Her hands fluttered to emphasize her words. And the beautiful diamond solitaire caught the girl's eye. She seized the hand. Having an affair of her own, it was natural that she should be interested in that of her friend.

"I never saw that ring before."

"A gift of yesterday." The countess assumed a shy air which would have deceived St. Anthony. She twisted the ring on her finger.

"Tell me," cried Florence. "You are engaged?"

"Mercy, no!"

"Is he rich?"

"No. Money should not matter when your heart is involved."

As this thought was in accord with her own, Florence nodded her head sagely.

"It's nothing serious. Just a fancy. I shall never marry again. Men are gay deceivers; they always have been and always will be. Perhaps I'm a bit wicked; but I rather like to prove my theory that all men are weak. If I had a daughter I'd rather have her be an old man's darling than a young man's drudge. I distrust every man I know. I came to ask you and Susan to go to the opera with me to-night. You will come to my apartments first. You will come?"

"To be sure we will!"

"Simple little fool!" thought the Russian on the way home. "She shall see."

"I believe the countess is engaged to be married," said Florence to Jones.

"Indeed, miss?"

"Yes. I couldn't get anything definite out of her, but she had a beautiful ring on her finger. She wants Susan and me to go to the opera with her to-night. Will that be all right?"

Jones gazed abstractedly at the rug. Whenever a problem bothered him he seemed to find the solution in the delicate patterns of the Persian rugs. Finally he nodded. "I see no reason why you should not go. Only, watch out."

"Jones, there is one thing that will make me brave and happy. Will you tell me if you are in direct communication with my father?"

"Yes, Miss Florence," he answered promptly. "But do not breathe this to a single soul, neither Susan nor Norton."

"I promise that. But, ah! hasten the day when he can come to me without fear."

"That is my wish also."

"You need not call me miss. Why should you?"

"It might not be wise to have any one hear me call you thus familiarly," he objected gravely.

"Please yourself about that. Now I must telephone Jim."

"Jim?" the butler murmured.

He caught the word which was not intended for his ears. But for once Jones had been startled out of himself.

"Is it wrong for me to call Mr. Norton Jim?" she asked with a bit of banter.

"It is not considered quite the proper thing, Miss Florence, to call a young man by his first name unless you are engaged to marry him, or grew up with him from childhood."

"Well, supposing I were engaged to him?" haughtily.

"That would be a very grave affair. What have you to prove that he may not wish to marry you for your money?"

"Why, Jones, you know that I haven't a penny in the

world I can call my own! There is nothing to prove, except your word, that I am Stanley Hargreave's daughter."

"No, there is nothing to prove that you are his daughter. But hasn't it ever occurred to you that there might be a purpose back of this? Might it not be of inestimable value that your father's enemies should be left in doubt? Might it not be a means of holding them on the leash? There is proof, ample proof, my child; and when the time comes these will be shown you. But meantime put all thought of marrying Mr. Norton out of your mind."

"That I refuse to do," quietly. "I am at least mistress of my heart; and no one shall dictate to me whom I shall or shall not marry. I love Mr. Norton and he loves me, knowing that I may not be an heiress after all. And some day I shall marry him."

Jones bowed. This seemed to appear final to him, and nothing more was to be said.

Norton did not return to his rooms till seven. He found the telephone call and also a note in a handwriting unfamiliar. He tore off the envelope and found the contents to be from the Countess Perigoff.

"Call at eight to-night," he read. "I have an important news story for you. Tell no one, as I can not be involved in the case. Cordially, Olga, Countess Perigoff."

Humph! Norton twiddled the note in his fingers and at length rolled it into a ball and threw it into the wastebasket. He, too, made a mistake; he should have kept that note. He dressed, dined, and hurried off to the apartments of the countess.

He arrived ten minutes before Florence and Susan.

And Jones did some rapid telephoning.

"How long, how long!" the butler murmured. How

long would this strange combat last? The strain was terrible. He slept but little during the nights, for his ears were always waiting for sounds. He had cast the chest into the sea, and it would take a dozen expert divers to locate it. And now, atop of all these worries, the child must fall in love with the first comer! It was heartbreaking. Norton, so far as he had learned, was cool and brave, honest and reliable in a pinch; but as the husband of Stanley Hargreave's daughter, that was altogether a different matter. And he must devise some means of putting a stop to it, but—

But he was saved that trouble.

Mongoose and cobra, that was the game being played; the cunning of the one against the deadly venom of the other. If he forced matters he would only lay himself open to the strike of the snake. He must have patience. Gradually they were breaking the organization, lopping off a branch here and there, but the peace of the future depended upon getting a grip on the spine of the cobra himself.

The trick was simple. The countess had news; trust her for that. She exhibited a cablegram, dated at Gibraltar, in which the British authorities stated definitely that no such a person as William Orts, aviator, had arrived at Gibraltar. And then, as Norton rose, she rose also and gently precipitated herself into his arms, just at the moment when Florence appeared in the doorway.

Very simple, indeed. When a woman falls toward a man there is nothing for him to do but extend his arms to prevent her from falling. Outwardly, however, to the eye which saw only the picture and comprehended not the cause, it had all the hallmarks of an affectionate embrace.

Florence stood perfectly still for a moment, then turned away.

"I beg your pardon," said the countess, "but a sudden fainting spell seized me. My heart is a bit weak."

"Don't mention it," replied the gallant Norton. He was as innocent as a babe as to what had really taken place.

Florence went back home. She wrote a brief note to Norton and inclosed the ring which she had secretly worn attached to a little chain around her neck.

When Norton came the next day she refused to see him. It was all over. She never wished to see him again.

"He says there has been some cruel mistake," said Jones.

"I saw him with the countess in his arms. I do not see any cruel mistake in that. I saw him. Tell him so. And add that I never wish to see him again."

Then she ran swiftly to her room, where she broke down and cried bitterly and would not be comforted by Susan.

"In heaven's name, what has happened?" demanded the frantic lover, "what has happened?"

The comedy of the whole affair lay in the fact that neither of the two suspected the countess, who consoled them both.

CHAPTER IX

S O FAR as Jones was concerned, he was rather pleased with the turn of affairs. This was no time for love-making; no time for silly, innocuous quarrels and bickerings, in which love must indulge or die. Florence no longer rode horseback, and Norton returned to his accustomed haunts, where no one made the slightest attempt upon his life. In his present state of mind he would have welcomed it.

"What's the matter with Jim?" asked the night city editor, raising his eye shade.

"I don't know," answered the copy reader.

"Goes around as if he'd been eating dope; bumped into the boss a while ago and never stopped to apologize."

"Perhaps he's mapping out the front page for that Hargreave stuff," laughed the copy reader. "Between you and me and the gate post, I don't believe there ever was a man by the name of Hargreave."

"Oh, there was a chap by that name, all right. He's dead. A man can't swim three hundred miles in rough water, life-buoy or no. They ought to have funeral services, and let it go at that."

"But what was the reason for that fake cable from Gibraltar saying that Orts was alive? I don't see any sense in that."

"The man who pulled it off did. I think, for my part,

116

that both Orts and Hargreave are dead, and that the man picked up by the tramp steamer *Orient* was riding some other balloon."

"You're wrong there. The description of it proved that it was Ort's machine. Oh, Jim probably has got a man's-size yarn up his sleeve, but he's a long time in delivering the goods. He's beginning to mope a good deal. Woman back of it somewhere. Haven't held down this copy job for twelve years without being able to make some tolerable guesses. Jim's a star man. When he gets started nothing can stop him. He covered the Chinese Boxer rebellion better than any other correspondent there. I wonder how old he is?"

"Oh, I should say about thirty-one or two. Here he comes now. 'Lo, Jim!'"

"Hello! Where's Ford? He gave me a ticket to the theater to-night, and I want to punch his head. What's drama coming to, anyhow? Cigarettes and booze and mismated couples. Can't they find good enough things out of doors? Oh, I know. They cater to a lot of fools who believe that what they see is an expression of high life in New York and London. And it's rot, plain rot. It's merely the scum of the boiling pot. Any old housewife would skim it off and chuck it into the slops. Life? Piffle!"

"What's the grouch?"

"Looking for the dramatic job?"

"No. I've just been wondering how far these theatrical managers can go without slitting the golden goose."

Norton sought his desk and began rummaging the drawers. He was not hunting for anything; he was merely passing away the time. By and by, when the pas-

time no longer served, he pulled his chair over to the
window and sat down, staring at stars such as Coperni-
cus never dreamed of. Ships going down to sea, ferries
swooping diagonally hither and thither, the clockwork
signs; but he took no note of these marvels of light.

"Not at home!" he muttered.

He had called, written, telephoned. No use. The door
remained shut, Jones answered the telephone, and the
letters came back. He began to think very deeply con-
cerning the Perigoff woman. Had she played a trick?
Had that fainting spell been buncombe for his benefit as
well as Florence's? But he had not a shadow of a proof.
The thing that puzzled him equally with this was that
all attempts against his life had miraculously ceased; no
safes thundered down in front of him, and no autos
tried to carve him in two. The only thing that kept him
active was the daily call of Jones by wire. Miss Florence
was well; that was all Jones was permitted to say.

Restlessly Norton spurned his chair and walked over
to the telephone booth. It was midnight. He might or
might not be able to get Jones. But almost instantly a
voice said, "What is it?"

"Jones?"

"Yes. Who is it?"

"Norton."

"Why, you called me up not ten minutes ago."

"Not I!"

"It was your voice, as plain as day."

"What did I want?" keen all at once.

The reply did not come immediately.   "You are certain it was not you?"

"Wait a moment and I'll call the editor. He will prove

to you that I've been here for an hour, and that this is the first call I've made. Some one has been imposing on you. What did they ask you to do?"

"You asked me to come down to the office at once, and I requested you to come to the house, and you said you could not. I declined to stir."

"What did you think?"

"Exactly what you're thinking—that they have come to life again."

"Jones, is Miss Florence awake?"

"No."

"Do you think there is any hope of having her understand what really happened?"

"I am only here to guard her. I can not undertake to read her thoughts."

"You're not quite in favor of a reconciliation?"

"Oh, yes, if it went no further. Young people are young people the world over."

"What does that mean?"

"That they would not create imaginary heartaches if they were not young. Better let things remain exactly as they are. When all these troubles are settled finally, the lesser trouble may be talked over sensibly. But this is not the time. There is no news. Good night."

Norton returned to his chair, gloomier than ever. With his feet upon the window sill he stared and stared and dreamed and dreamed till a hand fell upon his shoulder. It belonged to one of the office boys.

"Note f'r you, sir."

Norton read it and tore it into little pieces. Then he rose and distributed the pieces in the several yawning waste baskets which strewed the aisle leading to the city desk.

"I'm not wanted for anything?" he asked.

"No. Clear out!" laughed the night city editor. "The sight of you is putting everybody in the gloom ward."

Norton went down to the street. At the left of the entrance he was quietly joined by a man whose arm was carried in a sling. He motioned Norton to get into the taxicab. They were dropped in a deserted spot in River-dale. On foot they went forward to their destination, which proved to be the deserted hangar of the aviator, William Orts.

"I want you to tell Jones that a tub and several divers are at work on the spot where he threw the chest. That's all. Now, doctor, rewind this arm of mine."

The amateur surgeon made a very good job of it; not for nothing had he followed fighting armies to the front.

"Did they find anything?"

"Not up to date. But we might if we cared to. They have left a buoy over the spot they're exploring. But just now it floats a quarter of a mile to the east of the spot."

"Who were the men in the motor boat that chased Jones?"

"Only Jones can tell you. Queer old codger, eh?"

"A bit stubborn. He wants to handle it without police assistance."

"And he's right. We are not aiming to arrest any one," sinisterly. "There can't be any draw to this game. Here, no smoking. Too much gas afloat."

Norton put the cigarettes back into his pocket. "What's the real news?" he demanded. "You would not bring me out here just to rebandage that arm. It really did not need it. Come, out with it."

"You're sharp."

"I'm paid to be sharp."

"I've found where the Black Hundred hold their sessions."

"By George, that's news!"

"The room above is vacant. A little hole in the ceiling, and who knows what might happen?"

"What do you want me to do?"

"Tell Jones. When the next meeting comes around I'll advise you. I've stumbled upon a dissatisfied member. So, buck up, as they say. We've got two ends of the net down, and with a little care we'll have them all. Now let me have a hundred."

Norton drew out a packet of bills and counted off five twenties.

"Why don't you draw the cash yourself?"

"It happens to be in your name, son."

"I forgot," said Norton. "But what a chance for me! Nearly five thousand, all mine for a ticket to Algiers!"

A grunt was the only reply.

"I want you to tell me about the Perigoff woman."

"I know only one thing—that Braine is there every night."

"No!"

"The orders are for you to play the game just as you are playing it. When we strike, it must be the last blow. All this hide-and-seek business may look foolish to you. It's like that Japanese game called 'jo.' It looks simple, but chess is a tyro's game beside it. Can you find your way back all right?"

"I can."

"Well, you'd better be going. That's all the light I have, in this torch here. Got a lot to do to-morrow and need sleep."

Norton stole away with great caution. His first inten-

tion was to proceed straight to the city, but despite his
resolution he found himself within a quarter of an hour
gazing up at the windows of the Hargreave house. "Not
at home!"

Quite unconscious of the fact, he was as close to death
as any mortal man might care to be. The policeman suddenly looming up under the arc lamp proved to be his
savior.

The lull made Jones doubly alert. He was positive that
they were preparing to strike again. But from what
direction and in what manner? He had not met the gift
of clairvoyance so he had to wait; and waiting is a terrible game when perhaps death is balancing the scales. It
is always easier to make an assault than to await it; and
it is a good general who always finds himself prepared.

But it made his heart ache to watch the child. She
went about cheerfully—when any one was in the room
with her. Many a time, however, he had stolen to the
door of her bedroom and heard the heart-rending sobs, a
vain attempt being made to stifle them among the pillows.
She was only eighteen; it was first love; and first loves
are pale, evanescent attachments. It hurt now; but she
would get over it presently. Youth forgets. Time, like
water, smooths away the ragged places.

The countess called regularly. She was, of course,
dreadfully sorry over what had happened. She had heard
something about his character; newspaper men weren't
always the best. This one was a mere fortune hunter; a
two-faced one, at that. She was never more surprised in
her life than when he threw his arms around her. And so
on, and so forth, half lies and half truths, till the patient
Jones felt like wringing her neck.

From his vantage point the butler smiled ironically. He could read the heart of the Perigoff woman as he could read the page of a book. The effrontery! And all the while he must gravely admit her and pretend when the blood rioted in his veins at the sight of her. But he dared not swerve a single inch from the plans laid down. It was a cup of bitter gall, and there was no way of avoiding the putting of it to his lips. She emanated poison as nightshade emanates it, the upas tree. And he must bow when she entered and bow when she left! Still, she had done him an indirect favor in breaking up this love business.

One afternoon Braine summoned his runabout and called up two physicians. When he was ushered into the deserted office of the first he sent his card in. The doctor replied in person. His face was pale and his hands shook.

"Good afternoon," said Braine, smiling affably.

The doctor eyed him like a man hypnotized. "You . . . you wished to see me on some particular business?"

"Very particular," dryly. "My car is outside. Will you be so good as to accompany me?"

The doctor slowly went into the hall for his hat and coat. He left the house and got into the car with never a word of protest.

"Thinking?" said Braine.

"I am always thinking whenever I see your evil face. What devilment do you require of me this time?"

"A mere stroke of the pen."

"Where are we going?"

"To call on another physician of your standing," significantly. "It is a great thing to have friends like you two. Always ready to serve us, for the mere love of it."

"There's no need of using that kind of talk to me. You have me in the hollow of your hand. Why should I bother to deny it? I have broken the law. I broke it because I was starving."

"It is better to starve in freedom than to eat fat joints up the river. To-day it is a question of sanity."

"And you want me to assist in signing away the liberty of some person who is perfectly sane?"

"The nail on the head," urbanely.

"You're a fine scoundrel!"

"Not so loud!" warningly.

"As loud as I please. I am not forgetting that you need me. I'm no coward. I recognize that you hold the whip hand. But you can send me to the chair before I'll crawl to you. Now, leave me alone for a while."

The other physician had no such qualms of conscience. He was ready at all times for the generous emoluments which accrued from his dealings with the man Braine.

The Countess Perigoff was indisposed; so it was quite in the order of things that she should summon physicians.

There is a law in the state of New York—just or unjust, whichever you please—that reads that any person may be adjudged insane if the signatures of two registered physicians are affixed to the document. It does not say that these physicians shall have been proved reputable.

There were, besides the physicians, a motherly looking woman and a man of benign countenance. Their faces were valuable assets. To gain another person's confidence is, perhaps, among the greatest human achievements. A confidence man and woman in the real sense of the word. In your mind's eye you could see this man carrying the contribution plate down the aisle on Sunday mornings, and his wife Kate putting her mite on the plate for the benefit of some poor, untidy Hottentot.

On Tuesday of the following week Florence and Susan went shopping. The chauffeur was a strong young fellow whom Jones relied upon. If you pay a man well and hold out fine promises, you generally can trust him. As their car left the corner another followed leisurely. This second automobile contained Thomas Wendt and his wife Kate. The two young women stopped at the great dry goods shop near the public library, and for the time being naturally forgot everything but the marvels which had come from all parts of the world. It is as natural for a woman to buy as it is for a man to sell.

In some manner or other Florence became separated from Susan. She hunted through aisle after aisle, but could not find her; for the simple reason that Susan was hunting for her. It occurred to the girl that Susan might have wisely concluded the best place to wait would be in the taxicab. And so Florence hurried out into the street, into the arms of the Wendt family, who were patiently awaiting her.

The trusted chauffeur had been sent around to the side entrance by the major domo. The young lady had so requested, so he said.

Florence struggled and called for the policeman, who came running up, followed by the usual idle, curious crowd.

"The poor young woman is insane," said the motherly Kate, tears in her eyes. The benign Thomas looked at heaven. "We are her keepers."

"It is not true," cried Florence desperately.

"She has the hallucination that she is the daughter of the millionaire Stanley Hargreave." And Thomas exhibited his document, which was perfectly legal, so far as appearances went.

"Hurry up and get her off the walk. I can't have the crowd growing any larger," said the policeman, convinced.

So, despite her cries and protestations, Florence was hustled into the automobile, even the policeman lending a hand.

"Poor young thing!" he said to the crowd. "Come now, move on. I can't have the walk blocked up. Get a gait on you."

He was congratulating himself upon the orderliness of the affair when a keen-eyed young man in the garb of a chauffeur touched his shoulder.

"What's this I hear about an insane young woman?" he demanded.

"She was insane, all right. They had papers to prove it. She kept crying that she was Stanley Hargreave's daughter."

"My God!" The young man struck his forehead in despair. "You ass, she was Stanley Hargreave's daughter, and they've kidnaped her right under your nose! What was the number of that car?"

"Cut out that line of talk, young fellah; I know my business. They had the proper documents."

"But you hadn't brains enough to inquire whether they were genuine or not! You wait!" shrilled the chauffeur. "I'll have you broken for this work." He wheeled and ran back to his car, to find Susan and the countess in a great state of agitation. "They got her, they got her! And I swore on the book that they never should, so long as I drove the car."

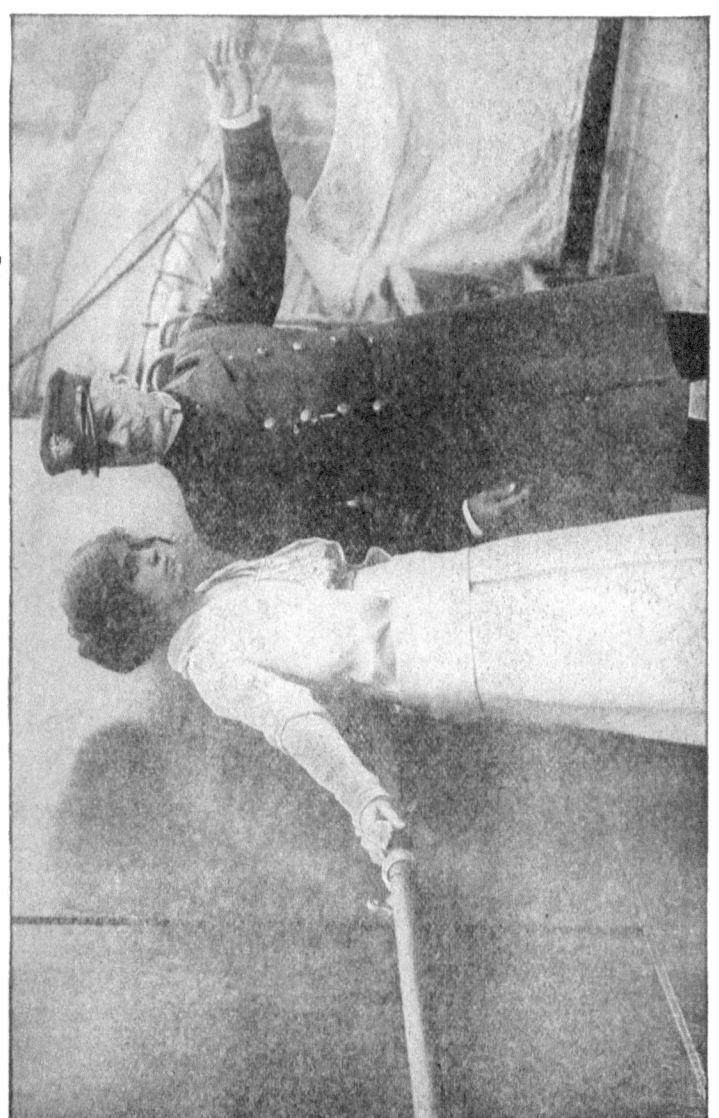

FLORENCE WAS PERMITTED TO WANDER ABOUT THE SHIP AS SHE PLEASED

Susan wept, and the countess tried in vain to console her.

And when Jones was informed he frightened even the countess with the snarl of rage which burned across his lips. He tore into the hall, seized his hat, and was gone. Not a word of reproach did he offer to the chauffeur. He understood that no one is infallible. He found the blundering policeman, who now realized that he stood in for a whiff of the commissioner's carpet. All he could do was to give a good description of the man and woman. Word was sent broadcast through the city. The police had to be informed this time.

Late in the day an officer whose beat included the ferry landing at Hoboken said he had seen the three. Everything had looked all right to him. It was the motherly face of the one and the benign countenance of the other that had blinded him.

At midnight Jones, haggard and with the air of one beaten, returned home.

"No wireless yet?" asked Norton.

"The *George Washington* of the North German Lloyd does not answer. Something has happened to her wires; tampered with, possibly."

"So long as we know they are at sea, we can remedy the evil. They will not be able to land at a single port. I have sent ten cables. They can't get away from the wire. If I could only get hold of the names of those damnable doctors who signed that document! Twenty years."

Jones bent his head in his hands, and Norton tramped the floor till the sound of his footsteps threatened to drive the moaning Susan into hysterics.

"It is only a matter of a few days."

"But can the child stand the terrors?" questioned Jones. "Who knows that they may not really drive her insane?"

On board the *George Washington* every one felt extremely sorry for this beautiful girl. It was a frightful misfortune to be so stricken at her age.

"She is certainly insane," said one of the passengers, who had known Hargreave slightly through some banking business. "Hargreave wasn't married. He lived alone."

After the second day out Florence was permitted to wander about the ship as she pleased.

A good many of the passengers were mightily worried when they learned that the wireless had in some mysterious way been tampered with after the boat had made the open sea. It was impossible to put about. The apparatus must be fixed at sea.

And when finally Norton's wireless caught the wires of the *George Washington* he was gravely informed that the young lady referred to had leaped the rail off the banks at night and had been drowned. She had not been missed till the following morning.

EVERYONE FELT EXTREMELY SORRY FOR THIS BEAUTIFUL GIRL

CHAPTER X

IT was perfectly true that Florence had cast herself into the sea. It had not been an act of despair, however. On the contrary, hope and courage had prompted her to leap. The night was clear, with only a moderate sea running. At the time the great ship was passing the banks, and almost within hail, she saw a fishing schooner riding gracefully at anchor. She quite readily believed that if she remained on board the *George Washington* she was lost. She naturally forgot the marvel of wireless telegraphy. No longer may a man hide at sea.

So, with that quick thought which was a part of her inheritance, she seized the life buoy, climbed the rail and leaped far out. As the great, dark, tossing sea swooped up to meet her she noted a block of wood bobbing up and down. She tried to avoid it, but could not, and struck it head on. Despite the blow and the shock of the chill water she instinctively clung to the buoy. The wash from the mighty propellers tossed her about, hither and yon, from one swirl to another, like a chip of wood. Then everything grew blank.

Fortunately for her the master of the fishing schooner was at the time standing on his quarterdeck by the wheel, squinting through his glass at the liner and envying the ease and comfort of those on board her. The mate, sitting on the steps and smoking his turning-in pipe, saw

129

the master lean forward suddenly, lower the glass, then raise it again.

"Lord A'mighty!"

"What's the matter, Cap'n?"

"Jake, in God's name, come 'ere an' take a peek through this glass. I'm dreamin'!"

The mate jumped and took the glass. "Where away, sir?"

"A p'int off th' sta'board bow. See somethin' white bobbin' up?"

"Yessir! Looks like some one dropped a bolster 'r a piller overboard. . . . Cod's whiskers!" he broke off.

"Then I ain't really seein' things," cried the master. "Hi, y' lubbers," he yelled to the crew; "lower th' dory. · They's a woman in th' water out there. I seen her leap th' rail. Look alive! Sharp's th' word! Mate, you go 'long."

The crew dropped their tasks and sprang for the davits, and the starboard dory was lowered in ship shape style.

It takes a good bit of seamanship to haul a body out of the sea, into a dancing, bobtailed dory, when one moment it is climbing frantically heavenward and the next heading for the bottomless pit. They were very tender with her. They laid her out in the bottom of the boat, with the life buoy as a pillow, and pulled energetically for the schooner. She was alive, because she breathed; but she did not stir so much as an eyelid. It was a stiff bit of work, too, to land her aboard without adding to her injuries. The master ordered the men to put her in his own bunk, where he nearly strangled her by forcing raw brandy down her throat.

"Well, she's alive, anyhow."

When Florence finally opened her eyes the gray of

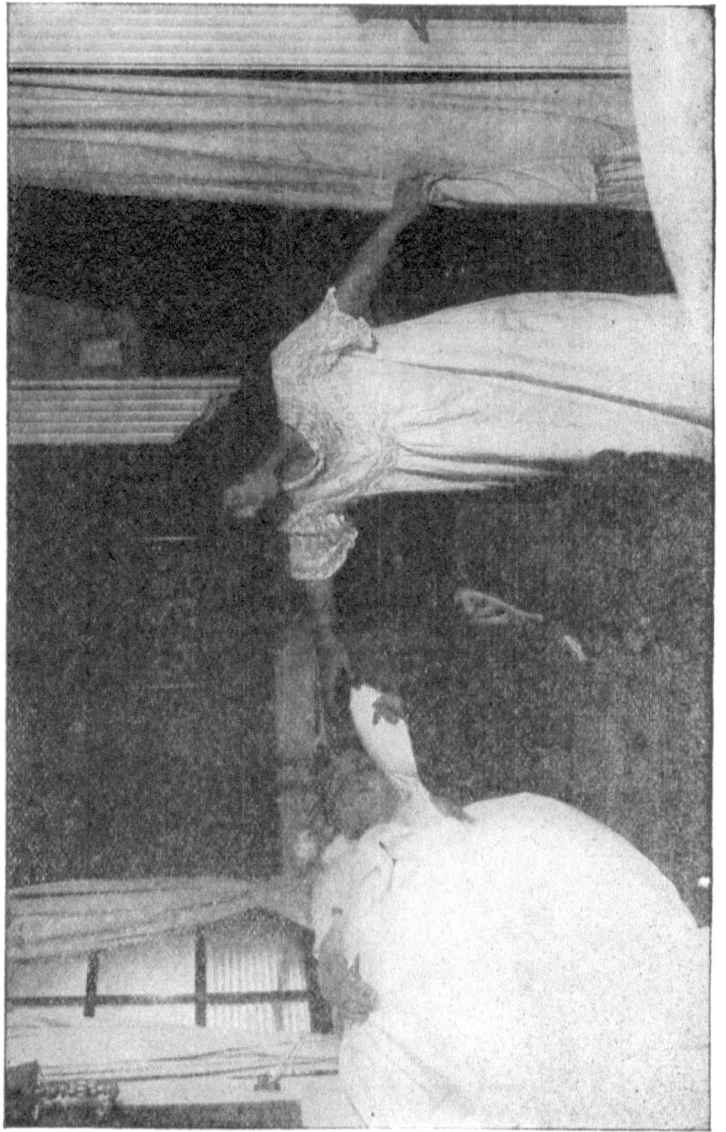

FLORENCE STEALS OUT IN THE NIGHT TO JUMP OVERBOARD

dawn lay upon the sea, dotted here and there by the schooners of the fleet, which seemed to be hanging in midair, as at the moment there was visible to the eye no horizon.

"Don't seem t' recognize nothin'."

"Mebbe she's got a fever," suggested the mate, rubbing his bristly chin.

"Fever nothin'! Not after bein' in th' water half an hour. Mebbe she hit one o' them wooden floats we left. Them dinged liners keep on crowdin' us," growled Barnes, with a fisherman's hate for the floating hotels. "Went by without a toot. See 'er, jes' like the banker's wife goin' t' church on Sunday? A mile a minute; fog or no fog, it's all the same t' them. They run us down and never stop. What th' tarnation we goin' to do? She'll haff t' stay aboard till th' run is over. I can't afford t' yank up my mudhook this time o' day."

"Guess she can stand three 'r four days in our company, smellin' oilcloths, fish, kerosene, an' punk t'bacco."

"If y' don't like th' kind o' t'bacco I buy buy your own. I ain't objectin' none."

The mate stepped over to the bunk and gingerly ran his hand over the girl's head. "Cod's whiskers, Cap'n, they's a bump as big's a cork on th' back o' her head! She's struck one o' them floats all right. Where's the arnica?"

Barnes turned to his locker and rummaged about, finally producing an ancient bottle and some passably clean cloth used frequently for bandages. Sometimes a man grew careless with his knife or got in the way of a pulley block. With blundering kindness the two men bound up the girl's head, and then went about their duties.

For three days Florence evinced not the slightest inclination to leave the bunk. She lay on her back either asleep or with her eyes staring at the beams above her head. She ate just enough to keep her alive; and the strong black coffee did nothing more than to make her wakeful. No one knew what the matter was. There was the bump, now diminished; but that it should leave her in this comatose state vastly puzzled the men. The truth is she had suffered a slight concussion of the brain, and this, atop of all the worry she had had for the last few weeks, was sufficient to cause this blankness of the mind.

The final cod was cleaned and packed away in salt, the mudhook raised, and the schooner *Betty* set her sails for the southwest. Barnes realized that to save the girl she must have a doctor who knew his business. Mrs. Barnes would know how to care for the girl, once she knew what the trouble was. There would be some news in the papers. A young and beautiful woman did not jump from a big Atlantic liner without the newspapers getting hold of the facts.

A fair wind carried the *Betty* into her haven, and shortly after Florence was sleeping peacefully in a feather bed, ancient, it is true, but none the less soft and inviting. In all this time she had not spoken a single word.

"The poor young thing!" murmured the motherly Mrs. Barnes. "What beautiful hair! Oh, John, I wish you would give up the sea. I hate it. It is terrible. I am always watching you in my mind's eye, in calm weather, in storms. Pieces of wrecks come ashore, and I always wonder over the death and terror back of them."

"Don't y' worry none about me, Betty. I never take

"A YOUNG AND BEAUTIFUL WOMAN DID NOT JUMP FROM A BIG ATLANTIC LINER WITHOUT THE NEWSPAPERS GETTING HOLD OF THE FACTS"

no chances. Now I'm goin' int' th' village an' bring back
th' sawbones. He'll tell us what t' do."

The village doctor shook his grizzled head gravely.

"She's been hurt and shocked at the same time. It
will be many days before she comes around to herself.
Just let her do as she pleases. Only keep an eye on her
so that she doesn't wander off and get lost. I'll watch
the newspapers and if I come across anything which
bears upon the case I'll notify you."

But he searched the newspapers in vain, for the simple
fact that he did not think to glance over the old ones.

The village took a good deal of interest in the affair.
They gossiped about it and strolled out to the Barnes'
cottage to satisfy their curiosity. One thing was certain
to their simple minds: some day Barnes would get a great
sum of money for his kindness. They had read about
such things in the family story paper. She was a rich
man's daughter; the ring on the unknown's finger would
have fitted out a fleet.

Florence was soon able to walk about. Ordinary conversation she seemed to understand; but whenever the
past was broached she would shake her head with frowning eyes. Her main diversion consisted of sitting on the
sand dunes and gazing out at sea.

One day a stranger came to town. He said he repre-
sented a life insurance company and was up here from
Boston to take a little vacation. He sat on the hotel
porch that evening surrounded by an admiring audience.
The stranger had been all over the world, so it seemed.
He spoke familiarly of St. Petersburg, Vladivostok,
Shanghai, as the villagers—some of them—might have
spoken of Boston.

There were one or two old-timers among the audience.

They had been to all these parts. The stranger knew what he was telling about. After telling of his many voyages he asked if there was a good bathing beach near by. He was told that he would find the most suitable spot near Captain Barnes' cottage just outside the village.

"An' say, Mister, seen anythin' in th' papers about a missin' young woman?" asked some one.

"Missing young woman? What's that?"

The man told the story of Florence's leap into the sea and her subsequent arrival at the cape.

"That's funny," said the stranger. "I don't recollect reading about any young woman being lost at sea. But those big liners are always keeping such things under cover. Hoodoos the ship, they say, and turns prospective passengers to other lines. It hurts business. What's the young girl look like?"

Florence was described minutely. The stranger teetered in his chair and smoked. Finally he spoke.

"She probably was insane. That's the way generally with insane people. They can't see water or look off a tall building without wanting to jump. My business is insurance, and we've got the thing figured pretty close to the ground. They used to get the best of us on the suicide game. A man would take out a large policy to-day and to-morrow he'd blow his head off, and we'd have to pay his wife. But nowadays a policy is not worth the paper it's written on if a man commits suicide under two years."

"You ain't tryin' to insure anybody in town, are you?"

"Oh, no. No work for me when I'm on my vacation. Well, I'm going to bed; and to-morrow morning I'll go out to Captain Barnes' beach and have a good swim. I'm no sailor, but I like water."

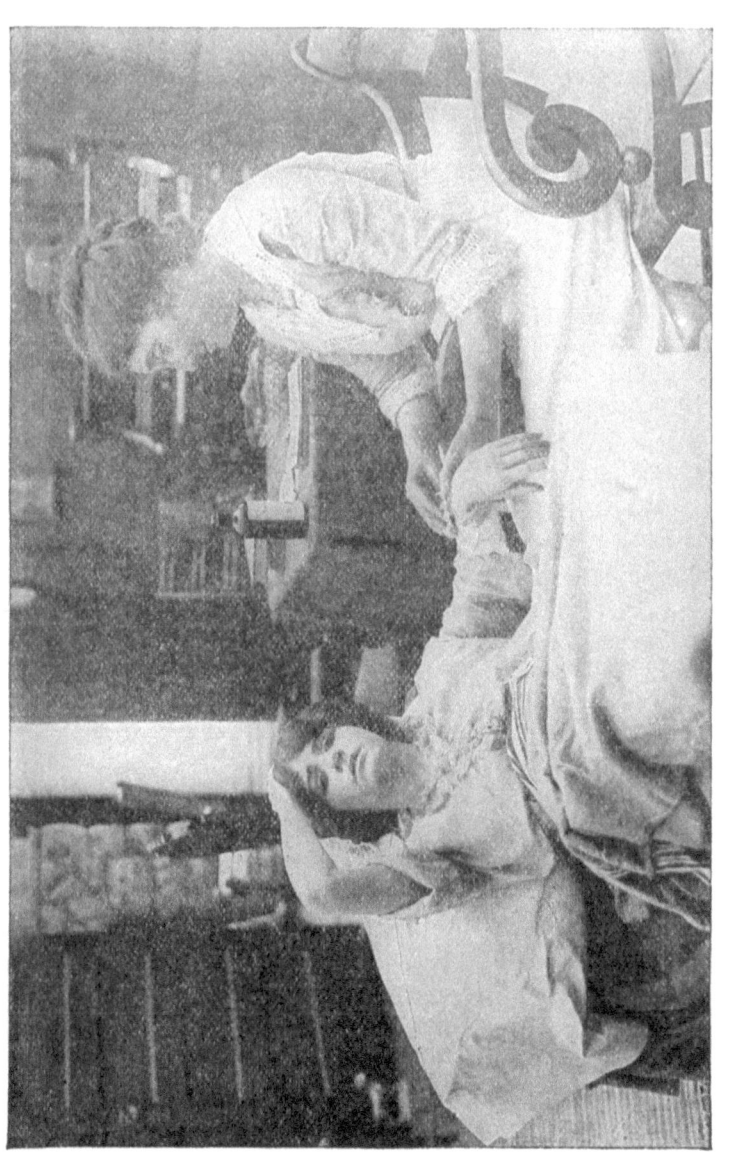

"THE POOR YOUNG THING," MURMURED THE MOTHERLY MRS. BARNES

He honestly enjoyed swimming. Early the next morning he was in the water, frolicking about as playfully as a boy. He had all the time in the world. Over his shoulder he saw two women wandering down toward the beach. Deeper he went, farther out. He was a bold swimmer, but that did not prevent a sudden and violent attack of cramps. And it was a rare piece of irony that the poor girl should save the life of that scoundrel who was without pity or mercy. As she saw his face a startled frown marred her brow. But she could not figure out the puzzle. Had she ever seen the man before? She did not know, she could not tell. Why could not she remember? Why must her poor head ache so when she tried to pierce the wall of darkness which surrounded her mentally?

The man thanked her feebly, but not in his heart. When he had sufficiently recovered he returned to the village and sought the railway station, where the Western Union had its office.

"I want to send a code message to my firm. Do you think you can follow it?"

"I can try," said the operator.

The code was really Slav; and when the long message was signed it was signed by the name Vroon.

The day after the news came that Florence had jumped overboard off the banks, Vroon with a dozen other men had started out to comb all the fishing villages along the New England coast. Somewhere along the way he felt confident that he would learn whether the girl was dead or alive. If she was dead then the game was a draw, but if she was alive there was still a fighting chance for the Black Hundred. He had had some idea of remaining in the village and accomplishing the work himself; but after deliberation he concluded that it was important enough for Braine himself to take a hand in. So the following night he departed for Boston, from there to New York. He proceeded at once to the apartment of the countess, where Braine declared that he himself would go to the obscure village and claim Florence as his own child. But to insure absolute success they would charter Morse's yacht and steam right up into the primitive harbor.

When Vroon left the apartment Norton saw him. He was a man of impulses, and he had found by experience that first impulses are generally the best. He did not know who Vroon was. Any man who called on the Countess Perigoff while Braine was with her would be worth following.

On the other hand, Vroon recognized the reporter instantly and with that ever-ready and alert mind of his set about to lure the young man into a trap out of which he might not easily come.

Norton decided to follow his man. He might be going on a wild-goose chase, he reasoned; still his first impulses had hitherto served him well. He looked careworn. He was convinced that Florence was dead, despite the assertions of Jones to the contrary. He had gone over all the mishaps which had taken place and he was now absolutely convinced that his whilom friend Braine and the Countess Perigoff were directly concerned. Florence had either been going to or coming from the apartment. And that memorable day of the abduction the countess had been in the dry goods shop.

Vroon took a down-town surface car, and Norton took the same. He sat huddled in a corner, never suspecting that Vroon was watching him from a corner of his eye. Norton was not keen to-day. The thought of Florence kept running through his head.

The car stopped and Vroon got off. He led Norton a winding course which at length ended at the door of a tenement building. Vroon entered. Norton paused wondering what next to do, now that his man had reached his destination. Well, since he had followed him all this distance he must make an effort to find out who he was and what he was going to do. Cautiously he entered the hallway. As he was about to lay his hand on the newel post of the dilapidated stairs the floor dropped from under his feet and he was precipitated into the cellar.

This tenement belonged to the Black Hundred; it concealed a thousand doors and a hundred traps. Its history was as dark as its hallways.

When Vroon and his companion, who had been waiting for him, descended into the cellar they found the reporter insensible. They bound, blindfolded, and gagged him.

"Saunders," said Vroon, "you tell Corrigan that I've a sailor for him to-night, and that I want this sailor booked for somewhere south of the equator. Tell him to say to the master that this fellow is ugly and disobedient. A tramp freighter, whose captain is a bully. Do you understand me?"

"I get you. But there's no need to go to Corrigan this trip. Bannock is in port and sails to-night for Norway. That's far enough."

"Bannock? The very man. Well, Mr. Norton, reporter and amateur detective, I guess we've got you fast enough this time. You may or may not come back alive. Go and bring around a taxi; some one you can trust. I'll dope the reporter while you're gone."

Long hours afterward Norton opened his aching eyes. He could hardly move and his head buzzed abominably. What had happened? What was the meaning of this slow rise and fall of his bed? Shanghaied?

"Come out o' that now, ye skulker!" roared a voice down the companionway.

"Shanghaied!" the reporter murmured. He sat up and ran through his pockets. Not a sou-markee, not a match even; and a second glance told him that the clothes he wore were not his own. "They've landed me this time. Shanghaied! What the devil am I going to do?"

"D'ye hear me?" bawled the strident voice again.

Norton looked about desperately for some weapon of defense. He saw an engineer's spanner on the floor by the bunk across the way, and with no small physical effort he succeeded in obtaining it. He stood up, his hand behind his back.

"All right, me bucko! I'll come down an' git ye!"

A pair of enormous boots began to appear down the companionway, and there gradually rose up from them a man as wide as a church door and as deep as a well.

"Wait a moment," said Norton, gripping the spanner. "Let us have a perfect understanding right off the bat."

"We're going to have it, matey. Don't ye worry none."

Norton raised the spanner, and, dizzy as he was, faced this seafaring Hercules courageously.

"I've been shanghaied, and you know it. Where are we bound?"

"Copenhagen."

"Well, for a month or more you'll beat me up whenever the opportunity offers. But I merely wish to warn you that if you do you'll find a heap of trouble waiting for

"COME OUT O' THAT NOW"

you the next time you drop your mudhook in North America."

"Is that so?" said the giant, eying the spanner and the shaking hand that held it aloft.

"It is. I'll take your orders and do the best I can, because you've got the upper hand. But, God is witness, you'll pay for every needless blow you strike. Now what do you want me to do?"

"Lay down that spanner an' come on deck, I'll tell ye what t' do. I was goin' t' whale th' daylights out o' ye; but ye're somethin' av a man. Drop the spanner first."

Norton hesitated. As lithe as a tiger the bulk of a man sprang at him and crushed him to the floor, wrenching away the spanner. Then the giant took Norton by the scruff of his neck and banged him up the steps to the deck.

"I ain't goin' t' hurt ye. I had t' show ye that no spanner ever bothered Mike Bannock. Now, d' know what a cook's galley is?"

"I do," said Norton, breathing hard.

"Well, hike there an' start in with peelin' spuds, an' don't waste 'em neither. That'll be all fer th' present. Ye were due for a wallopin' but I kinda like yer spunk."

So Jim stumbled down to the cook's galley and grimly set to work at the potatoes. It might have been far worse. But here he was, likely to be on the high seas for months, and no way of notifying Jones what had happened. The outlook was anything but cheerful. But a vague hope awoke in his heart. If they were still after him might it not signify that Florence lived.

Meantime Braine had not been idle. According to Vroon the girl's memory was in bad shape; so he had not the least doubt of bringing her back to New York without mishap. Once he had her there the game would begin in earnest. He played his cards exceedingly well. Steaming up into the little fishing harbor with a handsome yacht in itself would allay any distrust. And he wore a capital disguise, too. Everything went well till he laid his hand on Florence's shoulder. She gave a startled cry and ran over to Barnes, clinging to him wildly.

"No, no!" she cried.

"Now what, my child?" asked the sailor.

She shook her head. Her aversion was inexplicable.

"Come, my dear; can't you see that it is your father?" Braine turned to the captain. "She has been like this for a year. Heaven knows if she'll ever be in her right mind again," sadly. "I was giving her an ocean voyage, with the kindest nurses possible, and yet she jumped overboard. Come, Florence."

The girl wrapped her arms all the tighter around Barnes' neck.

An idea came into the old sailor's head. "Of course, sir, ye've got proof thet she's your daughter?"

"Proof?" Braine was taken aback.

"Yes; somethin' t' prove that you're her father. I got skinned out of a sloop once because I took a man's word at its face value. Black an' white, an' on paper, says I, hereafter."

"But I never thought of such a thing," protested Braine, beginning to lose his patience. "I can't risk sending to New York for documents. She is my daughter, and you will find it will not pay to take this peculiar stand."

"In black an' white, 'r y' can't have her."

Braine thereupon rushed forward to seize Florence. Barnes swung Florence behind him.

"I AIN'T GOIN' T' HURT YE"

"I guess she'll stay here a leetle longer, sir."

Time was vital, and this obstinacy made Braine furious. He reached again for Florence.

"Clear out o' here, 'r show your authority," growled Barnes.

"She goes with me, or you'll regret it."

"All right. But I guess th' law won't hurt me none. I'm in my rights. There's the door, mister."

"I refuse to go without her!"

Barnes sighed. He was on land a man of peace, but there was a limit to his patience. He seized Braine by the shoulders and hustled him out of the house.

"Bring your proofs, mister, an' nothin' more'll be said; but till y' bring 'em, keep away from this cottage."

And, simple-minded sailor that he was, he thought this settled the matter.

That night he kept his ears open for unusual sounds, but he merely wasted his night's rest. Quite naturally, he reckoned that the stranger would make his attempt at night. Indeed, he made it in broad daylight, with Barnes not a hundred yards away, calking a dory whose seams had sprung a leak. Braine had Florence upon the chartered yacht before the old man realized what had happened. He never saw Florence again; but one day, months later, he read all about her in a newspaper.

Florence fought; but she was weak, and so the conquest was easy. Braine was kind enough, now that he had her safe. He talked to her, but she merely stared at the receding coast.

"All right; don't talk if you don't want to. Here," to one of the men, "take her to the cabin and keep her there. But don't you touch her. I'll break you if you do. Put her in the cabin and guard the door; at least keep an eye on it. She may take it into her head to jump overboard."

Even the temporarily demented are not without a species of cunning. Florence had never seen Braine till he appeared at the Barnes cottage. Yet she revolted at the touch of his hand. On the second day out toward New York she found a box of matches and blithely set fire to her cabin, walked out into the corridor and thence to the deck. When the fire was discovered it had gained too much headway to be stopped. The yacht was doomed. They put off in the boats and for half a day drifted helplessly.

Fate has everything mapped out like a game of chess. You move a pawn, and bang goes your bishop, or your knight, or your king; or she lets you almost win a game, and then checkmates you. But there is one thing to be said in her favor—rail at her how we will, she is always giving odds to the innocent.

Mike Bannock was in the pilothouse, looking over his charts, when the lookout in the crow's nest sang out: "Two boats adrift off the port bow, sir!" And Bannock, who was a first-class sailor, although a rough one, shouted down the tube to the engine room. The freighter came to a halt in about ten minutes. The castaways saw that they had been noted, and pulled gallantly at the oars.

There are some things which science, well advanced as it is, can not explain. Among them is the shock which cuts off the past and the countershock which reawakens memory. They may write treatise after treatise and expound, but they never succeed in truly getting beyond that dark wall of mystery.

At the sound of Jim Norton's voice and at the sight

FLORENCE FOUGHT BUT SHE WAS WEAK AND SO THE CONQUEST WAS EASY

of his face—for subconsciously she must have been thinking of him all the while—a great blinding heat-wave
seemed to burn across her eyes, and when the effect
passed away she was herself again. A wild glance at
her surroundings convinced her that both she and her
lover were in danger. "Keep back," whispered Jim.
"Don't recognize me."

"They believe that I've lost my mind, and I'll keep that
idea in their heads. Sometime to-night I'll find a chance
to talk to you."

It took a good deal of cautious maneuvering to bring
about the meeting.

"They shanghaied me. And I thought you dead! It
was all wrong. It was a trick of that Perigoff woman,
and it succeeded. Girl, girl, I love you better than life!"

"I know it now," she said, and she kissed him. "Has
my father appeared yet?"

"No."

"Do you know anything at all about him?" sadly.

"I thought I did. It's all a jumble to me. But beware
of the man who brought you here. He is the head of
all our troubles; and if he knew I was on board he'd
kill me out of hand. He'd have to."

Braine offered Bannock $1,000 to turn back as far as
Boston; and as Bannock had all the time in the world,
carrying no perishable goods, he consented. But he
never could quite understand what followed. He had put
Florence and Braine in the boat and landed them; but
when he went down to see if Braine had left anything
behind, he found that individual bound and gagged in his
bunk.

CHAPTER XI

WHEN Jones received the telegram that Florence was safe, the iron nerve of the man broke down. The suspense had been so keenly terrible that the sudden reaction left him almost hysterically weak. Three weeks of waiting, waiting. Not even the scoundrel and his wife who had been the principal actors in the abduction had been found. From a great ship in midocean they had disappeared. Doubtless they had hidden among the immigrants, who, for little money, would have fooled all the officers on board. There was no doubt in Jones' mind that the pair had landed safely at Madrid.

As for Susan, she did have hysterics. She went about the room, wailing and laughing and wringing her hands. You would have thought by her actions that Florence had just died. The sight of her stirred the saturnine lips of the butler into a smile. But he did not remonstrate with her. In fact, he rather envied her freedom in emotion. Man can not let go in that fashion; it is a sign of weakness; and he dared not let even Susan see any sign of weakness in him.

So the reporter had found her, and she was safe and sound on her way to New York? Knowing by this time something of the reporter's courage, he was eager to learn how the event had come about. When he had not had a telephone message from Norton in forty-eight hours,

"I KNOW IT NOW," SHE SAID, AND SHE KISSED HIM

he had decided that the Black Hundred had finally succeeded in getting hold of him. It had been something of a blow; for while he looked with disfavor upon the reporter's frank regard for his charge, he appreciated the fact that Norton was a staff to lean on, and had behind him all the power of the press, which included the privilege of going everywhere even if one could not always get back.

As he folded the telegram and put it into his pocket, he observed the man with the opera glasses over the way. He shrugged. Well, let him watch till his eyes dropped out of his head; he would only see that which was intended for his eyes. Still, it was irksome to feel that no matter when or where you moved, watching eyes observed and chronicled these movements.

Suddenly, not being devoid of a sense of dry humor, Jones stepped over to the telephone and called up her highness the Countess Perigoff.

"Who is it?"

He was forced to admit, however reluctantly, that the woman had a marvelously fine speaking voice.

"It is Jones, madam."

"Jones?"

"Mr. Hargreave's butler, madam."

"Oh! You have news of Florence?"

"Yes." It will be an embarrassing day for humanity when some one invents a photographic apparatus by which two persons at the two ends of the telephone may observe the facial expressions of each other.

"What is it? Tell me quickly."

"Florence has been found, and she is on her way back to New York. She was found by Mr. Norton, the reporter."

"I am so glad! Shall I come up at once and have you tell me the whole amazing story?"

"It would be useless, madam, for I know nothing except what I learned from a telegram I have just received. But no doubt some time this evening you might risk a call."

"Ring up the instant she returns. Did she say what train?"

"No, madam," lied Jones, smiling.

He hung up the receiver and stared at the telephone as if he would force his gaze in and through it to the woman at the other end. Flesh and blood! Well, greed was stronger than that. Treacherous cat! Let her play; let her weave her nets, dig her pits. The day would come, and it was not far distant, when she would find that the mild-eyed mongoose was just as deadly as the cobra, and far more cunning.

The heads of the Black Hundred must be destroyed. Those were the orders. What good to denounce them, to send them to a prison from which, with the aid of money and a tremendous secret political pull, they might readily find their way out? They must be exterminated, as one kills off the poisonous plague rats of the Orient. A woman? In the law of reprisal there was no sex.

Shortly after the telephone episode (which rather puzzled the countess) she received a wire from Braine, which announced the fact that Florence and Norton had escaped and were coming to New York on train No. 25, and advising her to meet the train en route. She had to fly about to do it.

When Captain Bannock released Braine, he had been in no enviable frame of mind. Tricked, fooled by the girl, whose mind was as unclouded as his own! She had

HE HAD PUT FLORENCE AND BRAINE IN THE BOAT AND LANDED THEM

succeeded in bribing a coal stoker, and had taken him unawares. The man had donned the disguise he had laid out for shore approach, and the blockheaded Bannock had never suspected. He had not recognized Norton at all. It was only when Bannock explained the history of the shanghaied stoker that he realized his real danger. Norton! He must be pushed off the board. After this episode he could no longer keep up the pretense of being friendly. Norton, by a rare stroke of luck, had forced him out into the open. So be it. Self-preservation is in nowise looked upon as criminal. The law may have its ideas about it, but the individual recognizes no law but its own. It was Braine whom he loved and admired, or Norton whom he hated as a dog with rabies hates water. With Norton free, he would never again dare return to New York openly. This meddling reporter aimed at his ease and elegance.

He left the freighter as soon as a boat could carry him ashore. The fugitives would make directly for the railroad, and thither he went at top speed, to arrive ten minutes too late.

"Free!" said Florence, as the train began to increase its speed.

Norton reached over and patted her hand. Then he sat back with a sudden shock of dismay. He dived a hand into a pocket, into another and another. The price of the telegram he had sent to Jones was all he had had in the world; and he had borrowed that from a friendly stoker. In the excitement he had forgotten all about such a contingency as the absolute need of money.

"Florence, I'm afraid we're going to have trouble with the conductor when he comes."

"Why?"

He pulled out his pockets suggestively. "Not a postage stamp. They'll put us off at the next station. And," with a glance in the little mirror between the two windows, "I shouldn't blame them a bit." He was unshaven, he was wearing the suit substituted for his own; and Florence, sartorially, was not much better off.

She smiled, blushed, stood up, and turned her back to him. Then she sat down again. In her hand she held a small dilapidated roll of banknotes.

"I had them with me when they abducted me," she said. "Besides, this ring is worth something."

"Thank the Lord!" he exclaimed, relievedly.

So there was nothing more to do but be happy; and happy they were. They were quite oblivious to the peculiar interest they aroused among the other passengers. This unshaven young man, in his ragged coat and soiled jersey; this beautiful young girl, in a wrinkled homespun, her glorious blond hair awry; and the way they looked at each other during those lulls in conversation peculiar to lovers the world over, impressed the other passengers with the idea that something very unusual had happened to these two.

The Pullman conductor was not especially polite; but money was money, and the stockholders, waiting for their dividends, made it impossible for him to reject it. The regular conductor paid them no more attention than to grumble over changing a twenty-dollar bill.

So, while these two were hurrying on to New York, the plotters were hurrying east to meet them. The two trains met and stopped at the same station about eighty miles from New York. The countess, accompanied by Vroon, who kept well in the background, entered the car occupied by the two castaways.

In the mirror at the rear of the car Norton happened
to cast an idle glance, and he saw the countess. Vroon,
however, escaped his eye.

"Be careful, Florence," he said. "The countess is in
the car. The game begins again. Pretend that you suspect nothing. Pretty quick work on their part. And
that's all the more reason why we should play the comedy
well. Here she comes. She will recognize you, throw
her arms around you, and show all manner of effusive-
ness. Just keep your head and play the game."

"She lied about you to me."

"No matter."

"Oh!" cried the countess. She seized Florence in a
wild embrace. She was an inimitable actress, and Norton could not help admiring her. "Your butler telephoned me! I ran to the first train out. And here you
are, back safe and sound! It is wonderful. Tell me all
about it. What an adventure! And, good heavens, Mr.
Norton, where did you get those clothes? Did you find
her and rescue her? What a newspaper story you'll be
able to make out of it all! Now, tell me just what happened." She sat down on the arm of Florence's chair.
The girl had steeled her nerves against the touch of her.
And yet she was beautiful! How could any one so beautiful be so wicked?

"Well, it began like this," began Florence; and she described her adventures, omitting, to be sure, Braine's
part in it.

She had reached that part where they had been rescued
by Captain Bannock when a thundering, grinding crash
struck the words from her lips. The three of them were
flung violently to one side of the car amid splintering
wood, tinkling glass, and the shriek of steel against steel.

A low wail of horror rose and died away as the car careened over on its side. The three were rendered unconscious and were huddled together on the floor, under the uprooted chairs.

Vroon had escaped with only a slight cut on the hand from flying glass. He climbed over the chairs and passengers with a single object in view. He saw that all three he was interested in were insensible. He quickly examined them and saw that they had not received serious injuries. He had but little time. The countess and Norton would have to take their chance with the other passengers. Resolutely he stooped and lifted Florence in his arms and crawled out of the car with her. It was a difficult task, but he managed it. Outside, in the confusion, no one paid any attention to him. So he threw the unconscious girl over his shoulder and staggered on toward the road.

It was fortunate that the accident had occurred where it did. Five miles beyond was the station marked for the arrest of Norton as an abductor and the taking in charge of Florence as a rebellious girl who had run away from her parents. If he could only reach the Swede's hut, where his confederates were in waiting, the game would then be his.

After struggling along for half an hour a carriage was spied by Vroon, and he hailed it when it reached his side.

"What's the trouble, mister?" asked the farmer.

"A wreck on the railroad. My daughter is badly hurt. I must take her to the nearest village. How far is it?"

"About three miles."

"I'll give you twenty dollars for the use of that rig of yours."

"Can't do it, mister."

"But it's a case of humanity, sir!" indignantly. "You are refusing to aid the unfortunate."

The farmer thought it over for a moment. "All right. You can have the buggy for twenty dollars. When you get to the village take the nag to Doc Sanders' livery. He'll know what to do."

"Thank you. Help me in with her."

Vroon drove away without the least intention of going toward the village. As a result, when Florence came to her senses she found herself surrounded by strange and ominous faces. At first she thought they had taken her from the wreck out of kindness; but when she saw the cold, impassive face of the man Vroon she closed her eyes and lay back in the chair. Well, ill and weak as she was, they should find that she was not without a certain strength.

In the meantime Norton revived and looked about in vain for Florence. He searched among the crowd of terrified passengers, the hurt and the unharmed, but she was not to be found. He ran back to the countess and helped her out of the broken car.

"Where is Florence?" she asked dazedly.

"God knows! Here, come over and sit down by the fence till I see if there is a field telegraph."

They had already erected one, and his message went off with a batch of others. This time he was determined not to trust to chance. The shock may have brought back Florence's recent mental disorder, and she may have wandered off without knowing what she was doing. On the other hand, she may have been carried off. And against such a contingency he must be fortified. Money! The curse of God was upon it; it was the trail of the serpent, spreading poison in its wake.

By and by the countess was able to walk; and, sup-
porting her, he led her to the road, along which they
walked slowly for at least an hour. They might very
well have waited for the relief train. But he could not
stand the thought of inactivity. The countess had her
choice of staying behind or going with him. He hated
the woman, but he could not refuse her aid. She had a
cut on the side of her head, and she limped besides.

They stopped at the first farmhouse, explained what
had happened, and the mistress urged them to enter.
She had seen no one, and certainly not a young woman.
She must have wandered off in another direction. She
ran into the kitchen for a basin and towel and proceeded
to patch the countess' hurts.

The latter was extremely uneasy. That she should be
under obligation to Norton galled her. There was a spark
of conscience left in her soul. She had tried to destroy
him, and he had been kind to her. Was he a fool or was
he deep, playing a game as shrewd as her own? She
could not tell. Where was Vroon? Had he carried
Florence off?

An hour later a man came in.

"Hullo! More folks from the wreck?"

"Where's the horse and buggy, Jake?" his wife asked.

"Rented it to a man whose daughter was hurt. He
went to the village."

"Will you describe the daughter?" asked Norton.

The countess twisted her fingers.

The farmer rudely described Florence.

"Have you another horse and a saddle?"

"What's your hurry?"

"I'll tell you later. What I want now is the horse."

"What is to become of me?" asked the countess.

"You will be in good hands," he answered briefly. "I am going to find out what has become of Florence. Is there a deserted farmhouse hereabouts?" he asked of the farmer.

"Not that I recollect."

"Why yes, there is, Jake. There's that old hut about two miles up the fork," volunteered the wife. "Where the Swede died last winter."

"By jingo! I'm going into the village and see if that man brought in the rig."

"But get my horse first. My name is James Norton, and I am on the *Blade* in New York. Which way do I go?"

"First turn to the left. Come on; I'll get the horse for you."

Once the horse was saddled, Norton set off at a run. He was unarmed; he forgot all about this fact. His one thought was to find the woman he loved. He was not afraid of meeting a dozen men, not while his present fury lasted.

And he fell into an ambush within a hundred yards of his goal. They dragged him off the horse and buffeted and mishandled him into the hut.

"Both of them!" said Vroon, rubbing his hands.

"I know you, you Russian rat!" cried Norton. "And if I ever get out of this I'll kill you out of hand! Damn you!"

"Oh, yes; talk, talk; but it never hurts any one," jeered Vroon. "You'll never have the chance to kill me out of hand, as you say. Besides, do you know my face?"

"I do. The mask doesn't matter. You're the man who had me shanghaied. The voice is enough."

"Very good. That's what I wished to know. That's

your death warrant. We'll do it like they used to do at the old Academy; tie you to the railroad track. We shall not hurt you at all. If some engine runs over you heaven is witness we did not guide the engine. Remember the story of the boy and the cat?" with sinister amiability. "The boy said he wasn't pulling the cat's tail, he was only holding it; the cat did the pulling. Bring him along, men. Time is precious, and we have a good deal to do before night settles down. Come on with him. The track is only a short distance."

"Jim, Jim!" cried Florence in anguish.

"Never you mind, girl; they're only bluffing. They won't dare."

"You think so?" said Vroon. "Wait and see." He turned upon Florence. "He is your lover. Do you wish him to die?"

"No, no!"

"We promise to give him his freedom twelve hours from now on condition that you tell where that money is."

"Florence!" warned Norton.

Vroon struck him on the mouth. "Be silent, you scum!"

"It is in the chest Jones, the butler, threw into the sound," she said bravely. And so it might be for all she knew.

Vroon laughed. "We know about where that is."

"Florence, say nothing on my account. They are not the kind of men who keep their word."

"Eh?" snarled Vroon. "We'll see about that." He glanced at his watch. "In half an hour the freight comes along. It may become stalled at the wreck. But it will serve."

Norton knew very well that if need said must they

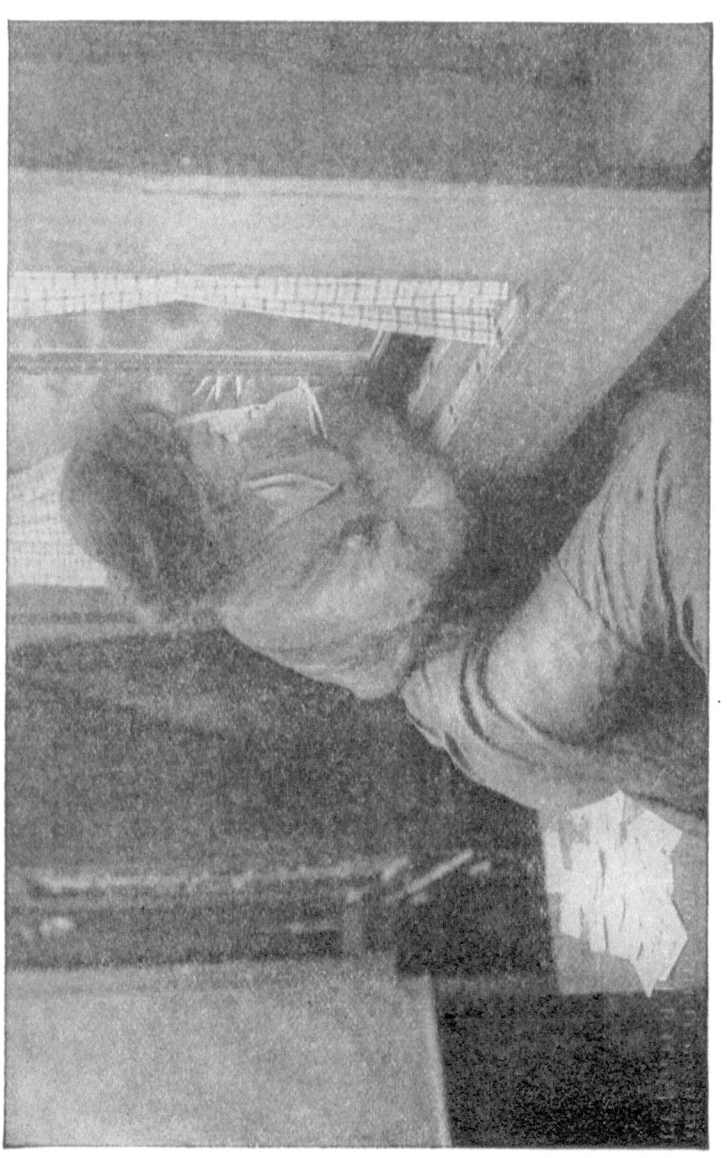

THEY BOUND FLORENCE AND LEFT HER SEATED IN THE CHAIR

would not hesitate to execute a melodramatic plan of this character. It was the way of the Slav; they had to make crime abnormal in order to enjoy it. They could very well have knocked him on the head then and there and have done with him. But the time used in conveying him to the railroad might prove his salvation. Nearly four hours had passed since the sending of the telegram to Jones.

They bound Florence and left her seated in the chair. As soon as they were gone she rolled to the floor. She was able to right herself to her knees, and after a torturous five minutes reached the fireplace. She burnt her hands and wrists, but the blaze was the only knife obtainable. She was free.

Jones arrived with half a dozen policemen. Vroon alone escaped.

The butler caught Florence in his arms and nearly crushed the breath out of her. And she was so glad to see him that she kissed him half a dozen times. What if he was her father's butler? He was brave and loyal and kind.

"They tied him to the track," she cried. "Look at my wrists!" The butler did so, and kissed them tenderly. "And I saved him."

Jones stretched out a hand over Florence's shoulder. "When the time comes," he said; "when the right time comes and my master's enemies are confounded. But always the rooks, never the hawks, do we catch. God bless you, Norton! I don't know what I should have done without you."

"When a chap's in love," began Norton, embarrassedly.

"I know, I know," interrupted Jones. "The second relief train is waiting. Let us hurry back. I shan't feel secure till we are once more in the house."

So, arm in arm, the three of them went down the tracks to the hand-car which had brought the police.

And now for the iron-bound chest at the bottom of the sea.

CHAPTER XII

A DIPSY-CHANTY, if you please; of sailormen in jerseys and tarry caps, of rolling gaits, strong tobacco and diverse profanity; of cutters, and blunt-nosed schooners, and tramps, canvas and steam, some of them honest, some of them shady, and some of them pirates of the first water who did not find it necessary to hoist aloft the skull and bones. The seas are dotted with them. They remind you of the once prosperous merchant, run down at the heel, who slinks along the side streets, ashamed to meet those he knew in the past. You never hear them mentioned in the maritime news, which is the society column of the ships; you know of their existence only by the bleached bones of them, strewn along the coast.

You who crave adventures on high seas, you purchase a ticket, a steamer chair, and a couple of popular novels, go on board to the blare of a very indifferent brass band, and believe you are adventuring; when, as a matter of fact, you are about to spend a dull week or a fortnight on a water hotel, where the most exciting thing is the bugle's call to meals or the discovery of a card sharp in the smoking-room. Take a real ship, go as supercargo, to the South Seas; take the side streets of the ocean, and learn what it can do with hurricanes, typhoons, blistering calms, and men's souls. There will be adventure

157

enough then. If you are a weakling, either you are made strong, or you die.

An honest ship, but run down at the heel, rode at anchor in the sound, a fourth-rater of the hooker breed; that is, her principal line of business was hauling barges up and down the coast. When she could not pick up enough barges to make it pay, why she'd go gallivanting down to Cuba for bales of tobacco or even to the Bermudas for the heaven-smelling onion. To-day she was an onion ship; which precludes any idea of adventure. She was about four thousand tons, and her engines were sternward and not amidship. She carried two masts and a half-dozen hoist booms, and the only visible sign of anything new on her was her bowsprit. This was new doubtless because she had poked her nose too far into her last slip.

Her crew was orderly and tractable. There were shore drunks, to be sure, because they were sailors; but they were at work. They moved about briskly, for they were on the point of sailing for the Bahamas—perhaps for more onions. Presently the windlass creaked and shrilled, and the blobby links, much in need of tar paint, red as fish gills, clattered down into the bow. Sometimes they painted the chain as it came over; but paint was costly, and this was done only when the anchor threatened to stay on the bottom.

There was a sailor among this crew, and he went by the name of Steve Blossom; and he was one of his kind. A grimy dime novel protruded rakishly from his hip pocket, and his right cheek was swollen as with the toothache, due, probably, to a generous "chaw" of Seaman's Delight. He was a real tobacco chewer, for he rarely spat. He was as peaceful as a backwater bay in summer; non-argumentative and passive, he stood his watch in fair weather and foul.

No one gave the anchor any more attention after it came to rest. The great city over the way was fairy-like in its haziness and softened lines. It was the poetry of angles, of shafts and spars of stone; and Steve Blossom, having a moment to himself, leaned against the rail and stared regretfully. He had been generously drunk the night before, and it was a pleasant recollection. Chance led his glance to trail down the cutwater. His neck stretched from his collar like a turtle's from its shell.

"Well, I'll be hornswoggled!" he murmured, shifting his cud from starboard to port.

Caught on the fluke of the anchor was the strangest looking box he had ever laid eyes on. There were leather and steel bands and diamond-shaped ivory and mother of pearl, and it hung jauntily on the point of the rusty fluke. Anybody would be hornswoggled to glimpse such a droll jest of fate. On the fluke of the old mudhook, by a hair, you might say. In all the wild sea yarns he had ever read or heard there was nothing to match this.

Treasure!

And Steve was destined never to be passive again. His first impulse was to call his companions; his second impulse was to say nothing at all, and wait for an opportunity to get the box to his bunk without being detected. Treasure! Diamonds and rubies and pearls and old Spanish gold; and all hanging to the fluke of the anchor.

"Hornswoggled!" in a kind of awesome whisper this time. "An' we a-headin' for th' Bahamas!" For under his feet he could hear the rhythm of engines. "What'll I do? If I leave it, some one else'll see it." He scratched his chin perplexedly; and the cud went back to starboard. "I got it!"

He took off his coat and carefully dropped it down over the mysterious box. It was growing darker and darker all the time, and shortly neither coat nor anchor would be visible without close scrutiny. Treasure: greed, cupidity, crime. Steve saw only the treasure and not its camp followers. What did they call them?—doubloons and pieces-of-eight?

He ate his supper with his messmates, and he ate heartily as usual. It would have taken something more vital than mere treasure to disturb Steve Blossom's appetite. He was one of those enviable individuals whose imagination and gastric juices work at the same time. And while he ate he planned. In the first place, he would buy that home at Bedford; then he would take over the Gilson House and live like a lord. If he wanted a drink, all he would have to do would be to turn the spigot or tip a bottle; and more than that, he'd have a bartender to do it. Onions! He swore he would not have an onion within a mile of the Gilson House. "Onions!" Quite unconsciously he spoke the words aloud.

"Huh? Well, if ye don't like onions, find a hooker that packs violets in her hold," was the cheerful advice of the man at Steve's elbow.

"Who's talkin' t' you?" grunted Steve. "Wha' did I say?"

"Onions, ye lubber! Don't we know whut onions is? Ain't we smelt 'em so long that ye could stick yer nose in th' starboard light an' never smell no kerosene? Onions! Pass th' cawffy."

Steve helped himself first. The man who spoke bunked over him, and they were not on the best of terms.

There was no real reason for this frank antagonism; simply, they did not splice any more effectually than cotton rope and hemp splice. Sailors are moody and superstitious; at least they generally are on hookers of the *Captain Manners* breed. Steve was superstitious and Jim Dunkers was moody and had no thumb on his left hand. Steve hated the sight of that red nubbin. He was quite certain that it had been a whole thumb once, on the way to gouge out somebody's eye, and had inadvertently connected with somebody's teeth.

Spanish doubloons and pearls and diamonds and rubies! It was mighty hard not to say these words out loud, too; blare them into the sullen faces grouped around the table. He was off watch till midnight; and he was wondering if he could get the box without attracting the attention of the lookout, who had a devilish keen eye for everything that stirred on deck or on water. Well, he would have to risk it; but he would wait till full darkness had fallen over the sea and the lookout would be compelled to keep his eyes off the deck. The boys wanted him to play cards.

"Not for me. Busted. How long d' y' think forty dollars 'll last in New York, anyhow?" And he stalked out of the forecastle and went down into the waist to enjoy his evening pipe, all the while keeping a weather eye forward, at the ratty old pilot house.

It was ten o'clock, land time, when he rammed his cutty into a pocket and resolutely walked forward. If any one watched him they would think he was only looking down the cutwater. The thought of money and the pleasures it will buy makes cunning the stupidest of dolts; and Steve was ordinarily a dolt. But to-night his brain was keen enough for all purposes. It was a hazardous job to get the box off the fluke without letting it slip back into the sea. Steve, however, accomplished the feat, climbed back on the rail and sat down, waiting. A quarter of an hour passed. No one had seen him. With his coat securely wrapped about his precious find he made for the forecastle. His mates, save those who were doing their watch, were all in their bunks. An oil lamp dimly illuminated the forward partition. Steve's bunk was almost in darkness. Very deftly he rolled back the bedding and secreted the box under his pillows, and then stretched himself out with the pretense of snoozing till the bell called him to duty.

He was rich; and the moment a man has money he has troubles; there is always some one who wants to take it away from you. His bunk was on the port side, and there was plenty of hiding space between the iron plates and the wooden partition. He intended to loosen three or four planks, and then when the time came, slip the box behind them. Some time during the morning the forecastle would be empty, and then would be his time.

But he suffered the agonies of damnation during the four-hours' watch. Supposing some fool should go rummaging about his bunk and discover the box? Suppose . . . But he dared not suppose. There was nothing to do but wait. If he created any curiosity on the part of his mates he was lost. He would have to divide with them all, from the captain down to the cook's boy. It was a heart-rending thought. From being the most open and frank man aboard, he became the most cunning. From being a man without enemies, he saw an enemy even in his shadow.

At four o'clock he turned in and slept like a log.

In the morning he found his opportunity. For half an hour the forecastle was empty of all save himself. Feverishly he pried back the boards, found the brace beam, and gently laid the box there. It was a mighty curious-looking box. Once he had stoked up the Chinese coast from the Philippines, and he judged it to be Chinese in origin. He tried to pry open the cover and feast his eyes upon the treasure; but under the leather and ivory and mother of pearl was impervious steel. It would take an ax or a crowbar to stir that lid. He sighed. He replaced the boards, and became to all appearances his stolid self again.

But all the way down to the Bahamas he was moody, and when he answered any questions it was with words spoken testily and jerkily.

"I know whut's th' matter," said Dunkers. "He's in love."

"Shut your mouth!"

"Didn't I tell yuh?" laughed the tantalizer, dancing toward the companionway. "Steve's in love, 'r he didn't git drunk enough on shore t' satisfy his whale's belly!"

A boot thudded spitefully against the door jamb.

"You fellahs let me alone, 'r I'll bash in a couple o' heads!"

"Oh, yuh will, will yuh?" cried Dunkers from the deck. "If yuh want a little exercise, yuh can begin on me, yuh moonsick swab! Whut's th' matter with yuh, anyhow? Where'd yuh git this grouch? Whut've we done t' yuh? Huh?"

"You keep out o' my way, that's all. I'm mindin' my watches, an' don't ask no odds of you duffers. What if I have a grouch? Is it any o' your business? All right. When we step ashore at th' Bahamas, Mister Jim Dunkers, I'll tear the ropes out o' your pulley blocks. But till we git there, you t' th' upper bunk an' me t' mine."

"Leave th' ol' grouch alone, Jim. Th' mate won't stand for no scrappin' aboard. We'll have th' thing done right in th' custom sheds. We'll have a finish fight, Queensberry rules, an' may th' best man win."

"I'm willin'," said Jim.

"So'm I," agreed Steve. But his intentions were not honorable. He proposed to desert before any fight took place. Not that he was physically afraid; no; he wanted to dig his hands deep into those doubloons and pieces-of-eight.

So the four days down passed otherwise uneventfully, amid paint pots and iron rust and three meals a day of pork, onion soup, potatoes, and strong, bitter coffee. The winds became light and balmy and the sea blue and gentle. The men went about in their undershirts and dungarees, barefooted. Of course the coming fight was the main topic of conversation. It promised to be a rattling good scrap, for both men were evenly matched, and both had a "kick" in either hand. Even the captain took a mild interest in the affair. He was an old sailor. He knew that there was no such word as arbitration in a sailor's vocabulary; his disputes could be settled only in one manner, by his calloused fists.

When the old mudhook (and some day Steve was going to buy it and hang it over the entrance to the Gilson House) slithered down into the smiling waters of the bay, Steve concluded that discretion was the better part of valor. He would steal ashore on the quarantine tug which lay alongside. He was willing to fight under ordinary circumstances, but he must get his treasure in safety first. They could call him a welcher if they wanted to; devil a bit did he care. So he pried back the boards of his bunk wall, took out the box, eyed it fondly, and noted for the first time the lettering on it:

STANLEY HARGREAVE.

He wrinkled his brow in the effort to recall a pirate by this name, but was unsuccessful. No matter. He hugged the box under his coat and made for the gang-way, and inadvertently ran into his enemy.

Dunkers caught a bit of the box peeping from under the coat.

"What 'a' yuh got there?" he demanded truculently.

"None o' your dam business! You lemme by; hear me?"

"Ain't none o' my business, huh? Where'd yuh git a box like that? Steal it? By cripes, I'm goin' t' have a look at that box, my hearty. It don't smell like honest onions."

"You lemme by!" breathed Steve, with murder in his heart.

Suddenly the two men closed, surged back and forth, one determined to take and the other to hold this mysterious box. Dunkers struggled to uphold his word: not that he really wanted the box but to prove that he was strong enough to take it if he wanted to. The name on the box flashed and disappeared. It was a kind of shock to him. He and Blossom went battering against the rail. Dunker's grip slipped and so did Blossom's. The result was that the box was catapulted into the sea. With an agonizing cry, Blossom leaned far over. He saw the box oscillate for a moment, then sink gracefully in a zigzag course, down through the blue waters. Fainter and fainter it grew, and at last vanished.

"I'm sorry, Steve; but yuh wouldn't let me look at it," said Dunkers, contritely.

"Damn you; I'm goin' t' kill y' for that!"

It became a real fight this time, fist and foot, tooth and nail; one mad with the lust to kill and the other desperately intent on living. It was one of those contests in which honor and fair play have no part. But for the timely arrival of the captain and some of the crew Dunkers would have been badly injured, perhaps fatally. They hauled back Blossom, roaring out his oaths at the top of his lungs. It took half an hour's arguing to calm him down. Then the captain demanded to know what it was all about. And blubbering, Steve told him.

"Six hundred feet of water, if I've got my reckoning right. The anchor lies in sixty feet, but the starboard side drops sheer six hundred. You swab! Why didn't you bring the box to me? A man has a right to what he finds. I'd have taken care of it for you till we got back to port. I know; you were greedy; you thought I might want to stick my fist into your treasure. And you'll never find it in six hundred feet of water and tangled, porous coral. That's what you get for being a blamed hog. As for you," and the captain turned to Dunkers, "get your dunnage and your pay and hunt for another boat back. I won't have no murder on board *Captain Manners*. And the sooner you go, the better."

"I'll go, sir," said Dunkers, readily enough. Had the misfortune happened to him and had Blossom been the aggressor, he would want his life. He understood. Like the valet in *Olivette,* it was the time for disappearing.

"An' keep out o' my way. I'll git y' yet," growled Blossom.

"Keep your mouth shut," said the mate, "or I'll have you put in irons, you pig!"

"All right, sir. I've said all I'm goin' t' say t'day;" and Blossom strode off.

"What was the box like?" asked the captain of Dunkers.

"Chinese contraption, sir; leastwise it looked that way to me. Didn't look as if it'd been in th' water long, sir. Somethin' lost overboard by some private yacht, t' my thinkin'. I'll keep out o' Steve's way. I'll lay low on shore, sir."

And though Steve made a perfect range of the spot, he never came back to find the mysterious box, never saw the Gilson House back home, nor did he ever see Dunkers again. On the voyage home he brooded continually, and was frequently found blubbering; and one night he skipped his watch and went to Davy Jones' locker.

Dunkers had not told about the name he had seen on the box; and Blossom had not thought to. The name Hargreave had instantly brought back to Dunkers' mind the newspaper stories he had recently read. There was no doubt in the world that this box belonged to the missing millionaire, who had drawn a million from his banks and vanished; and, moreover, there was no doubt in Dunkers' mind that this million lay in the Bahaman waters. It had been drawn up from the bottom of the sound, under the path of the balloon. He proceeded, then, to take a most minute range. It would require money and partners; but half a loaf would be far better than no loaf at all; and he was determined to return to New York to find backing. Finding is keeping, on land or sea.

Now it happened that his favorite grog shop was a cheap saloon across the way from the headquarters of the Black Hundred; and Vroon occasionally dropped in, for he often picked up a valuable bit of maritime news. Dunkers was an old friend of the barkeeper, and he proceeded to pour and guzzle down his throat a very poor substitute for whisky. He became communicative. He bragged. He knew where there was a million, and all he needed was a first-class diving bell. A year from now he would not be drinking cheap whisky; he'd be steering a course up and down Broadway and buying wine when he was thirsty. He was no miser. But he had to have a diving bell; and where the blue devil could he get one with twelve dollars and an Ingersoll watch in his pocket?

From his table Vroon made a sign which the bartender understood. Then he rose and approached Dunkers.

"I own a pretty good diving apparatus," he said. "If you've got the goods, I'll take a chance on a fifty-fifty basis." Vroon did not believe there was anything back of his talk; but it always paid to dig deep enough to find out. "Have a drink; and, Bill, give us a real whisky and none of your soap-lye. Now, let's hear your yarn."

"I don't know yuh," said Dunkers, with drunken caution. "How is it, Bill?" turning to the bartender.

"He's the goods, Jim. You've heard of Wyant & Co.?"

"Sure I've heard o' them. Best divin' app'ratus they is."

"Well, this gent here is Mr. Brooks, general manager for Wyant & Co. I can O. K. him."

Vroon threw an appreciative glance at the bartender. He was not affiliated with the Black Hundred, but he had often aided Vroon in minor affairs.

"All right, if yuh say so, Bill. Well, here's th' yarn."

And when he had done, Vroon smoked quietly without speaking.

"Don't yuh believe it?" demanded Dunkers, truculently.

"But six hundred feet of water, in a coral bottom, and no way of telling just where it fell overboard. That's a tough proposition."

"Oh, it is, is it? I'm a sailor. I can lay my hand right over th' spot. Do yuh think I'd be fool enough t' hunt for it without a perfect range?" Dunkers tapped his coat pocket suggestively.

And Vroon knew that the one thing he wanted was there, a plan or a drawing of the range. So there was another man shanghaied that night, and his destination was Cape Town, twenty-two days' voyage by the calendar.

Vroon carried his information to the organization that same night. They would start the expedition at once, and till this was accomplished, Hargreave's daughter was to be immune from attacks. Besides, it would give Hargreave (wherever he was) and the others the idea that the Black Hundred had concluded to give up the chase.

Above, with his ear to a small hole, skilfully bored through the ceiling without permitting the plaster to fall, knelt a man with a bandaged arm. He could never see any faces; no one ever took off a mask in this sinister chamber. But there were voices, and he was going to forget some of them. After the meeting came to an end, he waited an hour, and then stole down into the street by the aid of the fire-escape. Later, he entered a telephone booth and called up Jones.

Then, one leathern and steel box, dotted with bits of ivory and mother-of-pearl, became two; and the second one was soaked in mud and salt water for two weeks till you could not have told it from the original. And that is why Jones was able, some weeks later, to hide once more the original box. As for the substitute, just as Braine was about to use a mallet and chisel upon it, the lights went out. There was a wild scramble, a chair or two was overturned.

"The door, the door!" shouted Braine, furious.

It slammed the moment the words left his lips. And as suddenly as they had gone out the lights sprang up. The box was gone. There were evidently traitors among the Black Hundred.

CHAPTER XIII

THE Black Hundred, not as individuals but as an organization, began to worry. Powerful, and often reckless and daring because it was powerful, it began to look about for some basic cause for all these failures against Hargreave's daughter and Hargreave's ghost. They had tried to put the inquisitive reporter out of the way; they had laid every trap they could think of to catch the mysterious visitor at the Hargreave home; they had thrown out a hundred lures to bring Hargreave out of his lair, and failed; and they had lost a dozen valuable men and several thousand dollars. This must end somewhere, and quickly.

The one ray of hope for the conspirators lay in the fact that Florence had never seen her father and knew not in the least what he looked like. They determined to try again in this direction.

"Give it all up," said the countess to Braine. "I tell you, whatever is back of all this is stronger than we are. He knows the organization, and for all we know he may be a ghost."

"I never go back," smiled Braine. "There's something more than the million. There's the sport of the thing. We've been bested in a dozen bouts, and nearly always by a fluke. They have the breaks, as they say out at the Polo Grounds."

"But the time and expense when we might be getting results elsewhere! I tell you, Leo, I'm afraid. It's like always hearing some one behind you and never finding anybody when you turn. I have told you my doubts. I have also asked you to trap that butler, but you've always laughed."

"You are seeing ghosts, Olga. A new man from holy Russia," shrugging, "is coming to-night. Evidently the head over there thinks our contributions of late have not been up to the mark, and they are going to stir us up. I am willing to wager my soul, however, that that box is simply a hoax to befuddle us. Either that or it holds the key. But the rest of them insist that the box must be re-covered. When I leave this room to-night I am going over to Riverdale and stalk all by myself. I'm going to get a glimpse of that mysterious stranger. He carries a scar of mine somewhere, for I hit him that night."

The door opened and the executive chamber became silent.

"Count Paroff," boomed the voice of Vroon. "He will present his credentials."

This formality was executed as prescribed by the rules; and Count Paroff was given his chair. He spoke for a while, rather pompously.

"The head organization is not satisfied with its off-spring in this Hargreave affair," he said in conclusion. "You are slow."

"Then perhaps you have come with some suggestions for the betterment of our business?" asked Braine iron-ically.

"Sir, this is not the hour for flippancy," said the agent coldly.

Braine made a sign with his hand, a sign not observed

by every one. Instantly Paroff bent lowly. He recognized that the speaker was the actual, not the nominal, head of the American branch.

"What are your suggestions?" inquired the nominal head from his chair, anxious to avoid a clash between the newcomer and the truculent master of them all.

"I have been informed that Hargreave's daughter has never seen her father, not even a photograph of him," said Paroff, more amiably.

"We are absolutely certain that this is the case," said the nominal head, who was known as the president. "But we tried one play in that direction, and it failed miserably."

"I have the story," replied Paroff. "It was clumsily done. The ruse was an old one."

Braine was frank enough to admit the truth of this statement, however much he disliked the admission. He nodded.

"I have authority to take a hand in this affair. We can not waste all summer. Those government plans of the fortifications of the Panama are waiting. There's your millions. But the fact remains that it is the law of the Black Hundred never to step down till absolutely defeated. The hidden million is but half; we must find and break this renegade Hargreave."

"If he lives," said Braine.

"Who can say one way or the other?" bruskly asked Paroff. "The fact that all your plans and schemes have come to naught should prove to you that you are not fighting a ghost. There is but one way to bring out the truth."

"And that is to make a captive of his daughter," supplemented Braine. "And we have worked toward that

end ceaselessly. We are quite ready to listen to your suggestions, count."

"And so am I," thought the man with his ear to the
little hole in the ceiling above. "And some day, my ener-
getic friend, I'm going to pay you back for that bullet."

Count Paroff cleared his voice and laid his plans before
his audience.

"To act frankly and in the open, to go boldly to the
Hargreave home and proclaim myself Hargreave. I can
disguise myself in a manner that will at least temporarily
fool the butler."

"Who has been with his master for fourteen years,
knows every move, habit, gesture, inflection," interposed
Braine. "But proceed, count, proceed. You will remember the old adage; too many cooks."

"Ah," flashed back the count, "but a new cook?"

Olga touched Braine's arm warningly.

"You mean, then, that there has been talk in St. Petersburg of disposing of some one?"

"A good deal of talk, sir," haughtily, forgetting that he
had bent humbly enough but a few moments gone.

"Very well; go on."

Thought the man at the peephole above: "There's another adage. When thieves fall out, then honest men get
their dues. Yes, yes; proceed, proceed!"

Paroff went on. "I shall, then, go frankly to the Hargreave house and claim my own. Meantime I leave to
you the business of luring the butler away. Half an hour
is all I need to bring that child here, to break the wall
that stands between us and what we seek."

"Is that so?" murmured Braine. "Olga, I want you to
play a trick on this handsome delegate-at-large. I'm not
very enthusiastic over his talk. I want him humiliated.

All you have to do, he says, is to walk into the Hargreave house and walk out again. Well, let's you and I see that he does that and nothing else. I'll have no one meddling with my own game."

Some one sneezed, and everybody looked at his neighbor. The sneeze was repeated, but muffled, as if some one was desperately anxious to avoid sneezing.

"It came from above!" whispered Olga. "Don't look up!"

Braine was cool. He walked idly across the room to where Vroon sat. "Very well, Paroff; we give you free rein." To Vroon he said: "Some one is watching us from the room overhead. I thought that room belonged to us."

"It does," said Vroon stolidly.

"Then how is it that some one is watching from up there? No excitement. I'm going to bid every one good night, then I'm going to investigate. When I leave you will quietly send men to all exits to the building. I want the man who sneezed, and I want him badly."

Olga departed with Braine, only she immediately sought the taxi that brought her and was driven home. It was always understood that when any serious exploit was under way hereabouts she was to make her departure at once.

Vroon stationed his men at the several exits and Braine went up-stairs. The man who had sneezed, however, had vanished as completely as if he had worn that invisible cloak one reads about in the Persian tales. As a matter of fact, after the second sneeze he had gone up to the roof, got out by the trap, and jumped—rather risky business, too—to the next roof and had clambered down the fire-escape of the second building. He was swearing inaudibly. After all these days of care and planning, after all his cleverness in locating the rendezvous of the Black Hundred, and now to lose his advantage because of an uncontrollable sneeze! He would never dare go back, and just when he was beginning to pick up fine bits of information! So Florence Hargreave was going to have a new father in a day or so? There were some clever rogues among this band of theirs; but their cleverness was well offset by an equal number of fools.

Yes, there were some clever rogues, and to prove this assertion Braine secured a taxicab and drove furiously away, his destination the home of his ancient enemy. He dropped the cab a block or two away and presently stowed himself away in the summer house at the left of the lawn. It would have been a capital idea—that is, if the other man had not thought of and anticipated this very thing. So he used a public pay station telephone; and Braine waited in vain, waited till the lights in the Hargreave house went out one by one and it became wrapped in darkness within and moonshine without.

Braine was a philosopher. He returned to his waiting taxicab, drove home, paid the bill, smiling grimly, and went to bed. It was going to be a wonderful game of blind man's buff, and it was going to be sport to watch this fool Paroff blunder into a pit.

The next afternoon Florence and Norton sat in the summer house talking of the future. Lovers are prone to talk of that. As if anything else in the world ever equals the present! They talked of nice little apartments and vacations in the summer and how much they would save out of his salary, and a thousand and one other things which would not interest you at all if I recounted them in detail. But they did love each other, and they were going

THEY DID NOT CARE A SNAP OF THEIR FINGERS WHAT JONES THOUGHT

to be married; you may be certain of that. They did not care a snap of the finger what Jones thought. They were going to be married, and that was all there was to it. Of course, Florence couldn't touch a penny of her father's money. If he, Norton, couldn't take care of her without help, why, he wouldn't be worth the powder to blow him up with.

"But, my dear, you must be very careful," he said. "Jones and I will always be about somewhere. If they really get hold of you once, God alone knows what will happen. It is not you, it is your poor father they want to bring out into the open. If they knew where he was they would not bother you in the least."

"Have I really a father? Sometimes I doubt. Why couldn't he steal into the house and see me, just once?"

"Perhaps he dares not. This house is always watched, night and day, though you'll look in vain to discover any one. Your father knows best what he is doing, my dear girl. You see, I met him years ago in China; and when he started out to do a certain thing he generally did it. He never botched any of his plans. So we all must wait. Only I'm going to marry you all the same, whether he likes it or not. The rogues will try to impose upon you again; but do not pay any attention to notes or personals in the papers. And it was a lucky thing that I was on the freighter that picked you up at sea. I shall always wonder how that yacht took fire."

"So shall I," replied Florence, her brows drawing together in puzzlement. "Sometimes I think I must have done it. You know, people out of their heads do strange things. I seem to see myself as in a dream. And this man Braine is a scoundrel!"

"Yes; and more than that, he is the dear friend of the

countess. But understand, you must never let her dream
or suspect that you know. By lulling her into overconfi-
dence some day she will naturally grow careless, and then
we'll have them all. I think I understand what your
father's idea is: not to have them arrested for blackmail,
but practically to exterminate them, put them in prison
for such terms of years that they'll die there. When you
see a snake, a poisonous one, don't let it get away. Kill
it. Well, I must be off to work."

"And you be careful, too. You are in more danger
than I am."

"But I'm a man and can dodge quick," he laughed, pick-
ing up his hat.

"What a horrid thing money is! If I hadn't any money,
nobody would bother me."

"I would," he smiled. He wanted to kiss her, but the
eternal Jones might be watching from the windows; and
so he patted her hand instead and walked down the
graveled path to the street.

It was difficult work for Florence to play at friendship. She was like her father; she did not bestow it on
every one. She had given her friendship to the Russian,
the first real big friendship in her life, and she had been
roughly disillusioned. But if the countess could act, so
could she; and of the two her acting was the more con-
summate. She could smile and laugh and jest, all the
while her heart was burning with wrath.

One day, a week or so after her meeting with Norton
in the summer house, Olga arrived, beautifully gowned,
handsome as ever. There was not the least touch of the
adventuress in her makeup. Florence had just received
some mail, and she had dropped the letters on the library

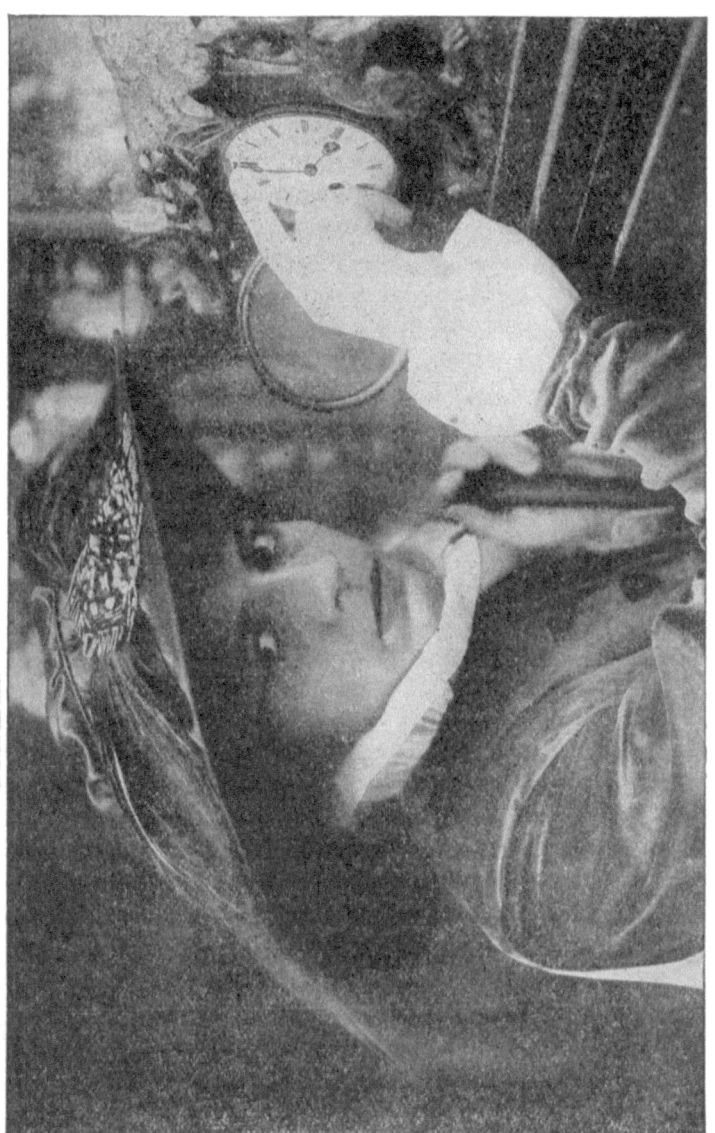

SHE FIRST THOUGHT OF CHANGING THE CLOCK

table to greet the countess. She had opened them, but had not yet looked at their contents.

They were chatting pleasantly about inconsequent things, when the maid came in and asked Florence to come to Miss Susan's room for a moment. Florence excused herself, wondering what Susan could want. She, forgot the mail.

As soon as she was gone the countess, certain that Jones was not lurking about, picked up the letters and calmly examined their contents; and among them she found this remarkable document: "Dear daughter I have never seen: I must turn the treasure over to you. Meet me at eight in the summer house. Tell no one, as my life is in danger. Your loving father."

The countess could have laughed aloud. She saw this man Paroff's hand; and here was the chance to befool and humiliate him and send him off packing to his cold and miserable country. She had made up once as Florence, and she could easily do so again. The only thing that troubled her was the fact that she did not know whether Florence had read the letter or not. Thus, she did not dare destroy it. She first thought of changing the clock; then she concluded to drop the letter exactly where she found it and trust to luck.

When Florence returned she explained that her absence had been due to some trifling household affair.

Said the Russian: "I come primarily to ask you to tea to-morrow, where they dance. If you like, you may ask Mr. Norton to go along. I begin to observe that you two are rather fond of each other."

"Oh, Mr. Norton is just a valuable friend," returned Florence with a smile that quite deceived the other woman. "I shall be glad to go to the tea. But I shall not promise to dance."

"Not with Mr. Norton?" archly.

"Reporters never dance themselves; they make others dance instead."

"I shall have to tell that," declared the countess; and she laughed quite honestly.

"Then I have said something witty?"

"Indeed you have; and it is not only witty but truthful. I'm afraid you're deeper than the rest of us have any idea of."

"Perhaps I am," thought Florence; "at least deeper than you believe."

When the countess fluttered down to her limousine—Florence hated the sight of it—and drove away, Florence remembered her letters. And when she came to the one purporting to be from her father, she read it carefully, bent her head in thought, and finally destroyed the missive, absolutely confident that it was only a trap, and not very well conceived at that. Norton had given her plenty of reason for believing all such letters to be forgeries. Her father, if he really wished to see her, would enter the house; he would not write. Ah, when would she see that father of hers, so mysterious, always hovering near, always unseen?

It must have been an amusing adventure for the countess. To steal into the summer house and wait there, not knowing if Florence had advised Jones or the reporter. If caught, she had her excuses. Paroff, the confident, however, appeared shortly after.

"My child!" whispered the man.

And Olga stifled a laugh; but to him it sounded like a sob.

HE TOOK HER STRAIGHT TO THE EXECUTIVE CHAMBER OF THE BLACK HUNDRED

"I am worn out," he said. "I am tired of the game of hide and seek."

"You will not have to play the game long," thought Olga.

"The money is hidden in my office down-town. And we must go there at once. When we return we will pack up and leave for Europe. I've longed to see you so!"

"You poor fool! And they sent you to supersede Leo!" she mused.

She played out the farce to the very end. She permitted herself to be pinioned and jogged; and for what unnecessary roughness she suffered at the hands of Paroff he would presently pay. He took her straight to the executive chamber of the Black Hundred and pushed her into the room, exclaiming triumphantly:

"Here is Hargreave's daughter!"

"Indeed!" said Olga, throwing back her veil and standing revealed in her mask.

"Olga!" cried Braine, laughing.

And that was the inglorious end of the secret agent from Russia.

CHAPTER XIV

PERHAPS the most amusing phase of the secret
agent's discomfiture was the fact that neither Jones
nor Florence had the least idea what had happened.
Florence regretted a hundred times during the evening
that she had not gone out to the summer house. It might
really have been her father. Her regret grew so deep in
her that just before going to bed she confessed to Jones.

"You received a letter of that sort and did not show
it to me?" said Jones, astonished.

"You warned me never to pay any attention to them."

"No; I warned you never to act upon them without
first consulting me. And we might have made a capture!
My child, always show me these things. I will advise you
whether to tear them up or not."

"Jones, I believe you are going a little too far," said
Florence haughtily. "It might have been my father."

"Never in this world, Miss Florence. Still, I beg your
pardon for raising my voice. What I do and have done
is only for your own sake. There are two things I wish to
impress upon your mind before I go. This can be made
a comedy or a terrible tragedy. You have already had a
taste of the latter; and each time you escaped because
God was good to us. But He is rarely kind to thoughtless

182

people. They have to look out for themselves. I am acting under orders; always remember that."

"Forgive me; I acted wrongly. But I'm so weary and
tired of this eternal suspicion of everybody and everything. Can't I go somewhere, some place where I can
have rest?"

"If I thought for a single moment it was possible to
take you thousands of miles from this spot, it would be
done this very night. But this is our fortress. So far
it has been impregnable. The police are watching it; and
that prevents a general assault by the scoundrels. If we
tried to leave we would be followed; and they play the
game exceedingly well. Now, good night. We'll have
you out of all this doubt and suspicion one of these days.
There will not be any past; that will be lopped off as
you'd lop a limb from a tree."

"Please let it be quick. I want to see my father."

Jones' eyes sparkled. "And you have my word that
he wants to see you. But I dare not tell you."

"Do you think he would object to Mr. Norton?" she
asked, studying the rug.

"In what capacity?" he countered, forcing her hand.

"As—as a husband?" bravely.

Jones in turn studied the patterns in the rug. "It is
only natural for a father to look high for his daughter's
husband. But, after all, an honest man is worth as much
as anything I know of. And Norton is honest and loyal
and brave."

"Thank you, Jones. I intend to marry him when the
time comes; so you may as well prepare father for this
eventuality."

"There is an old adage—"

But she interrupted him. "If you have a new adage,

Jones, I shouldn't mind hearing it. But I'm only just out of school, where old adages are served from soup to pudding. Good night."

And Jones went to the rear of the house, chuckling.

In the passing it might well be observed that the Hargreave house had a remarkable menage. There was a gardener, a cook, and a maid; and the three of them reported to Jones each night before going to bed. They were all three detectives from one of the greatest organizations in America.

Finding themselves unable to lure Florence away from the environs of the Hargreave home, the Black Hundred set some new machinery in motion. They proposed to rid the house of every one in it by a perfectly logical device. But the first step in this new move was going to be extremely delicate and risky. It was no small adventure to enter the Hargreave home; and yet this must be done. So finally "Spider" Beggs was selected for the work. The man could practically walk over crockery without causing a sound; he could climb a house by the window ledges; and he could hold his breath like those professional tank swimmers.

Three or four nights after the Paroff fiasco, Jones started the rounds, putting out the lights. He left the one in the hall till the last, for it was his habit, after having turned off that light, to stand by the door for several minutes, watching. One never could tell.

On the other hand, "Spider" Beggs never approached a house till an hour after the lights went out. Persons were likely to move about for some minutes later; they might want something to eat, a drink of water. So he remained hidden behind the summer house till long after midnight. When at last he felt assured that all in the

HERE WAS AN OPERATION THAT NEEDED ALL HIS CARE AND SKILL

Hargreave house were asleep, he moved out cautiously. Both his future and his pocketbook depended upon the success of this venture. It took him ten minutes to crawl from the summer house to the veranda, and to have detected this approach Jones, had he been watching, would have needed a searchlight. Beggs hugged the lattice-work for another ten minutes and then drew himself up and wriggled to one of the windows. Here was an operation that needed all his care and skill; to lift this window without sound. But he was an old hand and windows with ordinary locks were playthings under his deft touch. He raised the window, stepped over the sill into the library, and crouched down. He did not close the window; house thieves never do. They leave windows and doors open, because sooner or later they have to make their escape that way.

Presently he stood up, flashed his torch, found the library shelves, and tiptoed toward them. He then selected three or four volumes, opened them at random and laid neat packages of money between the leaves. It was not real money, but only a bank clerk could have told that. This done, he moved toward the window again.

"Stop!" said Jones quietly.

"Spider" Beggs gasped, it was so unexpected; but at the same time almost instinctively he plunged headlong through the window, and the bullet which followed snipped a lock of his hair. He threw himself off the veranda and scurried across the lawn, zigzag fashion. But no more bullets followed.

Jones turned on the lights and investigated the room, but he could not find anything disturbed, and naturally came to the conclusion that the intruder had been in-

terrupted before he had begun his work. He turned off
the lights and sat up the major part of the night. Nothing more happened. Florence came down, but he sent
her back to bed, explaining that some one had attempted
to enter the house and he had taken a shot at him.

"Spider" Beggs had a letter to write. He was in
high feather. He had tackled a difficult job and had
come away without a scratch. But he had the misfortune to write his letter to the secret service officials in a
hotel often frequented by Norton. And so Jim, on finish-
ing his own letter, blotted it and casually glanced at the
blotter. A single word caught his eye. Being an alert
newspaper man, always on the hunt for stories, he examined the blotter with care. It was an easy matter
for him to read writing backward, having fooled away
many an hour in the composing rooms. The word which
had awakened the reportorial sense in him was "counterfeit." He held the blotter toward the mirror and read
enough to satisfy himself that the Black Hundred had
become active once more. And this was one of the best
ideas they had yet conceived.

Hargreave had always been something of a mystery
to his neighbors. Where he had lived in other days was
unknown; neither had any one the remotest idea from
what source his riches had been obtained. And nothing
was known of Jones or the daughter. It was a very
shrewd method of clearing every one out of the house
and leaving it to be examined at leisure. And he had
fallen upon this thing; he, Norton, all because his tailor
had written him a sharp note about his bill and he had
been provoked to reply in kind! Counterfeit money.
There was quite a flurry these days over certain issues
of spurious paper. It was so good that only experts could

HE EXAMINED THE BLOTTER WITH CARE

detect it. There were two plates, one for a ten and another for a twenty. For a while he was pulled between duty and love. Well, it would only add another interesting chapter to the general story when he published it. He started out to Riverdale to acquaint Jones with the discovery.

"Humph!" said Jones; "not a bad idea this. So that's what the sneak was doing here last night. I've been wondering and wondering. Let's have a look."

He went through the books and at length came across the three volumes. These held a thousand in excellent counterfeit.

"Mighty good work that. What are you going to do?" asked the reporter.

Jones rubbed his chin reflectively. "How long may a counterfeiter be sent up?"

"Anywhere from ten to twenty years."

"That will serve. My boy, this time we'll go and take Mr. Black Hundred right in his cubby-hole."

"You know where it is?"

"Every nook and corner of it. Now you go at once to the chief of the local branch of the secret service and put the matter to him frankly. I, Florence, Susan, and the rest of us must be arrested. The wretches must believe that the house is empty. They'll rove about fruitlessly and will return to their den to report the success of the coup. All the while you and some detectives will be in hiding up-stairs, dictagraph and all that. When the time comes you will follow. This will not reach the heads, perhaps, but it will demoralize the organization in such a way as to make it helpless for several months to come. There is a tunnel from the stables to this house."

"What, a tunnel?"

"Yes, Mr. Hargreave had it built several years ago. I don't know what his idea was; possibly he anticipated an event like this. You and your men will find entrance by this method. It can be done without exciting the suspicions of the watchers."

"Looks as if my yarn wasn't going to be delayed so long after all. Jones, you ought to have been in the secret service yourself," admiringly.

Jones smiled and shrugged. "I am perfectly satisfied with my lot—or would be if the Black Hundred could be wiped out of existence."

"I'll see the secret service people at once. I stand in well with them all."

"And good luck to you. We'll need good luck."

Norton was welcomed cordially by the chief. The secret service men trusted him and told him lots of tales that never saw light on the printed page. The reporter went directly to the point of his story, without elaboration, and the chief smiled and handed him the original letter.

"Norton, I've been after this gang of counterfeiters for months and they are clever beyond words. I've never been able to get anywhere near their presses. And for a moment I thought this note was from a squealer. I've a dozen men scouring the country. They find the bogus notes, but never the men who pass them. You see, it's new stuff. I know what all of the old-timers are at; none of them has had a hand in this issue. Some foreigners, I take it, under the leadership of a man I'd very much like to know. Now, what's your scheme?"

Jim outlined it briefly.

"It all depends," said the chief, "upon the fact that they will be impatient. If they have the ability to wait, we lose. But we can afford to risk the chance. The man who wrote this letter is not a counterfeiter. He's an old yeggman. We haven't heard anything of him lately. We tried to corner him on a post-office job, but he slipped by. He may be a stool. Anyhow, I'll draw him in somehow."

"There'll be some excitement."

"We're used to that; you too. All we've got to do is to locate this man Beggs. There are signs of spite in this letter. Very well played, if you want my opinion. What's this Black Hundred?"

"I'm not at liberty to tell just yet. It's a strange game; half political, half blackmail. It's a pretty strong organization. But if they're back of this counterfeiting, there's a fine chance of landing them all."

Here the chief's assistant came in. "Got Beggs on the wire. Says he'll conduct you to the home if you'll promise him immunity for some other offenses."

"Tell him he shall have immunity on the word of the chief. But also say that he must come to see me in person."

"All right, sir."

"I don't believe it would be wise for Beggs to see me here. I gave him a good send-off—Sing Sing—five years ago. He may recollect," said Norton.

"Suit yourself about that. Only, keep in communication with me by telephone and I'll tip you off as to when the raid shall take place. Lucky you came in. I should have honestly gone there and arrested innocent people, and they would have had a devil of a time explaining. It would have taken them at least a week to clear themselves. That would leave the house empty all that time."

Norton did not reply, but he put the blotter away carefully. There was no getting away from the fact, but the god of luck was with him.

"Do you know what's back of it all?"

"I can't tell you any more than I have," said Norton.

"Then I pass. I know you well enough. If you've made up your mind not to talk a man couldn't get anything out of you with a can-opener. And that's why we trust you, my boy. Don't forget the telephone."

"I shan't. So long."

That same night Braine paid the Russian woman a brief visit.

"I think that here's where we go forward. The secret service will raid the house to-morrow and then for a few days we'll roam about as we bally please. I'm hanged if I don't have every plank torn up and the walls pulled down. More and more I'm convinced that the money is in that house."

"Don't be too confident," warned Olga. "So many times we have been tripped up when everything seemed in our hands. The house should be guarded but not entered for a day or two; at least not till after the raid is cold. I'm beginning to see traps everywhere."

"Nonsense! Leave it to me. We shan't stick our heads inside the Hargreave house till we are dead certain that it is absolutely empty. Olga, you're a gem. I don't think Russia will bother us for a while. Eh? Paroff will not dare tell how he was flimflammed. The least he can do to save his own skin is to say that we are fully capable of taking care of ourselves."

Olga laughed. "To think of his writing a note like that! Florence would have recognized—and no doubt did—a palpable attempt to play an old game twice."

"How does she act toward you?"

"Cordial as ever; and yet . . ."

"Yet what?"

"I thought her an ordinary schoolgirl, and yet every once in a while she makes what you billiard players call a professional shot. What matter? So long as they do not shut the door in my face, I ask nothing more. But do you want my opinion? I feel it in my bones that something will go wrong to-morrow."

"Good lord, are you losing your nerve?" cried Braine impatiently. "The secret service has the warning; they find the green stuff, and Jones & Co. will mog off to the police station. And there'll be a week of red tape before they are turned loose again. They'll dig into Hargreave's finances and all that. We'll have all the security in the world to find out if the money is in the house or not. Why worry?"

"It's only the way I feel. There is something uncanny in the regularity of that girl's good luck."

"Ah, but we're not after her this time; it's the whole family."

"The servants too?"

"Everybody in the house will be under suspicion."

"And can you trust Beggs?"

"His life is in the hollow of my hand. You can always trust a man when you hold the rope that's around his neck."

Still the frown did not leave Olga's brow. With all her soul she longed to be out of this tangle. It had all looked so easy at the start; yet here they were, weeks later, no further forward than at the beginning, and added to this they had paid much in lives and money. Well, if she would be fool enough to love this man she must abide with the consequences. She wanted him all by herself, out of danger, in a far country. He might tire, but she knew in her heart that she never would. This was her one great passion, and while her mode of living was not as honest as might be, her love was honest enough and unswerving, though it was not gilded by the pleasant fancies of youth.

"Of what are you thinking?" he asked when he concluded that the pause had been long enough.

"You."

"H'm. Complimentary?"

"No; just ordinary every-day love."

"Ah, Olga, why the deuce must you go and fall in love with a bundle of ashes like myself? Ashes, and bitter ashes, too. Sometimes I regret. But the regretting only seems to make me all the more savage. What opium and dope are to other men, danger and excitement are to me. It is not written that I shall die in bed. I have told you that already. There is no other woman—now. And I do love you after a fashion, as a man loves a comrade. Wait till this dancing bout is over and I may talk otherwise. And now I am going to shake hands and hobnob with the elite—beautiful word! And while I bow and smirk and crack witticisms, I and the devil will be chuckling in our sleeves. But this I'll tell you, while there's a drop of blood in my veins, a breath in my body, I'll stick to this fight if only to prove that I'm not a quitter."

He caught her suddenly in his arms, kissed her, ran lightly to the door, and was gone before she could recover from her astonishment.

The affair went smoothly, without a hitch. Norton and his men gained the house through the tunnel without attracting the least attention. The Black Hundred, watching the front and rear of the house, never dreamed that there existed another mode of entrance or that there was a secret cabinet room.

Half an hour later the head of the secret service, accompanied by his men, together with "Spider" Beggs, who was in high feather over his success, arrived, demanded admittance, and went at the front of the business at once.

"Your name is Jones?" began the chief.

The butler nodded, though his face evinced no little bewilderment at the appearance of these men.

"What is it you wish, sir?"

"I am from the secret service and I have it from a pretty good source that there is counterfeit money hidden in this house. More than that, I can put my hand on the very place it is hidden."

"That is impossible, sir," declared Jones indignantly.

"I am an old hand, Mr. Jones. It will not do you a bit of good to put on that bold front."

Beggs smiled. How was he to know that this was a comedy set especially for his benefit?

"I should like to see that money," said Jones, not quite so bravely.

"Come with me," said the secret service man. "Where's the library?"

"Beyond that door, sir."

The chief beckoning to his men, entered the library, went directly to a certain shelf, extracted three volumes, and there lay the money in three neat packages.

"Good heavens!" gasped Jones.

"I shall have to request you and the family to accompany me to the station."

"But it is all utterly impossible, sir! I know nothing of that money nor how it got there. It's a plot. I declare on my oath, sir, that I am innocent, that Miss Florence and her companion know nothing about it."

"You will have to tell that to the federal judge, sir. My duty is to take you all to the station. It would be just as well not to say anything more, sir."

"Very well; but some one shall smart for this outrage."

"That remains to be seen," was the terse comment of the secret service man.

He led his prisoners away directly.

Norton and his men had to wait far into the night. The Black Hundred did not intend to make any mistake this time by a hasty move. At quarter after ten they descended. Braine was not with them. This was due to the urgent request of Olga, who still had her doubts. The men rioted about the house, searching nooks and corners, examining floors and walls, opening books, pulling out drawers, but they found nothing. They talked freely, and the dictagraph registered every word. The printing plant, which had so long defied discovery, was in the cellar of the house occupied by the Black Hundred. Norton and his men determined to follow and raid the building. And the reporter promised himself a good front-page story without in any way conflicting with his promises to Jones.

Events came to pass as they expected. The trailing was not the easiest thing. Norton knew about where the building was, but he could not go to it directly. He was quite confident that its entrance was identical with that which had the trap door through which he had been flung that memorable day when he had been shanghaied.

When they reached the building he warned the men to

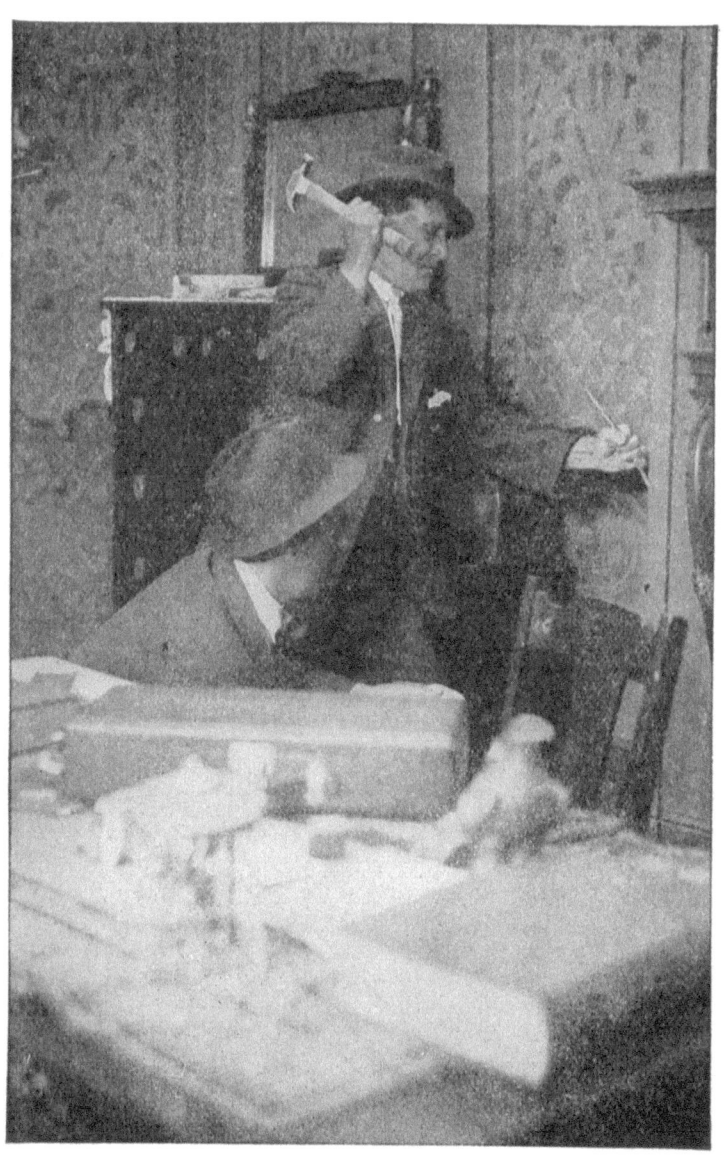

THE MEN RIOTED ABOUT THE HOUSE SEARCHING NOOKS AND CORNERS

hug the wall to the stairs. The trap yawned, but no one was hurt. They scampered up the stairs like a lot of eager boys; broke the door in—to find the weird executive chamber dark and empty and an acrid smoke in their nostrils. This latter grew stifling as they blundered about in the dark. By luck Norton found the exit and called to the men to follow. They saw Beggs at the top of the stairway and called out to him to surrender. He held up his hands and the stairs collapsed. Real fire burst out and Norton and his companions had a desperate battle with flame and smoke to gain the street.

The fire was put out finally, but there was nothing in the ruins to prove that there had been a counterfeiting den there. There was, however, at least one consoling feature: in the future the Black Hundred would have to hold their star-chamber elsewhere.

It was checkmate; or, rather, it was a draw.

CHAPTER XV

IF the truth is to be told, Jones was as deeply chagrined over the outcome of the counterfeit deal as was Braine. They had both failed signally to reach the goal sought. But this time the organization had broken even with Jones, and this fact disturbed the butler. It might signify that the turning point had been reached, and that in the future the good luck might swing over to the side of the Black Hundred. Jones redoubled his cautions, reiterated his warnings, and slept less than ever. Indeed, as he went over the ground he conceded a point to the Black Hundred. He would no longer be able to keep tab on the organization. They had deserted their former quarters absolutely. The agent of whom they had leased the building knew nothing except that he would have to repair the place. The rent had been paid a year in advance, as it had been these last eight years. He had dealt through an attorney who knew no more of his clients than the agent. So it will be seen that Jones had in reality received a check.

More than all this, it would give his enemies renewed confidence; and this was a deeper menace than he cared to face. But he went about his affairs as usual, giving no hint to any one of the mental turmoil which had possession of him.

It is needless to state Norton did not scoop his rivals on

196

the counterfeit story. But he set to work exploring the cellar of the gutted building, and in one corner he found a battered die. He turned this over to the secret service men. There was one man he wanted to find—Vroon. This man, could he find him, should be made to lead him, Norton, to the new stronghold. He saw the futility of trying to trap Braine by shadowing him. He desired Braine to believe that his escape from the freighter had been a bit of wild luck and not a preconceived plan. Braine was out of reach for the present, so he began to search for the man Vroon. He haunted the water front saloons for a week without success.

He did not know that it was the policy of the Black Hundred to lay low for a month after a raid of such a serious character. So the Hargreave menage had thirty days of peace; always watched, however. For Braine never relaxed his vigilance in that part of the game. He did not care to lose sight of Jones, who he was positive was ready for flight if the slightest opportunity offered itself.

Norton went back to the primrose paths of love; and sometimes he would forget all about such a thing as the Black Hundred. So the summer days went by, with the lilacs and the roses embowering the Hargreave home. But Norton took note of the fact that Florence was no longer the light-hearted schoolgirl he had first met. Her trials had made a serious woman of her, and perhaps this phase was all the more enchanting to him, who had his serious side also. Her young mind was like an Italian garden, always opening new vistas for his admiring gaze.

He went about his work the same as of old, interviewing, playing detective, fattening his pay envelope by specials to the Sunday edition and some of the lighter magazines. Sometimes he had vague dreams of writing a play, a novel, and making a tremendous fortune like that chap Manders, who only a few years ago had been his desk mate. He really began the first chapter of a novel; but that has nothing to do with this history.

All ready, then. The chess are once more on the board, and it is the move of the Black Hundred.

The day was rather cloudy. Jones viewed the sky wearily. He could hear Florence playing rather a cheerless nocturne by Chopin. Fourteen weeks ago this warfare had begun, and all he had accomplished, he and those with him, was the death or incarceration of a few inconsequent members of the Black Hundred. Always they struck and always he had to ward off. He had always been on the defensive; and a defensive fighter may last a long while, but he seldom wins; and the butler knew that they must win or go down in bitter defeat. There was no half-way route to the end; there could be no draw. It all reminded him of thunderbolts; one man knew where they were going to strike.

The telephone rang; at the same moment Florence left the piano. She stopped at the threshold.

"Hello! You? Where have you been? What has happened?"

"Who is it?" asked Florence, stepping forward.

Jones held up a warning hand, and Florence paused.

"Yes, yes; I hear perfectly. Oh! You've been working out their new quarters? Good, good! But be very careful, sir. One never knows what may happen. They have been quiet for some time now. . . . Ah! You can't work the ceiling this time? . . . Window over the way. Very good, sir. But be careful."

The word "sir" caught Florence's attention. She ran to Jones and seized him by the arm.

"Who was that?" she cried, as he turned away from the telephone.

"Why?"

"You said 'sir.'"

Jones' eyes widened. "I did?"

"Yes, and it's the first time I ever heard you use it over the telephone. Jones, you were talking to my father!"

"Please, Miss Florence, do not ask me any questions. I can not answer any. I dare not."

"But if I should command, upon the pain of dismissal?" coldly.

"Ah, Miss Florence," and Jones tapped his pocket, "you forget that you can not dismiss me by word. I am legally in control here. I am sorry that you have made me recall this fact to you."

Florence began to cry softly.

"I am sorry, very sorry," said the butler, torn between the desire to comfort her and the law that he had laid down for himself. "It is very gloomy to-day, and perhaps we are a little depressed by it. I am sorry."

"Oh, I realize, Jones, that all this unending mystery and secrecy have a set purpose at back. Only, it does just seem as if I should go mad sometimes with waiting and wondering."

"And if the truth must be told, it is the same with me. We have to wait for them to strike. Shall I get you something to read? I am going down to the drug store and they have a circulating library."

"Get me anything you please. But I'd feel better with a little sunshine."

"That's universal," replied Jones, going into the hall for his hat.

Had the telephone rung again at that moment it is quite probable that the day would have come to a close as the day before had, monotonously. But the ring came five minutes after Jones had left the house.

"Is this the Hargreave place?"

"Yes," said Florence. "Who is it?"

"This is Miss Hargreave talking?"

"Yes."

"This is Doctor Morse. I am at the Queen Hotel. Mr. Norton has been badly hurt, and he wants you and Mr. Jones to come at once. We can not tell just how serious the injury is. He is just conscious. Shall I tell him you will come immediately?"

"Yes, yes!"

Florence snapped the receiver on the hook. She wanted to fly, fly. He was hurt. How, when, where?

"Susan! Susan!" she called.

"What is it?" asked Susan, running into the room.

"Jim is badly hurt. He wants me to come at once. Oh, Susan! I've been dreading something all day long." Florence struck the maid's bell. "My wraps. You will go with me, Susan."

"Where, Miss Florence," asked the maid, alive to her duty.

"Where? What is that to you?" demanded Florence, who did not know that this maid was a detective.

"Why not wait till Mr. Jones returns?" she suggested patiently.

"And let the man I love die?" vehemently.

"At least you will leave word where you are going, Miss Florence."

"The Queen Hotel. And if you say another word I'll discharge you. Come, Susan."

There happened to be a taxicab conveniently near (as Vroon took care there should be), and Florence at once engaged it. She did not see the man hiding in the bushes. The two young women stepped into the taxicab and were driven off. They had been gone less than five minutes when Jones returned with his purchase, to find the house empty of its most valuable asset. He was furious, not only at the maid, who, he realized, was virtually helpless, but at his own negligence.

In the midst of his violent harangue the bell sounded. In his bones he knew what was going to be found there. It was a letter on the back of which was drawn the fatal black mask. With shaking fingers he tore open the envelope and read the contents:

"Florence is now in our power. Only the surrender of the million will save her. Our agent will call in an hour for an answer.   THE BLACK HUNDRED."

As a matter of fact, they had wanted Jones almost as badly as Florence, but her desire for a book—some popular story of the day—had saved him from the net. The letter had been written against this possibility.

Jones became cool, now that he knew just what to face. The Queen Hotel meant nothing. Florence would not be taken there. He called up Norton. It took all the butler's patience, however, as it required seven different calls to locate the reporter.

Meantime the taxicab containing Florence and Susan spun madly toward the water front. Here the two were separated by an effective threat. Florence recognized

the man Vroon and knew that to plead for mercy would
be a waste of time. She permitted herself to be led to a
waiting launch. Always when she disobeyed Jones something like this happened. But this time they had cun-
ningly struck at her heart, and all thought of her personal safety became as nothing. For the present she
knew that she was in no actual physical danger. She
was merely to be held as a hostage. Would Susan have
mentality enough to tell Jones· where the taxicab had
stopped? She doubted. In an emergency Susan had
proved herself a nonentity, a bundle of hysterical thrills.

As a matter of fact, for once Florence's deductions
were happily wrong. When the chauffeur peremptorily
deposited Susan on the lonely country road, several miles
from home, she ran hot-foot to the nearest telephone and
sent a very concise message home. Susan was becoming
acclimated to this strange, exciting existence.

Norton arrived in due time, and he and Jones were
mapping out a plan when Susan's message came.

"Good girl!" said Jones. "She's learning. Can you
handle this alone, Norton? They want me out of the
house again, for I believe they were after me as well as
Florence. Half an hour gone!"

"Trust me!" cried Norton.

And he ran out to his auto. It was a wild ride. Several policemen shouted after him, but he went on un-
mindful. They could take his license number a hundred
times for all he cared. So they had got her? They could
wait till their enemy's vigilance slacked and then would
strike? But Susan! The next time he saw Susan he
was going to take her in his arms and kiss her. It might
be a new sensation to kiss Susan, always so prim and
offish. Corey Street—that had been her direction. They

THEY WERE MAPPING OUT A PLAN WHEN SUSAN'S MESSAGE CAME

had put Florence in a motor boat at the foot of Corey Street. He was perhaps half an hour behind.

Florence never opened her lips. She stared ahead proudly. She would show these scoundrels that she was her father's daughter. They plied her with questions, but she pretended not to hear.

"Well, pretty bird, we'll make you speak when the time comes. We've got you this trip where we want you. There won't be any jumping overboard this session, believe me. We've wasted enough time. We've got you and we're going to keep you."

"Let her be," said Vroon morosely. "We'll put all the questions we wish when we're at our destination." And he nodded significantly toward the ships riding at anchor.

Florence felt her heart sink in spite of her abundant courage. Were they going to take her to sea again? She had acquired a horror of the sea, so big, so terrible, so strong. She had had an experience with its sullen power. They had gone about four miles down when she looked back longingly toward shore. Something white seemed to be spinning over the water far behind. At first she could not discern what it was. As she watched it it grew and grew. It finally emerged from the illusion of a gigantic bird into the actuality of an every-day hydroplane. Her heart gave a great bound. This flying machine was coming directly toward the launch; it did not deviate a hair's breadth from the line. Fortunately the men were looking toward the huge freighter a quarter of a mile farther on, and from their talk it was evident that the freighter was to be her prison—bound for where? Nearer and nearer came the hydroplane. Was it for her?

It was impossible for the men not to take notice of the barking of the engines at last.

"The thing's headed for us!"

Vroon stared under his palm. It was not credible that pursuit had taken place so quickly. To test yonder man-bird he abruptly changed the course of the launch. The hydroplane veered its course to suit.

Florence heard her name called faintly. One of the men drew his revolver, but Vroon knocked it out of his hand.

"There's the police boat, you fool!"

"Jump!" a voice called to Florence.

She flung herself into the water without the slightest hesitation.

All this came about something after this fashion. When Norton arrived at the foot of Corey Street a boatman informed him that a young woman of his description had got into a fast motor boat and had gone down the river.

"Was there any struggle?"

"Struggle? None that I could see. She didn't make no fuss about going."

"Have you a launch?"

"Yes, but the other boat has half an hour's start, and I'd never catch her in a thousand years. But there's a hydroplane a little above here. You might interest the feller that runs it."

"Thanks!"

But the aviator would not listen.

"A life may hang in the balance, man!" expostulated Norton, longing to pommel the stubborn man.

"What proof have I of that?"

Norton showed his card and badge.

"Oh, I see!" jeered the aviator. "A little newspaper

stunt in which I am to be the goat. It can't be done, Mr. Norton; it can't be done."

"A hundred dollars!"

"Not for five hundred," and the aviator callously turned away toward the young woman with whom he had been conversing prior to Norton's approach. The two, walked a dozen yards away.

Norton had not served twelve years as a metropolitan newspaper man for nothing. He approached the mechanics who were puttering about the machine.

"How about twenty apiece?" he began.

"For what?" the men asked.

"For sending that paddle around a few times."

"Get into that seat, but don't touch any of those levers," one of them warned. "Twenty is twenty, Jack, and the boss is a sorehead to-day anyhow. Give her a shove for the fun of it."

It was a dumfounded aviator who saw his hydroplane skim the water and a moment later sail into the air. These swift moving days a reporter of the first caliber is supposed to be able to run railroad engines, submarines, flying machines, conduct a war, able to shoot, walk, run, swim, fight, think, go without food like a python, and live without water like a camel. Norton had flown many times in the last four years. At the moment he called out to Florence to jump he dropped to the water with all the skill of an old-timer and took her aboard. And he could not use a line of this exploit for his paper!

Jones heard the bell. It was the agent from the Black Hundred. He smiled jauntily.

"Well, old fox, we've cornered you at last, haven't we?

I want that money, or Hargreave's daughter takes another sea voyage, and this time she will not jump overboard. A million; and no more nonsense."

"Give me fifteen minutes to decide," begged Jones, hoping against hope.

"Fifteen seconds!"

"Then we can't do business. What! Give you a million, knowing you all to be a pack of liars? Bring Miss Florence back and the money is yours. We are tired of fighting." As indeed Jones really was. The strain had been terrific for weeks.

"The money first. We don't lie any better than you do. Fork over. You'll have to trust us. We have no use for the girl once we get the cash."

"And you'll never touch a penny of it, you blackguard!" cried Norton from the doorway.

The agent turned to behold the reporter and the girl. He did not stop to ask questions, but bolted. He never got beyond the door, however.

"Always the small fry," sighed Jones. "And if I could have put my hands on the money I'd have given it to him! Ah, girl, it doesn't do any good to talk to you, does it?"

"But they told me he was dying!"

Jones shrugged.

CHAPTER XVI

T HE maid stole into the house, wondering if she had been seen. She wanted to be loyal to this girl, but she was tired of the life; she wanted to be her own mistress, and the small fortune offered her would put her on the way to realize her ambition. What had she not seen and been of life since she joined the great detective force! Lady's maid, cook, ship stewardess, flash woman, actress, clerk, and a dozen other employments. Her pay, until she secured some fat reward, was but twelve hundred a year; and here was five thousand in advance, with the promise of five thousand more the minute her work was done. And it was simple work, without any real harm toward Florence as far as she was concerned. The whole thing rested upon one difficulty; would Jones permit the girls to leave the house?

One day Florence found Susan sitting in a chair, her head in her hands.

"Why, Susan, what's the matter?" cried Florence.

"I don't know what is the matter, dear, but I haven't felt well for two or three days. I'm dizzy all the time; I can't read or sew or eat or sleep."

"Why didn't you tell me?" said Florence, reproachfully. She rang for the detective-maid. "Ella, I don't know anything about doctors hereabouts."

207

"I know a good one, Miss Florence. Shall I send for him?"

"Do; Susan is ill."

Jones was not prepared for treachery in his own household; so when he heard that a doctor had been called to attend Susan he was without the least suspicion that he had been betrayed. More than this, there had been no occasion to summon a doctor in the seven years Mr. Hargreave had lived there. So Jones went about his petty household affairs without more thought upon the matter. The maid had been recommended to him as one of the shrewdest young women in the detective business.

The doctor arrived. He was a real doctor; no doubt of that. He investigated Susan's condition—brought about by a subtle though not dangerous poison—and instantly recommended the seashore. Susan was not used to being confined to the house; she was essentially an out-of-doors little body. The seashore would bring her about in no time. The doctor suggested Atlantic City because of its mildness throughout the year and its nearness to New York.

"I'm afraid she'll have to go alone," said Jones gravely.

"I shan't stir!" declared Susan. "I shan't leave my girl even if I am sick." Susan caught Florence's hand and pressed it.

"Would you like to go with her, Florence?" asked Jones, with a shy glance at the strange doctor. The shy glance was wasted. The doctor evinced no sign that it mattered one way or the other to him.

"It is nothing very serious now," he volunteered. "But it may turn out serious if it is not taken care of at once."

"What is the trouble?" inquired Jones, who was growing fond of Susan.

"Weak heart. Sunshine and good sea air will strengthen her up again. No, no!" as Jones drew forth his wallet. "I'll send in my bill the first of the month. Sunshine and sea air; that's all that's necessary. And now, good day."

All very businesslike; not the least cause in the world for any one to suspect that a new trap was being set by the snarers. The maid returned to the sewing-room, while Florence coddled her companion and made much of her.

Jones was suspicious, but dig in his mind as he would he could find no earthly reason for this suspicion save that this attribute was now instinctive, that it was always near the top. If Susan was ill she must be given good care; there was no getting around this fact. Later, he telephoned several prominent physicians. The strange doctor was recommended as a good ordinary practitioner and in good standing; and so Jones dismissed his suspicions as having no hook to hang them on.

His hair would have tingled at the roots, however, had he known that this same physician was one of the two who had signed the document which had accredited Florence with insanity and had all but succeeded in making a supposition a fact. Nor was Jones aware of the fact that the telephone wire had been tapped recently. So when he finally concluded to permit Florence to accompany Susan to Atlantic City he telephoned to the detective agency to send up a trusty man, who was shadowed from the moment he entered the Hargreave home till he started for the railway station. He became lost in the shuffle and was not heard from till weeks later, in Havana. The Black Hundred found a good profit in the shanghaing business.

Susan began to pick up, as they say, the day after the

arrival at Atlantic City, due, doubtless, to the cessation of the poison she had been taking unawares. The two young women began to enjoy life for the first time since they had left Miss Farlow's. They were up with the sun every day and went to bed tired but happy. No one bothered them. If some stray reporter encountered their signatures on the hotel register, he saw nothing to excite his reportorial senses. All this, of course, was due to Norton's policy of keeping the affair out of the papers.

Following Jones' orders, they made friends with none. Those about the hotel—especially the young men—when they made any advances were politely snubbed. Every night Florence would write to her good butler to report what had taken place during the day, and he was left to judge for himself if there was anything to arouse his suspicions. He, of course, believed the two were covertly guarded by the detective he had sent after them.

When Braine called on Olga he found his doctor there.

"Well, what's the news?" he asked.

"I had better run down and inquire how the young lady is progressing," said the doctor, who was really a first-rate surgeon and who had performed a number of skilled operations upon various members of the Black Hundred anent their encounters with the police. "I've got Miss Florence where you want her. It's up to you now."

"She ought to be separated from her companion. We have left them alone for a whole week, so Jones will not worry particularly. A mighty curious thing has turned up. Before Hargreave's disappearance not a dozen persons could recollect what Jones looked like. He was rarely ever in sight. What do you suppose that signifies?"

"Don't ask me," shrugged the man of medicine. "I shouldn't worry over Jones."

"But we can't stir the old fool. We can't get him out of that house. I've tried to get that maid to put a little something in his coffee, but she stands off at that. She says that she did as she agreed in regard to Florence, but her agreement ended there. We have given the jade five thousand already and she is clamoring for the balance."

"Have you threatened her?" asked Olga.

Braine smiled a little. "My dear woman, it is fifty-fifty. While I have a hold on her, it is not quite so good as she has on me. We are not dealing with an ordinary servant we could threaten and scare. No, indeed; a shrewd little woman who desperately wanted money. And she will be paid; no getting out of it. She will not move another step, one way or the other, after she receives the balance. Hargreave will have a pretty steep bill to pay when the time comes."

"She has no idea where the million is?"

"If she had, she's quite capable of lugging it off all by herself," said Braine.

The doctor laughed.

"Olga," went on Braine, "you must look at it as I do; that it is still in the middle of the game, and we have neither lost nor won."

"How do you know that Hargreave may not have at his beck and call an organization quite as capable if not as large as ours?" suggested the physician.

"That is not possible," Braine declared without hesitation.

"Well, it begins to look that way to me. We've never made a move yet that hasn't been blocked."

"Pure luck each time, I tell you; the devil's own luck always at the critical moment, when everything seems to be in our hands. Now, we want Florence, and we've tried a hundred ways to accomplish this fact and failed. The question is, how to get her away from her companion?"

"Simple enough," said the doctor complacently.

"Out with it, if you have an idea."

The doctor leaned forward and whispered a few words.

"Well, I'm hanged!" Braine laughed and slapped the doctor on the shoulder. "The simplest thing in the world. Mad dog wouldn't be in it. I always said that you had gray matter if you cared to exert yourself."

"Thanks," replied the doctor dryly. "I'll drop down there to-morrow, if you say so, ostensibly to see the other patient. It will make a deuce of a disturbance."

"Not if you scare the hotel people."

"That is what I propose to do. They will not want such a thing known. It would scare every one away for the rest of the season. But of course this depends upon whether they are honest or in the hotel business to make money."

Again Braine laughed. "Bring her back to New York alone, Esculapius, and a fat check is yours. Nothing could be simpler than an idea like this. It's a fact; no man can think of everything, and you've just proved it to me. I've tried to do a general's work without aids. Olga, does any one watch me come and go any more?"

"No; I've watched a dozen nights. The man has gone. Either he found out what he wanted or he gave up the job. To my mind he found out what he wanted."

"And what's that?"

"Heaven knows!" discouragedly.

"Come, doctor, suppose you and I go down to Daly's for a little turn at billiards?"

"Nothing would suit me better."

"All aboard, then! Good night, Olga, keep your hair on; I mean your own hair. We're going to win out, don't you worry. In all games the minute you begin to doubt you begin to lose."

That same night Norton sat at his desk, in his shirt sleeves, pounding away at his typewriter. From time to' time he paused and teetered his chair and scowled over his pipe at the starlit night outside. Bang! would go his chair again, and clickity-click would sing the keys of the machine. The story he was writing was in the ordinary routine; the arrival of a great ocean liner with some political notables who were not adverse to denouncing the present administration. You will have noticed, no doubt, that some disgruntled politician is always denouncing the present administration, it matters not if it be Republican or Democratic. When you are out of a good job you are always prone to denounce. The yarn bored Norton because his thoughts were miles southward.

He completed his story, yanked out the final sheet, called for a copy boy, rose and sauntered over to the managing editor's door, before which he paused indecisively. The "old man" had been after him lately regarding the Hargreave story, and he doubted if his errand would prove successful.

However, he boldly opened the door and walked in.

"Humph!" said the "old man," twisting his cigar into the corner of his mouth. "Got that story?"

Norton sat down. "Yes, but I have not got it for print yet. Mr. Blair, when you gave me the Hargreave job you gave me carte blanche."

"I did," grimly. "But, on the other hand, I did not give you ten years to clear it up in."

"Have I ever fallen down on a good story?" quietly.

"H'm, can't remember," grudgingly.

"Well, if you'll have patience I'll not fall down on this one. It's the greatest criminal story I ever handled, but it's so big that it's going to take time."

"Gimme an outline."

"I have promised not to," with a grimness equal to the "old man's." "If a line of this story trickles out it will mean that every other paper will be moving around, and in the end will discover enough to spoil my end of it. I'll tell you this much: The most colossal band of thieves this country ever saw is at one end of the stick. And when I say that counterfeiting and politics and millions are involved, you'll understand how big it is. This gang has city protection. We are running them all into a corner; but we want that corner so deep that none of them can wriggle out of it."

"Umhm. Go on."

"I want two months more."

The "old man" beat a tattoo with his fat pencil. "Sixty days, then. And if the yarn isn't on my desk at midnight, you—"

"Hunt for another job. All right. I came in to ask for three days' leave."

"You're your own boss, Jim, for sixty days more. Whadda y' mean counterfeiting?"

"Those new tens and twenties. If I stumble on that right, why, I can turn it over without conflicting with the other story."

"Well, go to it."

"I'm turning in my regular work, day in and day out, and while doing it I've gone through more hairbreadth escapes than you ever heard of. They have been after me. I've dodged falling safes; I've been shanghaied, poisoned; but I haven't said a word."

"Good lord! Do you mean all that?"

"Every word, sir."

"I'll make it ninety days, Jim; and if this story comes in I'll see that you get a corking bonus."

"I'm not looking for bonuses. I'm proud of my work. To get this story is all I want. That'll be enough. Thanks for the extension of time. Good night."

So Florence received a long night letter in the morning.

And the doctor arrived at about the same time. And called promptly upon his patient.

"Fine!" he said. "The sea air was just the thing. A doctor always likes to find his advice turning out well."

He glanced quizzically at Florence, who was the picture of glowing health. Suddenly he frowned anxiously.

"You need not look at me," she laughed. "I never felt better in all my life."

"Are you sure?"

"Why, what in the world do you mean?"

He did not speak, but stepped forward and took her by the wrist, holding his watch in his other hand. He shook his head. He looked very solemn, indeed.

"What is it?" demanded Susan, with growing terror.

"Go to your own room immediately and remain there for the present," he ordered. "I must see Miss Hargreave alone."

He opened the door and Susan passed out bewilderedly. He returned to Florence, who was even more bewildered than her companion. The doctor began to ask her questions; how she slept, if she was thirsty, felt pains in her back. She answered all these questions vaguely. Not the slightest suspicion entered her head that she was being hoodwinked. Why should she entertain any suspicion? This doctor, who seemed kindly and benevolent, who had prescribed for Susan and benefited her, why should she doubt him?

"In heaven's name, tell me what is the matter?" she pleaded.

"Stay here for a little while and I'll be back. Under no circumstances leave your room till I return."

He paced out into the hall, to meet the frantic Susan.

"We must see the manager at once," he replied to her queries. "And we must be extremely quiet about it. There must be no excitement. You had better go to your room. You must not go into Miss Hargreave's. Tell me, where have you been? Have you been trying to do any charitable work among the poorer classes?"

"Only once," admitted Susan, now on the verge of tears.

"Only once is sufficient. Come; we'll go and see the manager together."

They arrived at the desk, and the manager was summoned.

"I take it," began the doctor lowly, "that a contagious disease, if it became known among your guests, would create a good deal of disturbance?"

"Disturbance! Good heavens, man, it would ruin my business for the whole season!" exclaimed the astounded manager.

"I am sorry, but this young lady's companion has been stricken with smallpox—"

The manager fell back against his desk, his jaw fallen. Susan turned as white as the marble top.

"The only way to avoid trouble is to have her conveyed immediately to some place where she can be treated properly. Not a word to any one now; absolute secrecy or a panic."

The manager was glad enough to agree.

"She is not dangerous at present, but it is only a matter of a few hours when the disease will become virulent. If you will place a porter before Miss Hargreave's door till I make arrangements to take her away, that will simplify matters."

Smallpox! Susan wandered aimlessly about, half out of her mind with terror. There was no help against such a dreaded disease. Her Florence, her pretty rosy-cheeked Florence, disfigured for life. . . . !

"Miss Susan, where is Florence?"

"Oh, Mr. Norton!" she gasped.

"What's the trouble?" instantly alert.

"Florence has the smallpox!"

"Impossible! Come with me."

But the porter having had the strictest orders from the manager, refused to let them into Florence's room.

"Never mind, Susan. Come along." Out of earshot of the porter, he said: "My room is directly above Florence's. We'll see what can be done. This smells of the Black Hundred a mile off. Smallpox! Only yesterday she wrote me that she never felt better. Have you wired Jones?"

"I never thought to!"

"Then I shall. Our old friends are at work again."

"But it's the same doctor who sent me down here."

Norton frowned.

What followed all appeared in the reporter's story, as written three months later. He and Susan went up to his room, raised the flooring, cut through the ceiling, and with the fire-escape rope dropped below. One glance at Florence's tear-stained face was enough for him. Norton's subsequent battle with the doctor and his accomplices made very interesting reading. Their escape from the hotel, their flight, their encounter with one of the gang in the road, and Florence's blunder into the bed of quicksand, gave a succession of thrills to the readers of the *Blade.*

And all this while the million accumulated dust, layer by layer. Perhaps an occasional hardy roach scrambled over the packets, no doubt attracted by the peculiar odor of the ink.

CHAPTER XVII

THE Black Hundred possessed three separate council chambers, always in preparation. Hence, when the one in use was burned down they transferred their conferences to the second council chamber appointed identically the same as the first. As inferred, the organization owned considerable wealth, and they leased the buildings in which they had their council chambers, leased them for a number of years, and refurnished them secretly with trap floors, doors and panels and all that apparatus so necessary to men who are sometimes compelled to make a quick getaway.

When the Atlantic City attempt was turned into a fiasco by Norton's timely arrival Braine determined once more to rid himself of this meddling reporter. He knew too much, in the first place, and in the second place Braine wanted to learn whether the reporter bore a charmed life or was just ordinarily lucky. He would attempt nothing delicate, requiring finesse. He would simply waylay Norton and make a commonplace end of him. He would disappear, this reporter, that would be all; and when they found him he might or might not be recognizable.

So Braine called a conference and he and his fellow rogues went over a number of expedients and finally agreed that the best thing to do would be to send a man

219

to the newspaper, ostensibly as a reporter looking for a situation. With this excuse he would be able to hang around the city room for three or four days. The idea back of this was to waylay Norton on his way to some assignment which took him to the suburbs.

All this was arranged down to the smallest detail; and a man whom they were quite certain Norton had not yet seen was selected to play the part. He had been a reporter once, more's the pity; so there was no doubt of his being able to handle his end of the game.

"I want Norton, I want him badly," declared Braine, "and woe to you if you let booze play in between you and the object of this move."

The man selected to act the reporter hung his head. Whisky had been the origin of his fall from honest living, and he was not so calloused as not to feel the sting of remorse at times.

"More," went on Braine, "I want Norton brought to 49. It's a little off the beat, and we can handle Norton as we please. When we get rid of this newspaper ferret there'll be another to eliminate. But he's a fox, and a fox must be set to trail him."

"And who is that?"

"Jones, Jones, Jones!" thundered Braine. "He's the live wire. But the reporter first. Jones depends a lot on him. Take away this prop and Jones will not be so sure of himself. There's a man outside all this circle, and all these weeks of warfare have not served to bring him into the circle."

"Hargreave is dead," said Vroon stolidly.

"As dead as I am," snarled Braine. "Two men went away in that balloon; and I'll wager my head that one man came back. I am beginning to put a few things together that I have not thought of before. Who knows? That balloon may have been carried out to sea purposely. The captain on that tramp steamer may have lied from beginning to end. I tell you, Hargreave is alive, and wherever he is he has his hand on all the wires. He has agents, too, whom we know nothing about. Hang the million! I want to put my hands on Hargreave just to prove that I am the better man. He communicates with Jones, perhaps through the reporter; he has had me followed; it was he who changed the boxes, bored the hole in the ceiling of the other quarters and learned heaven knows what."

"If that's the case," said Vroon, "why hasn't he had us apprehended?"

Braine laughed heartily. "Haven't you been able to see by this time what his game is? Revenge. He does not want the police to meddle only in the smaller affairs. He wants to put terror into the hearts of all of us. Keep this point in your mind when you act. He'll never summon the police unless we make a broad daylight attempt to get possession of his daughter. And even then he would make it out a plain case of kidnaping. Elimination, that's the word. All right. We'll play at that game ourselves. No. 1 shall be Mr. Norton. And if you fail I'll break you," Braine added to the ex-reporter.

"I'll get him," said the man sullenly.

Later, when he applied for a situation on the *Blade,* it happened that there were two strikes on hand, and two or three extra men were needed on the city staff. The man from the Black Hundred was given a temporary job and went by the name of Gregg.

For three days he worked faithfully, abstaining from his favorite tipple. He had never worked in New York, so his record was unknown. He had told the city editor that he had worked on a Chicago paper, now defunct.

He paid no attention whatsoever to Norton, a sign of no little acumen. On the other hand Norton never went forth on an assignment that Gregg did not know exactly where he was going. But all these stories kept Norton in town; and it would be altogether too risky to attempt to handle him anywhere but outside of town. So Gregg had to abide his time.

It came soon enough.

Norton was idling at his desk when the city editor called him up to the wicket.

"General Henderson has just returned to America. Get his opinion on the latest Balkan rumpus. He's out at his suburban home. Here's the address."

"How long will you hold open for me?" asked Norton, meaning how long would the city editor wait for the story.

"Till one-thirty. You ought to be back by midnight. It's only eight now."

"All right; Henderson's approachable. I may get a good story out of him."

"Maybe," thought Gregg, who had lost nothing of this conversation.

It was his opportunity. He immediately left the zone of the city desk for a telephone booth. But as he passed the line of desks and busy reporters he did not note the keen scrutiny of a smooth-faced, gray-haired man who stood at the side of Norton's desk awaiting the reporter's return.

"Why, Jones," cried the surprised Norton. "What are you doing all this way from home?"

NORTON WAS IDLING AT HIS DESK WHEN THE CITY EDITOR CALLED HIM
UP TO THE WICKET

"Orders," said Jones, smiling faintly as he delivered a note to the reporter.

"Anything serious?"

"Not that I am aware of. Miss Florence was rather particular. She wanted to be sure that the note reached your hands safely."

"And do you mean to say that you came away and left her alone in that house?"

Again Jones smiled. "I left her well guarded, you may be sure of that. She will never run away again." He waited for Norton to read the note.

It was nothing more than one of those love orders to come and call at once. And she had made Jones venture into town with it! The reporter smiled and put the note away tenderly. And then he caught Jones smiling, too.

"I'm going to marry her, Jones."

"That remains to be seen," replied the butler, not unkindly.

"Well, anyhow, thanks for bringing the note. But I've got to disappoint her to-night. I'm off in a deuce of a hurry to interview General Henderson. I'll be out to tea to-morrow. You can find your way out of this old firetrap. By-by!"

The moment he turned away the smile faded from Jones' face, and with the quickness and noiselessness of a cat he reached the side of the booth in which Gregg believed himself so secure from eavesdropping. The half dozen words Jones heard convinced him that Norton was again the object of the Black Hundred's attention. He had seen the man's face that memorable night when the balloon stopped for its passenger. Before Gregg came out of the booth Jones decided to overtake Norton and

forewarn him, but unfortunately the reporter was nowhere in sight.

There was left for Jones nothing else but to return
home or follow when Gregg came out. As this night he
knew Florence to be exceptionally well guarded, both
within and without the house, he decided to wait and
follow the spy.

When Braine received the message he was pleased.
Norton's assignment fitted his purpose like a glove. Before midnight he would have Mr. Meddling Reporter
where he would bother no one for some time—if he
proved tractable. If not, he would never bother any one
again. Braine gave his orders tersely. Unless Norton
met with unforeseen delay, nothing could prevent his
capture.

When Norton arrived at the Henderson place, a footman informed him from the veranda that General Henderson was at 49 Elm Street for the evening, and it would
be wise to call there. Jim nodded his thanks and set off
in haste for 49 Elm Street. The footman did not enter
the house, but hurried down the steps and slunk off
among the adjacent shrubbery. His mission was over
with.

The house in Elm Street was Braine's suburban estab-
lishment. He went there occasionally to hibernate, as it
were, to grow a new skin when close pressed. The care-
taker was a man rightly called Samson. He was a bruiser
of the bouncer type.

It was fast work for Braine to get out there. If the
man disguised as a footman played his cards badly Braine
would have all his trouble for nothing. He disguised
himself with that infernal cleverness which had long since
made him a terror to the police, who were looking for ten

different men instead of one. He knew that Norton would understand instantly that he was not the general; but on the other hand he would not know that he was addressing Braine.

So the arch-conspirator waited; and so Norton arrived and was ushered into the room. A single glance was enough to satisfy the reporter, always keen-eyed and observant.

"I wish to see General Henderson," he said politely.

"General Henderson is doubtless at his own house."

"Ah!"

"Don't be alarmed—yet," said Braine smoothly.

"I am not alarmed," replied Norton. "I am only chagrined. Since General Henderson is not to be found here I must be excused."

"I will excuse you presently."

"Ah! I begin to see."

"Indeed!" mocked Braine.

"I have tumbled or walked into a trap."

"A keen mind like yours must have recognized that fact the moment you discovered that I was not the general."

"I am indebted to the Black Hundred?" coolly.

"Precisely. We do not wish you ill, Mr. Norton."

"To be sure, no!" ironically. "What with falling safes, poisoned cigarettes, and so forth, I can readily see that you have my welfare at heart. What puzzled me was the suddenness with which these affectionate signs ceased."

"You're a man of heart," said Braine with genuine admiration. "These affectionate signs, as you call them, ceased because for the time being you ceased to be a menace. You have become that once more, and here you are!"

"And what are you going to do with me now that you have got me?"

"There will be two courses." Braine reached into a drawer and drew out a thick roll of bills. "There are here something like $5,000."

"Quite a tidy sum; enough for a chap to get married on."

The two eyed each other steadily. And in his heart Braine sighed. For he saw in this young man's eyes incorruptibility.

"It is yours on one condition," said Braine, reaching out his foot stealthily toward the button which would summon Samson.

"And that is," interpolated Norton, "that I join the Black Hundred."

"Or the great beyond, my lad," took up Braine, his voice crisp and cold.

Norton could not repress a shiver. Where had he heard this voice before? . . . Braine! He stiffened.

"Murder in cold blood?" he managed to say.

"Indefinite imprisonment. Choose."

"I have chosen."

"H'm!" Braine rose and went over to the sideboard for the brandy. "I'm going to offer you a drink to show you that personally there are no hard feelings. You are in the way. After you, our friend, Jones. This brandy is not poisoned, neither are the glasses. Choose either and I'll drink first. We are all desperate men, Norton; and we stop at nothing. Your life hangs by a hair. Do you know where Hargreave is?"

Norton eyed his liquor thoughtfully.

"Do you know where the money is?"

Norton smelt of the brandy.

"I am sorry," said Braine. "I should have liked to win over a head like yours."

Norton nonchalantly took out his watch, and that bit of bravado perhaps saved his life. In the case of his watch he saw a brutal face behind him. Without a tremor, Norton took up his glass.

"I am sorry to disappoint you," he said, "but I shall neither join you nor go to by-by."

Quick as a bird shadow above grass, he flung his brandy over his shoulder into the face of the man behind. Samson yelled with pain. Almost at the same instant Norton pushed over the table, upsetting Braine with it. Next he dashed through the curtains, slammed the door, and fled to the street, very shaky about the knees, if the truth is to be told.

General Henderson's views upon the latest Balkan muddle were missing from the *Blade* the following morning. Norton, instead of returning to the general's and fulfilling his assignment like a dutiful reporter, hurried out to Riverside to acquaint Jones with what had happened. Jones was glad to see him safe and sound.

"That new reporter started the game," he said. "I overheard a word or two while he was talking in the booth. All your telephone booths are ramshackle affairs, you use them so constantly. I tried to find you, but you were out of sight. Now, tell me what happened."

"Sh!" warned Norton as he spied Florence coming down the stairs.

"I thought you couldn't come!" she cried. "But ten o'clock!"

"I changed my mind," he replied, laughing.

He caught her arm in his and drew her toward the library. Jones smiled after them with that enigmatical

smile of his, which might have signified irony or affec-
tion. After half an hour's chat, Florence, quite unaware
that the two men wished to talk, retired.

At the door Norton told Jones what had taken place
at 49 Elm Street.

"Ah! we must not forget that number," mused Jones.
"My advice is, keep an eye on this Gregg chap. We may
get somewhere by watching him."

"Do you know where Hargreave is?"

Jones scratched his chin reflectively.

Norton laughed. "I can't get anything out of you."

"Much less any one else. I'm growing fond of you, my
boy. You're a man."

"Thanks ; and good night."

When Olga Perigoff called the next day Jones divested
himself of his livery, donned a plain coat and hat, and left
the house stealthily. To-day he was determined to learn
something definite in regard to this suave, handsome Russian. When she left the house Jones rose from his hiding place and proceeded to follow her. The result of
this espionage on the part of Jones will be seen presently.

Meantime Jim went down to the office and lied cheerfully about his missing the general. Whether the city
editor believed him or not is of no matter. Jim went
over to his desk. From the corner of his eye he could
see Gregg scribbling away. He never raised his head as
Jim sat down to read his mail. After a while Gregg rose
and left the office ; and, of course, Jim left shortly afterward. When the newcomer saw that he was being followed, he smiled and continued on his way. This Norton
chap was suspicious. All the better ; his suspicions should
be made the hook to land him with. By and by the man
turned into a drug store and Jim loitered about till he

reappeared. Gregg walked with brisker steps now. It was his intention to lead Norton on a wild goose chase for an hour or so, long enough to give Braine time to arrange a welcome at another house.

Norton kept perhaps half a block in the rear of his man all the while. But for this caution he would have witnessed a little pantomime that would have put him wholly upon his guard. Turning a corner, Gregg all but bumped into the countess. He was quick enough to place a finger on his lips and motion his head toward a taxicab. Olga hadn't the least idea who was coming around the corner, but she hailed the cab and was off in it before Jim swung around the corner.

Jones, who had followed the countess for something over an hour and a half, hugged a doorway. What now? he wondered. The countess knew the man. That was evidence enough for the astute butler. But what meant the pantomime and the subsequent hurry? He soon learned. The man Gregg went his way, and then Jim turned the corner. Jones cast a wistful glance at the vanishing cab of the Russian, and decided to shadow the shadower—in other words, to follow the reporter, to see that nothing serious befell him.

The lurer finally paused at a door, opened it with a key and swung it behind him, very careful, however, not to spring the latch. Naturally Jim was mightily pleased when he found the door could be opened. When Jones, not far behind, saw him open the door, he started to call out a warning, but thought the better of it. If Norton was walking into a trap it was far better that he, Jones, should remain outside of it. If Jim did not appear after a certain length of time, he would start an investigation on his own account.

No sooner was Jim in the hallway than he was set upon and overpowered. They had in this house what was known as "the punishment room." Here traitors paid the reckoning and were never more heard of. Into this room Jim was unceremoniously dropped when Braine found that he could get no information from the resolute reporter.

The room did not look sinister, but for all that it possessed the faculty of growing smaller and smaller, slowly or swiftly, as the man above at the lever willed. When Jim was apprised of this fact, he ran madly about in search of some mode of escape, knowing full well in his heart that he should not find one.

Presently the machinery began to work, and Norton's tongue grew dry with terror. They had him this time; there was not the least doubt of it. And they had led him there by the nose into the bargain.

Twenty minutes passed, and Jones concluded it was time for him to act. He went forward to try the door, but this time it was locked. Jones, however, was not without resource. The house next door was vacant, and he found a way into this, finally reaching the roof. From this he jumped to the other roof, found the scuttle open, and crept down the stairs, flight after flight, till the whir of a motor arrested him.

Conspirators are often overeager, too. So intent were the rascals upon the business at hand that they did not notice the door open slowly. It did not take the butler more than a moment to realize that his friend and ally was near certain death. With an oath he sprang into the room, gave Braine a push which sent him down to join the victim, and pitched into the other two. It was a battle royal while it lasted. Jones knocked down one of them, yelled to Norton, and kicked the rope he saw down into the pit. One end of this rope was attached to a ring in the wall. And up this rope Norton swarmed after he had disposed of Braine. The tide of battle then swung about in favor of the butler, and shortly the fake reporter and his companion were made to join their chief.

Jones stopped the machinery. He could not bring himself to let his enemies die so horribly. Later he knew he would regret this sentiment.

When the people came, summoned by some outsider who had heard the racket of the conflict, there was no one to be found in the pit. Nor was there any visible sign of an exit.

There was one, however, built against such an hour and known only to the chiefs of the Black Hundred.

And still the golden-tinted banknotes reposed tranquilly in their hiding place!

CHAPTER XVIII

ABOUT this time—that is to say, about the time the Black Hundred was stretching out its powerful secret arms toward Norton—there arrived in New York city a personage. This personage was the Princess Parlova, a fabulously rich Polish Russian. She leased a fine house near Central Park and set about to conquer social New York. This was not very difficult, for her title was perfectly genuine and she moved in the most exclusive diplomatic circle in Europe, which, as everybody knows, is the most brilliant in the world. When the new home was completely decorated she gave an elaborate dinner, and that attracted the newspapers. They began to talk about her highness, printed portraits of her, and devoted a page occasionally in the Sunday editions. She became something of a rage. One morning it was announced that the Princess Parlova would give a masked ball formally to open her home to society; and it was this notice that first brought the Princess Parlova under Braine's eyes. He was at the Perigoff apartment at the time.

"Well, well," he mused aloud.

"What is it?" asked Olga, turning away from the piano and ending one of Chopin's mazurkas brokenly.

"Here is the Princess Parlova in town."

"And who is she?"

232

"She is the real thing, Olga; a real princess with vast estates in Poland with which the greedy Slav next door has been very gentle."

"I haven't paid much attention to the social news lately. What about her?"

"She is giving a masked ball formally to open her house on the West Side. And it's going to cost a pretty penny."

"Well, you're not telling me this to make me want to know the princess," said Olga, petulantly.

"No. But I'm going to give you a letter of introduction to her highness."

"Oh!"

"And you are going to ask her to invite two particular friends of yours to this wonderful ball of hers."

"Indeed," ironically. "That sounds all very easy."

"Easier than you think, my child."

"I will not have you call me child."

"Well, then, Olga."

"That's better. Now, how will it be easier than I think?"

"Simply this; the Princess Parlova is an oath-bound member, but has not been active for years."

"Oho!" Olga was all animation now. "Go on!"

"You will go to her with a letter of introduction—no! Better than that, you will make a formal call and show her this ring. You know the ring," he said, passing the talisman to the countess. "Show this to her and she will obey you in everything. She will have no alternative."

"Very good," replied Olga. "And then the program is to insist that she invite Florence and that fool of a reporter to this ball. Then what?"

"You can leave that to me."

"Haven't all these failures been a warning?"

"No, my dear. I was born optimistic; but there's a jinx somewhere in one of my pockets. Time after time I've had everything just where I wanted it, and then— poof! It's pure bald luck on their side, but sooner or later the wheel will turn. And any chance that offers I am bound to accept. Somehow or other we may be able to trap Florence and Norton. I want both of them. If I can get them, Jones will be forced to draw in Hargreave."

"Is there such a man?"

"You saw him that night at the restaurant."

"I have often thought that perhaps I just dreamed it." She turned again to the piano and began humming idly.

"Stop that and listen to me," said Braine, not in quite the best of tempers. "I'm in no mood for whims."

"Music does not soothe your soul, then?" cynically.

"If I had one it might. You will call on the Princess Parlova to-morrow afternoon. It depends upon you what my plans will be. I think you'll have little trouble in getting into the presence of her highness, and once there she will not be able to resist you."

"I'll go."

And go she did. The footman in green livery hesitated for a moment, but the title on the visiting card was quite sufficient. He bowed the countess into the reception room and went in search of his distinguished mistress.

The Princess Parlova was a handsome woman verging upon middle age. She was a patrician; Olga's keen eye discerned that instantly. She came into the reception room with that dignified serenity which would have impressed any one as genuine. She held the card in her fingers and smiled inquiringly toward her guest.

"I confess," she began, "that I recall neither your face

nor your name. I am sorry. Where have I had the honor of meeting you before?"

"You have never met me before, your highness," answered Olga sweetly.

"You came on a charity errand, then?"

"That depends, your highness. Will you be so good as to glance at this?" Olga asked, holding out her palm upon which the talisman lay.

The princess shrank back, paling.

"Where did you get that?" she panted.

"From the head," was the answer.

"And you have followed me from Russia?" whispered the princess, her terror growing.

"Oh, no. The Black Hundred is as strongly organized here as in St. Petersburg. But we always keep track of old members, especially when they stand so high in the world as yourself."

"But I was deceived and betrayed!" exclaimed the princess. "They urged me to join on the ground that the organization was to attempt to bring about the freedom of Poland."

Olga shrugged. "You were rich, highness. The Black Hundred needed money!"

"And you need it now?" eagerly, believing that she saw a loophole. "How much? Oh, I will give a hundred thousand rubles on your promise to leave me alone. Tell me!"

"I am sorry, your highness, but I have no authority to accept such an offer. Indeed, my errand is far from being expensive. All the Black Hundred desires is four invitations to this ball which you are soon to give. That should not cause you any alarm. We shall not interfere with your sojourn in America in any way whatsoever, provided these invitations are issued."

"You would rob my guests?" horrified.

"Positively no! Here is a list of four names. Invite them; that is all you have to do. Not so much as a silver spoon will be found missing. This is on my word of honor, and I never break that word, if you please."

"Give me the list," said the princess wearily. "Who gave you that ring?"

"The head."

"In Russia?"

"No; here in America." Olga dipped into her hand-bag and produced a slip of paper. This she handed to the princess. "Here is the list, highness."

"Who is Florence Hargreave?"

"A friend of mine," evasively.

"Does she belong to the organization?"

"No."

"Then you have some ulterior purpose in having me invite her?"

"I have," answered Olga sharply; "but that does not concern your highness in the least."

The princess bit her lips. "I see your name here also; a man named Braine, and another, Norton."

"Say at once that you do not care to execute the wishes—the commands—of the order," said Olga coldly.

"I will do as you wish. And I beg you now to excuse me. But if anything happens to any of my personal friends—"

"Well?" haughtily from Olga.

"Well, I will put the matter in the hands of the police."

"But so long as your personal friends are not concerned?"

"I shall then of necessity remain deaf and blind. It is one of the penalties I must pay for my folly. I wish you good day."

"And also good riddance," murmured Olga under her breath, as she arose and started for the hallway.

Thus it was that when Norton went to the office the next afternoon he found a broad white envelope on his desk. Indifferently he opened the same and his eyes bulged. "Princess Parlova requests" and so forth and so on. Then he shrugged. The chief had probably asked for the invitation and he would have to write up the doings, a phase of reportorial work eminently distasteful to him. He went up to the city desk.

"Can't you find some one else to do this stuff?" he growled to the city editor.

The city editor glanced at the card and crested envelope. "Good lord, man! Nobody in this office had anything to do with that. What luck! Our Miss Hayes tried all manner of schemes, but was rebuffed on all sides. How the deuce did you chance to get one?"

"Search me," said the bewildered Norton.

"If I were you I'd sit tight and take it all in," advised the editor. "It's going to be the biggest splurge of its kind we've had in years. We've been working every wire we know to get Miss Hayes inside, but it was no go. This princess is not on to the game yet. In this country you get into society or you don't through the Sundays."

"Hanged if I know who wished this thing on me."

"Take it philosophically," said the editor sarcastically. "The princess won't bite you. She may even have seen your picture—"

"Get out!" grumbled Norton, turning away.

He would go out and see Florence. On the way out

to Riverdale he came to the conclusion that the list of the princess fell short and some friend of his who was helping the woman out suggested his name. It was the only way he could account for it.

But when he learned that Florence had an invitation exactly like his own and that she received it that morning he became suspicious.

"Jones, what do you think of it?" he questioned.

"I think it was very kind of the Countess Perigoff suggesting your name and that of Florence," said the butler urbanely.

"Olga?" cried Florence disappointedly.

"It is the only logical deduction I can make," declared Jones. "They are both practically Russians."

"And what would you advise?" asked Norton.

"Why, go and enjoy yourselves. Forewarned is forearmed. The thing is, be very careful not to acquaint any one with the character of your disguise, least of all the Countess Perigoff. Besides," Jones added smiling, "perhaps I may go myself."

"Goody! I've read about masked balls and have always been crazy to go to one," said Florence with eagerness.

"Suppose we go at once and pick out some costumes?" suggested Norton.

"Just as soon as I can get my hat on," replied Florence, happy as a lark.

"But mind," warned Jones; "be sure that you see the costumer alone and that no one else is about."

"I'll take particular care," agreed Norton. "We've got to do some hustling to find something suitable. For a big affair like this the town will be ransacked. All aboard! There's room for two in that car of mine; and we can have a spin besides. Hang work!"

Florence laughed, and even Jones permitted a smile (which was not grim this time) to stir his lips.

A happy person is generally unobservant. Two happy persons together are totally unobservant of what passes around them. In plainer terms this lack is called love. And being frankly in love with each other, neither Norton nor Florence observed that a taxicab followed them into town. Jones, not being in love, was keenly observant; but the taxicab took up the trail two blocks away, so the matter wholly escaped Jones' eye.

The two went into several costumers', but eventually discovered a shop on a side street that had been overlooked by those invited to the masquerade. They had a merry time rummaging among the camphory-smelling boxes. There were dominoes of all colors, and at length they agreed upon two modest ones that were evenly matched in color and design. Florence ordered them to be sent home. Then the two of them sallied up to the Ritz-Carleton and had tea.

The man from the taxicab entered the costumer's, displayed a detective's shield and demanded that the proprietor show him the costumes selected by the two young people who had just left. The man obeyed wonderingly.

"I want a pair exactly like these," said the detective. "How much?"

"Two dollars each, rental; seven apiece if you wish to buy them."

"I'll buy them."

The detective paid the bill, nodded curtly, and returned to his taxicab.

"Now, I wonder," mused the costumer, "what the dickens those innocent-looking young people are up to?" He never found out.

On the night of the ball Norton dined with Florence for the first time; and for once in his life he experienced that petty disturbance of collective thought called embarrassment. To talk over war plans with Jones was one thing, but to have Jones serve soup was altogether another. All through dinner Jones replied to questions with no more and no less than "Yes, sir," and "No, sir." Norton was beginning to learn that this strange man could put on a dozen kinds of armor and always retain his individuality. And to-night there seemed something vaguely familiar about the impassive face of the butler, as if he had seen it somewhere in the past, but could not tell when or where. As he and Florence were leaving for the automobile which was to take them to the princess', the truth came home to him with the shock of a douche of ice-cold water. Under his breath he murmured: "You're a wonderful man, Jones; and I take my hat off to you with the deepest admiration. Hang me!"

"What are you mumbling about?" asked the happy girl.

"Was I mumbling? Perhaps I was going over my catechism. I haven't been out in society in so long that I've forgotten how to act."

"I believe that. We've been in here for five minutes and you haven't told me that you love me."

"Good heavens!" And his arms went around her so tightly that she begged for quarter.

"How strong you are!"

The splendor of the rooms, the dazzling array of jewels, the kaleidoscopic colors, the perfume of the banked flowers and the music all combined to put Florence into a pleasurable kind of trance. And it was only when the first waltz began that she became herself and surrendered to the arms of the man she loved.

And they were waltzing over a volcano. She knew and he knew it. From what direction would the blow come? Well, they were prepared for all manner of tricks.

In an alcove off the ballroom sat Braine and Olga, both dressed exactly like Norton and Florence. Another man and woman entered presently, and Braine spoke to them for a moment, as if giving instructions, which was indeed the case.

The band crashed into another dance, and the masqueraders began swirling hither and thither and yon. A gay cavalier suddenly stopped in front of Florence.

"Enchantress, may I have the pleasure of this dance?"

Jim touched Florence's hand. But she turned laughingly toward the stranger. What difference did it make? The man would never know who she was nor would she know him. It was a lark, that was all; and despite Jim's warning touch she was up and away like the mischievous sprite that she was. Jim remained in his chair, twisting his fingers and wondering whether to laugh or grow angry. After all, he could not blame her. To him an affair like this was an ancient story; to her it was the door of fairyland swung open. Let her enjoy herself.

Florence was having a splendid time. Her partner was asking her all sorts of questions and she was replying in kind, when out of the crowd came Norton (as she supposed), who touched her arm. The cavalier stopped, bowed and made off.

Norton whispered: "I have made an important discovery. We must be off at once. Come with me."

Florence, without the least suspicion in the world, followed him up the broad staircase. What with the many sounds it was not to be wondered at that the difference in the quality of voices did not strike Florence's ear as odd. The result of her confidence was that upon reaching the upper halls, opposite the dressing rooms, she was suddenly thrust into a room and made prisoner. When the light was turned up she recognized with horror the woman who had helped to kidnap her and take her away on the *George Washington* weeks ago. She could not have cried out for help if she had tried.

Meantime Jim got up and began to wander about in search of Florence.

Braine played a clever game that night. He and the Russian, still dominoed like Norton and Florence, ordered the Hargreave auto, by number, entered it and were driven up to the porte-cochère of the Hargreave house. The two alighted, the chauffeur sent the car toward the garage, and Braine and his companion ran lightly down the path to the street where the cab which had followed picked them up.

It grew more and more evident to Jim that something untoward had taken place. He could not find Florence anywhere, in the alcoves, in the side rooms, the supper or card room. Later, to his utter amazement, he was informed that the Hargreave auto had some time since been called and its owner taken home. Some one had taken his place.

His first sensation was impotent fury against Jones, who had permitted them to play with fire. He flung out of the mansion unceremoniously, commandeered a cab, and flew out to Riverdale. And when Jones came to the door he was staggering with sleep.

"What's the matter with you?" demanded Jim roughly. "Where's Florence?"

"Isn't she with you?" cried Jones, making an effort to dispel the drowsiness. "What time is it?" suddenly.

"Midnight! Where is she?"

"Midnight? I've been drugged!"

Without a word Jones staggered off to the kitchens, Jim at his heels.

There was always hot water, and within five minutes Jones had drunk two cups of raw strong coffee.

"Drugged!" he murmured. "Some one in the house! I'll attend to that later. Now, the chauffeur."

But the chauffeur swore on his oath that he had left Jim and Florence on the steps of the porte-cochère.

"Get in!" said Jones to Norton, now fully alive. He could not get it out of his head that some one in the house had drugged him.

The events which followed were to both Jones and Norton something like a series of nightmares. In the new home of the Princess Parlova a bomb had exploded and fire followed the explosion. From pleasure to terror is only a step. The wildest confusion imaginable ensued. Most of the guests were of the opinion that some anarchist had attempted to blow up the house of the rich Pole. Jones and Norton arrived just as the smoke began to pour out from the windows. A crowd had already collected.

Then Jim overheard a woman masquerader say: "The fool made the bomb too strong. She is in the room on the second floor. The game is up if she suffocates——" The voice trailed off and the woman became lost in the crowd. But it was enough for the reporter, who pushed his way roughly through the excited masqueraders and entered the house. The rescue was one of the most exciting to be found in the newspaper files of the day.

So Braine in his effort to scare everybody from the house had overreached himself once more.

CHAPTER XIX

FLORENCE was a fortnight in recovering from the
shock of her experience at the masked ball of the
Princess Parlova, who, by the way, disappeared from
New York shortly after the fire, no doubt because of her
fear of the Black Hundred. The fire did not destroy the
house, but most of the furnishings were so thoroughly
drenched by water that they were practically ruined. Her
coming and going were a nine-days' wonder, and then
the public found something else to talk about.

Norton was a constant visitor at the Hargreave place.
There was to him a new interest in that mysterious
house, with its hidden panels, its false floors, its secret
tunnels; but he treated Jones upon the same basis as hitherto. One thing, however: He felt a sense of security
in regard to Florence such as he had not felt before. So,
between assignments, he ran out to Riverdale and did
what he could to amuse his sweetheart. Later they took
short rides in the runabout, and at length she became as
lively as she had ever been.

But often she would catch Norton brooding.

"What makes you frown like that?"

"Was I frowning?" innocently enough.

"I find you this way a dozen times in an afternoon.
What is the matter? Are they after you again?"

"Heavens, no! I'm only a vague issue. They will

244

not bother me so long as I do not bother them. It has dwindled into a game of truce."

"Do you think so?" eying him curiously.

"Why, yes."

"What's the use of trying to fool me, Jim? If they haven't been after you, you are sensing a presage of evil. I'm not a child any longer. Haven't I been through enough to make me a woman? Sometimes I feel very old."

"To me you are the most charming in all this wide world. No, you're not a child any longer. You are a woman, brave and patient; and I know that I could trust you with any secret I have or own. But sometimes a person may have a secret which is not his and which he hasn't any right to disclose."

She became silent for a while. "I hate money," she said. "I hate it, hate it!"

"It's mighty comfortable to have it around sometimes," he countered.

"As in my case, for instance. If I were poor and had to work no one would bother me."

"I would!" he declared, laughing. "Come; let's throw off moods and go into town for tea at the Rose Garden; and if you feel strong enough we'll trip the light fantastic."

They had been gone from the house less than an hour when a man ran up the steps of the veranda and rang the bell. Jones being busy at the rear of the house, the maid came to the door.

"Is Miss Hargreave in?" the stranger asked.

"No," abruptly. The door began to close ever so slowly.

"Do you know where I can find her?"

The maid eyed him with covert keenness; then, remembering that the reporter was with Florence, said: **"I** believe she is at the Rose Garden this afternoon."

"That is in town?"

"Yes."

"Thanks." The man turned abruptly and ran down the steps.

The maid ran back to Jones.

"Why didn't you call me?" he demanded impatiently.

"There wasn't time."

"Did you tell him where she was?"

"Yes. But I shouldn't have told him if Mr. Norton had not been with Miss Florence."

Jones ran to the front, dashed out, eyed the back of the man hastening down the street, smiled, and returned to his work, or, rather, to the maid. He took her by the shoulder, whirled her about, and shot a look into her eyes that quailed her.

"Always call me hereafter, no matter what I'm doing. That man has never laid eyes on Florence and has no idea what she looks like. Why did you drug my coffee the night of that ball?"

She stepped back.

"And how much did they pay you for letting that doc-tor send Florence to Atlantic City? I know everything. Hereafter, walk straight. If you play another trick I'll kill you with these two hands. And listen and tell this to your confederates: I always know every move they make; that is why no one is missing from this house. There is a traitor. Let them find him if they can. Will you walk straight, or will you leave?"

"I—I will walk straight," she faltered. "The money was too big a temptation."

"Did they give it to you?"

"Yes. And more to stay here. But this is the first bit of dishonest work I ever did."

"Well, remember what I have said. Another misstep and I'll make an end to you. Don't think I'm trying to scare you. You have witnessed enough to know that it's life and death in this house. Now run along."

At the garden Jim and Florence sauntered among the crowd, not having any particular objective point in view.

"Sh!" whispered Jim.

"What is it?"

"Olga Perigoff is yonder in a box."

"Very well; let us go and sit with her. Is she alone?"

"Apparently. But don't you think we'd better go elsewhere?"

"My dear young man," said Florence with mock loftiness, "Olga Perigoff has written me down as a simple young fool, and that is why, sooner or later, I'm going to put the shoe on the other foot. You and Jones have coddled me long enough. Inasmuch as I am the stake they are playing for, I intend to have something more than a speaking part in the play."

"All right; you're the admiral," he said with pretended lightness.

So the two of them joined their subtle enemy, conscious of a tingle of zest as they did so. On her part, the countess was always suspicious of this sleepy-eyed reporter. She never could tell how much he knew. But of Florence she was reasonably certain; and so long as she could fool the pretty infant the suspicions of the reporter were a negligible quantity. She greeted them effusively and offered them chairs. For half an hour they sat there, chatting inanities, all the while each mind was busy with deeper concerns.

When the man in search of Florence eventually arrived and asked the manager of the garden if he knew Miss Hargreave by sight the manager pointed toward the box. The man wound his way in and out of the idlers and by the time he reached the box Jim and Florence had made their departure. The man bowed, approached, and asked the countess if she was Miss Hargreave. For a moment Olga suspected a trap. Then it appealed to her mind that if there was no trap it might be well to pose as Florence, if only to learn what the outcome might be.

"Yes. What is wanted?" she asked.

The man took a letter from his pocket and handed it to Olga, saying: "Give this to your father. He knows how to read it."

Before she could reply the man had turned and was hurrying away.

Olga opened the note, her heart beating furiously. It was utterly blank. At first she thought it was a hoax. Then she happened to remember that there was such a thing as invisible ink. At last! Hargreave was alive; this letter settled all doubt in her mind on this question. Alive! And not only that, but the girl and Jones were evidently in communication with him. She summoned a waiter, made a secret sign, and he bowed and approached. She slipped the letter into his hand and whispered: "Show that at the cave to-morrow. It is in invisible ink and meant for Hargreave."

"He's alive?"

"Positively."

"Very well." The waiter bowed and strolled away nonchalantly.

Braine was in Boston over night, otherwise the countess would have taken the mysterious note at once to him.

"GIVE THIS TO YOUR FATHER. HE KNOWS HOW TO READ IT"

She remained for perhaps a quarter of an hour longer and then left the garden. She would have taken the letter to her own apartment but for the fact that the chemicals needed were hidden in the cave.

Now it happened that Florence went out for her early ride the next morning, and crossing a field she saw a man with a bundle under his arm. The sun struck his profile and limned it plainly, and Florence uttered a low cry. The man had not observed her. So, very quietly, she slipped from the horse, tethered it to a tree, and started after the man to learn what he was doing so far from the city. She would never forget that face. She had seen it that dreadful night when the note had lured her into the hands of her enemies. The face belonged to the man who had impersonated her father.

It occurred to her that she might just as well do a little detective work on her own hook. She had passed through so many terrifying episodes that she was beginning to crave for the excitement, strange as this may seem. Like a gambler who has once played for high stakes, she no longer found pleasure in thimbles and needles and pins. She followed the man with no little skill and at length she saw him approach a knoll, stoop, apparently press a spring, and a hole suddenly yawned. The man vanished quickly, and the spot took on again its virginal appearance. A cave. Florence had the patience to wait. By and by the man appeared again and slunk away.

When she was sure that he was beyond range, she came out from the place of concealment, crept up the knoll, and searched about for the magic handle of this strange door. Diligence rewarded her, and she soon found herself in a large, musty, earth-smelling cave. Loot was scattered about, and there were boxes and chairs and a large chest. Men evidently met here, possibly after some desperate adventure against society. She found nothing to reward her hardihood, and as she was in the act of moving toward the cave's door she beheld with terror that it was moving!

She was near the chest at that moment. The cave was not a deep one. There was no tunnel, only a wall. Resolutely she raised the lid of the chest, stepped inside, and drew the lid down. She was just in time. The door opened and three men entered, talking volubly. They felt perfectly secure in talking as loudly as they pleased. To Florence it seemed almost impossible that they did not hear the thunder of her heart? Strain her ears as she might, she could gather but little of what they said, except:

"If Hargreave had this paper we might all be put on the defensive. To an outsider it is a blank paper. But the boss will be able to read it. . . ." The speaker moved away from the vicinity of the chest and she heard no more.

Very deftly Florence raised the lid just enough to peep out. The man who had been talking was putting the note in his hip pocket. As he turned toward the chest he sat down on the soap-box immediately in front of the chest. An inspiration came to the girl, an exceedingly daring one. She took her liberty in her hands as she executed the deed. But the dimness of the cave aided her. When she crouched down again the magic paper was hers.

It seemed hours to her before the men left the cave. As she heard the hidden door jar in closing she raised the lid and stepped out, breathing deeply. The paper she had purloined was indeed blank, but Jones or Jim would

FLORENCE DISCOVERS THE CAVE

know what to do with it. And wouldn't they be surprised when she told them what she had accomplished all alone? Her exultation was of short duration. She heard the whine of the door on its hinges. The men were returning. Why?

They were returning because they had discovered a woman's shoeprint outside. It pointed toward the cave, freshly, and there was none coming away. To re-enter the chest would be foolhardy. It would be the first place the men would look. She glanced about desperately. She saw but one chance, the well. And even while the door was swinging inward, letting the brilliant sunshine enter, she summoned up the courage and let herself down into the well, which proved to be nothing more nor less than an underground river!

The men came in with a rush. They upset boxes, looked into the chest, and the man who was evidently in command, gazed down the well, shaking his head. Their search was thorough, but they found no one. And at length they began to reason that perhaps a woman had got as far as the door and then turned away, walking on the turf.

Meantime Florence was borne along by the swift current of the river, which gained in swiftness every moment. From time to time she bumped along the rocky walls, but she clung to life valiantly. In ten minutes she was swept to the other side of the hill, into the rapids; but the blue sky was overhead, she was out in the familiar world again. On, on she was carried. Even though she was half dead, she could hear the roar of a falls somewhere in advance.

Braine thought he really had a clue to the treasure,

and with his usual promptness he set about to learn if it was worth anything. He procured a launch and began to prowl about, using a pole as a feeler. All the while he was being closely watched by Norton, who had concluded to hang on to Braine's trail till he found something worthy of note. Braine was disguised, but this time Jim was not to be fooled. But what was he looking for, wondered the reporter? Braine continued to pole along, sometimes pausing to look over the gunwale down into the water. In raising his head after the last investigation, he discerned something struggling in the water, about three hundred yards away. The current leisurely brought the object into full view. It was a young woman with just power enough to keep herself afloat. The golden head roused something in him stronger than curiosity. It might be!

Braine proceeded to move the launch in the direction of the girl. It was this movement that turned the reporter's gaze. He, too, now saw the woman in the water and wondered how she had come there. When Braine reached the girl and pulled her into the launch Jim saw her face plainly.

He flew from his vantage point, found a skiff and started after Braine.

"By the Lord Harry!" murmured the rogue. "Well, they can talk of manna from heaven, but this is what I call luck. Florence Hargreave, out of nowhere, into my arms! The god of luck has cast another horseshoe and it's mine."

He had a flask in his pocket, and he forced some of the biting spirits down the girl's throat. She opened her eyes.

"Well, my beauty?"

FLORENCE STEALS THE PAPERS FROM BRAINE'S POCKET

Florence eyed him wildly, not quite understanding where he had come from.

"I don't know how you got here," he said, "and I don't care. But here we are together at last. Where is your father?"

"I—I don't know," dazedly.

"Better think quickly," he warned; "I want lucid answers to my questions or back you go into the water. I'm about at the end of my rope. I've been beaten too many times, my girl, to have any particular love for you. Now, where is your father?"

"I don't know; I have never seen him."

Braine laughed.

And Jim's boat ran afoul some rocks and into the water he went. He had not attracted Braine's attention, fortunately. He began to swim toward the drifting launch.

"Where have they hidden that money?"

"I don't know."

"Well, well; I've given you your chance. You'll have to try your luck with the water again."

Florence, weak as she was, set her lips.

"You don't ask for mercy?" he said banteringly.

"I should be wasting my breath to ask for mercy from such a monster as you are," she answered quickly.

"That damned Hargreave nerve!" he snarled.

He rolled up his sleeves and stepped toward her. She braced herself but did not turn her eyes from his. Suddenly, from nowhere at all, came a pair of hands. One clutched the gunwale and the other laid hold of Braine. A quick pull followed, and Braine began to topple. But even as he fell he managed to fling himself atop his assailant; and it was only when the struggle began in the water

that he recognized the reporter. All the devil in him came
to the surface and he fought with the fierceness of a tiger
to kill, kill, kill. In nearly every instance this meddling
reporter had checkmated him. This time one or the other
of them should stay in the water.

Norton recognized that he had a large order before him
to disable Braine. The recognition between them was
now frank and absolute; there could never again be any
diplomatic sidestepping.

"You're a dead man, Norton!" panted Braine, as he
reached for the reporter's throat.

Norton said nothing, but struck the hand aside. For a
moment they both went under. They came up sputtering,
each trying for a hold. It was a terribly enervating
struggle.

Florence could do nothing. The boat in which she
sat continued to drift away from the fighting men. Once
she tried to reach Braine with the pole he had been using,
but failed.

From the shore came another boat. For a while she
could not tell whether it contained friends or enemies. It
was terrible to be forced to wait, absolutely helpless.
When she heard the newcomers call encouragingly to
Braine she knew then that the brave fight of her sweetheart was going to come to naught. She knew a little
about motors. She threw on the power and headed
straight toward the rowboat. The men shouted at her,
but she did not alter her course. The rowboat had its
sides crushed in and the men went piling into the water.

"Jim," she cried.

Norton suddenly flung off Braine and began to swim
madly for the motor boat, which Florence had brought
about. Even then it was only by the barest luck in the

BRAINE PROCURED A LAUNCH AND BEGAN TO PROWL ABOUT

world that Norton managed to catch the gunwale. The rest of it was simple. When they finally reached a haven, Florence, oddly enough, thought of the horse she had left tethered nine miles from the stables. She laughed hysterically.

"I guess he won't die. We can send some one out for him. Now, for heaven's sake, how did you get into this? Where were you? What have you been up to?" with tender bruskness.

"I wanted to do a little detective work of my own," she faltered.

"It looks as if you had done it. You infant! Will you never learn to keep outside this muddle? It's a man's work."

Florence, thoroughly weakened by her long immersion in the water, began to weep silently.

"You poor child. I'm a brute!" And he comforted her.

Later that day, at home, she remembered the blank paper.

"I stole this from one of the men in the cave. He said this blank paper would probably save father."

Jim took it. "H'm! Invisible ink, and it's had a fine washing."

"But maybe it is waterproof."

"Maybe it is. Anyhow, Miss Sherlock, we'll show it to Jones and see what he says."

CHAPTER XX

"WHAT I want now," said Braine, as he paced the living-room of the apartment of the countess, "is revenge. I've been checkmated enough, Olga; they're playing with us."

"That is nothing new," she replied, shrugging. "At the beginning I warned you. I never liked this affair after the first two or three failures. But you would have your way. You wanted revenge at that early date; but I can not see that you've gone forward. Has it ever occurred to you that the organization may be getting tired, too? They depend solely upon your invention, and each time your invention has resulted in touching nothing but zero."

"Thanks!"

"Oh, I'm not chiding you. I've failed, too."

"Are you turning against me?" he demanded bitterly.

"Do my actions point that way?" she countered. "No. But the more I view what has passed, the more disheartened I grow. It has been a series of blind alleys, and all we have succeeded in doing is knocking our heads. I can see now that all our failures are due to one mistake."

"And what the devil is that?" he asked irritably.

"We were in too much of a hurry at the beginning. Hargreave prepared himself for quick action on your part."

"And if I had not acted quickly he would have started

BRAINE REACHED THE GIRL AND PULLED HER INTO THE BOAT

successfully on one of his world tours again, and that would have been the last of him, and we should never have learned of the girl's existence. So there's your argument."

"Perhaps you are right. But for all that we have not played the game with any degree of finesse."

"Bah!" Braine lit a cigarette and smoked nervously. "I can't even get rid of that meddling reporter. He has been as much to blame for our failures as either Jones or Hargreave. I admit that in his case I judged hastily. I believed him to be just an ordinary newspaper man, and he was clever enough to lull my suspicions. But I'm going to get him, Olga, even if I have to resort to ordinary gunman tricks. If there's any final reckoning, by the Lord Harry, he shan't get a chance in the witness stand."

"And I begin to think that that little chit of a girl has been hoodwinking me all along. By the way, did you find out what that letter said?" she asked after a pause.

"Letter? What letter?"

She sprang from her chair. "Do you mean to say that they have not told you about that?" Olga became greatly excited.

"Explain," he said.

"Why, I was at the garden day before yesterday, and a man approached and asked if I was Miss Hargreave. Becoming at once suspicious that something very important was about to happen I signified that I was Miss Hargreave. The man slipped a paper into my hand and hurried off. I took a quick glance at it and was dumfounded to find it utterly blank of writing. At first I thought some joke had been played on me, then I chanced to remember the invisible ink letters you always wrote me. Understanding that you were to visit the cave in the morning, I had one man at the garden take the note. And you never got it!"

"Some one shall certainly pay for this carelessness. I'll call up Vroon and Jackson at once. Wait just a moment."

He went to the telephone. A low muttering conversation took place. Olga could hear little or none of it. When Braine put the receiver back on the hook his face was not pleasant to see.

"That girl!"

"What now?"

"It seems she had been out horseback riding that morning. She had seen one of the boys cross the field and suddenly disappear; and she was curious to learn what had become of him. With her usual luck she stumbled on the method of opening the door of the cave and went in. She must have been nosing about. She didn't have much time, though, as the boys came up to await me. Evidently she crawled into that old chest and in some inexplicable manner purloined the letter from Jackson's pocket. They left to reconnoiter; and it was then that Jackson discovered his loss. When Florence heard them returning she jumped into the well. And lived through that tunnel! The devil is in it!"

"Or out of it, since we consider him our friend."

"And I had her in my hands, note and all!"

"But with all that water there will not be any writing left on the letter."

"Invisible ink is generally indelible and impervious to the action of water; at least the kind I use is. I'd give a thousand for a sight of that letter."

"And it might be worth a million," Olga suggested.

FROM THE SHORE CAME ANOTHER BOAT

"Not the least doubt of it in my mind. Olga, old girl, it does look as if my star was growing dim. We'll never get our hands on that million. I feel it in my bones. So let's settle down to a campaign of revenge, without any furbelows. I want to twist Hargreave's heart before the game winds up."

"You wish really to injure her?"

"I do not wish to injure her. Far from it," he replied, smiling evilly.

"You want her . . . dead?" whispered Olga, paling.

"Exactly. I want her dead. And so if all my efforts here come to nothing, so shall Hargreave's. His millions will become waste paper to him. That's revenge. The Persian peach method."

"Poison? You shall not! You shall not kill her!" vehemently.

"Tender-hearted?"

"No. If I must in the end go to prison, so be it; but I refuse to die in the chair."

"Very well, then. We shan't kill her, but we'll make her wish she was dead. I was only trying to see how far you would go. The basket of peaches is in the hallway. Every peach is poisoned. No man in the country knows more about subtle poisons than I do. Have I not written books on that subject?" ironically.

"And they will trace it back to you in a straight line," she warned. "I will not have it!"

"I can go elsewhere," he replied coldly.

"You would leave me?"

"The moment you cross my will," emphatically.

It became her turn to pace. Torn between her love of the man and the danger which stared her in the face, she was for the time being distracted. All the time he watched her with malevolent curiosity, knowing that in the end she would concur with his evil plans.

"Very well," she said finally. "But listen; we shall be found out. Never doubt that. Your revenge will cost us both our lives. I feel it."

"Bah! The law will have no hand in my end. I always carry a pellet; and that ring of yours would suffice a regiment. She will not die. She will merely become a kind of paralytic; the kind that can move a little but not enough; always wheeled about in a chair. I'll bring in the peaches; rosy and downy. One bite, after a given time, will do the trick. If they suspect and throw them out we have lost nothing but the peaches. A trusted messenger will carry them to the Hargreave house. And then we'll sit down and wait."

Meantime, in the library of the Hargreave house, Florence and Jim were puzzling over the blank sheet of paper.

"I'll wager," said Jim, "the water washed all the writing away. The fire does not seem to do any good. We'll turn it over to Jones. Jones'll find a way to solve it. Trust him."

"What are you two chattering about?" asked Susan, who was arranging some flowers on the table.

"Secrets," said Jim, smiling.

"Humph!"

Susan puttered about for a few minutes longer, then crossed to the reception room, intending to go up-stairs. At that moment the maid was admitting a messenger with a basket of fruit.

"For Miss Hargreave," said he. He gave the basket to the maid, touched his cap awkwardly, and swung on his heel, closing the door behind him. He was in a hurry to deliver another message.

"Oh, what lovely fruit!" cried Susan, pausing. "I'm going to steal one," she laughed. She selected a peach and began eating it on the way up to her room.

The maid passed on into the library.

"What's this?" inquired Florence, as the maid held out the basket. She selected a peach and was about to set her white teeth into it when Jim interposed.

"Wait a moment, dear." Florence lowered the peach. Jim turned to the maid. "Who sent it?"

"I don't know, sir. A messenger brought it, saying it was for Miss Hargreave."

"Let me see if there is a card." But Jim searched in vain for the card of the donor. All at once his suspicions arose. "Don't touch them. Better let the maid throw them out. Fruit from unknown persons might not be the healthiest thing in the world."

"What do you think?"

"That in all probability they are poisoned. But there's no need trying to prove my theory right or wrong. Ask Jones. He'll tell you to throw them away."

"Horrible!" Florence shuddered. "But they do not want to poison me. I'm too valuable. They want me alive."

"Who can say?" returned Jim gloomily. "They may have learned that they can not beat us, no matter what card they turn up. I may be wrong, but take my advice and throw them away. . . . Good lord, what's that?" startled.

"Some one cried!"

"Oh, Miss Florence!" exclaimed the maid, terror-stricken as she recalled Susan's act. "Miss Susan took a peach from the basket and was eating it on the way to her room!"

"Good heavens!" gasped Jim. "I was right. The fruit was poisoned."

Jim had heard enough to send for a specialist he knew. The specialist arrived about twenty minutes after Susan's first cry. To his keen eye it looked like a certain poison which had for its basis the venom of the cobra.

"Will she live?"

"Oh, yes. But she'll be a wreck for some months. Send her to the hospital where I can visit her frequently. And I'll take that peach along for analysis. No police affair?"

"No. We dare not call them in," said Jim.

"That's your affair. I'll send down the ambulance. Keep her quiet. She'll have a species of paralysis; but that'll work off under treatment. A strange business."

"So it is," agreed Jim grimly.

Florence knelt beside her friend's bed and cried softly.

"You called me just in time. An hour later, nothing would have saved her. She would have been paralyzed for life."

Jim accompanied the doctor to the door and went in search of Jones. He found the taciturn butler eying the fruit basket, his face gray and drawn, though his eyes blazed with fury.

"Poison!"

"A pretty bad poison, too," said Jim. "We can't do anything. We've just got to sit still. But in the end we'll get them. That she devil. . . ."

"No, my friend; that he devil. The woman is mad over him and would commit any crime at his bidding. But this is his work. We want him. He wasn't without courage to send this fruit, knowing that I would instantly suspect the sender. Yet, I have no definite proof. I could not hold him in court in law. He will have bought the fruit piece by piece, the basket in a basket shop. He will have injected the poison himself when alone. Poor Susan! That messenger was without doubt some one over whom he holds the threat of the death chair. That's the way he works."

Jim tramped the room while Jones carried the fruit to the kitchen. The butler returned after a while.

"What about that blank sheet of paper?"

"It has to be dipped into a solution; after that you can read it by heating. I have already dipped it into the solution. The moment the heat leaves the sheet the writing disappears again. The ink is waterproof. I'll show you."

Jones got a candle from the mantel, lit it, and held the sheet of paper very close to the flame. Gradually, almost imperceptibly, letters began to form on the blank sheet. At length the message was complete.

"Dear Hargreave—The Russian minister of police is at the Blank Hotel under the name of Henri Servan. He is investigating the work of the Black Hundred in this country and can free you from their vengeance if you supply the evidence needed."

"Now, what evidence can he want?" asked Jim.

"Such as will prove Braine an undesirable citizen."

"And then?"

"Quietly pack him off to Russia, where he is badly wanted."

"Who sent this message?"

"One of our mysterious friends. We have a few, as you already know. But I'll go and make this man Servan a visit. I have seen the real minister, and if this man is the same one, something of importance may turn up. I shall want you somewhere about. Here, I'll let you have this letter. Remember, heat brings it out and cold air makes it vanish. Now I'll go up for a moment to see how that poor girl is getting along. We are lucky; there's no gainsaying that."

"You're a clever man, Jones," said Jim.

Jones turned upon him, his face grave. The two men looked steadily into each other's eyes. Jones was first to turn aside his glance, as he had something to conceal and Jim had nothing.

When the ambulance took the tortured Susan away, Jones addressed Florence gravely.

"I am going out, and so is Mr. Norton. Do not leave the house; not even if you have a telephone call from me or Norton. Both of us will return; so don't let anything bother or confuse you."

"I promise," said Florence, struggling with a sob.

Jones went down-stairs again, paused by a window as if cogitating, and suddenly threw it up and looked abroad. A rustle among the lilacs caused a smile to flit across his face. So they had sent some one to learn the effect of the poison? Or to follow him should he leave the house? He retired to the kitchen and gave some explicit orders to the chef, orders which did not in any way refer to cooking. Then Jones and the reporter left the house, each quite aware that they were being followed. Near the Blank Hotel they separated in order to confuse the stalker. He might dodder and follow the wrong man. But it was evident that this time he had been directed to follow Jones; for he entered the hotel a minute after Jones.

Meantime a second spy, whom Jones had not seen, had observed the transfer of the invisible writing and had immediately informed Braine, who was not far away.

That his poisoned fruit had stricken down an outsider troubled him none at all. But that mysterious message he meant to have; it might be a life and death affair, it might be a clue to the treasure, or the whereabouts of Hargreave.

Thus, while only one man followed Jones, several kept a far eye on Jim.

Jones scribbled his name on a blank card and had it taken to the Russian's room. The page eyed that card curiously. It was different from anything he had ever seen before. In one corner were written three or four words which resembled a cross between Hebrew and Greek.

"Humph!" muttered the boy. "Whadda y' know about that? Chicken scratches; but I guess the bell rings Roosian. On your way, Hortense," he cried to the hall maid, who wanted a look at the card. "Up t' th' room, sir. He'll see yuh!" The boy kept the silver salver extended expectantly, but Jones went past without apparently noticing the hint.

The Russian was standing by a window when Jones knocked and was bidden to enter.

"You are not Hargreave."

"Neither are you the Russian minister of police," urbanely.

"Who are you?"

"I am Hargreave's confidential man, sir."

The two men eyed each other cautiously.

"You speak Russian?"

"No. I am able to scribble a few words; that is all."

The Russian lit a cigarette and smoked leisurely. He was in no hurry.

"No, I am not the minister; but I am his accredited

agent. I am empowered to bring back to Russia a man who is known here by the name of Braine, another by the name of Vroon, and a woman who calls herself a countess and unfortunately is one. All I desire is some damaging proof against them that they are outlaws in this country. The rest will be simple."

"They have all three taken out naturalization papers."

The Russian waved his hand airily. "Once they are in Russia those documents will never come to light. This man Braine, it has been learned, has long been in the pay of Prussia, and has given the general staff of that country many plans of our frontier fortifications. I do not know what any one of the three looks like. That is why I sought Hargreave."

"I will gladly point them out to you," said Jones, rubbing his hands together, a sign that he was greatly pleased.

"That will be very good of you, I'm sure," in a rumbling but perfectly intelligible English.

"And suddenly they all three will disappear."

"Suddenly; and you may believe me that from that time on they'll be heard of never more."

"All this sounds extremely agreeable to me. Mr. Hargreave will be happy to hear that his long enforced hiding will soon come to an end."

"All you have to do, sir, is to point them out to me."

"It may take a week or ten days."

"My government has waited for ten years to gather in this delectable trio. A month, if you like."

"The sooner the better. I shall call this evening after dinner. We shall begin with Mr. Braine; and generally where he is is the woman. Vroon will be the most difficult."

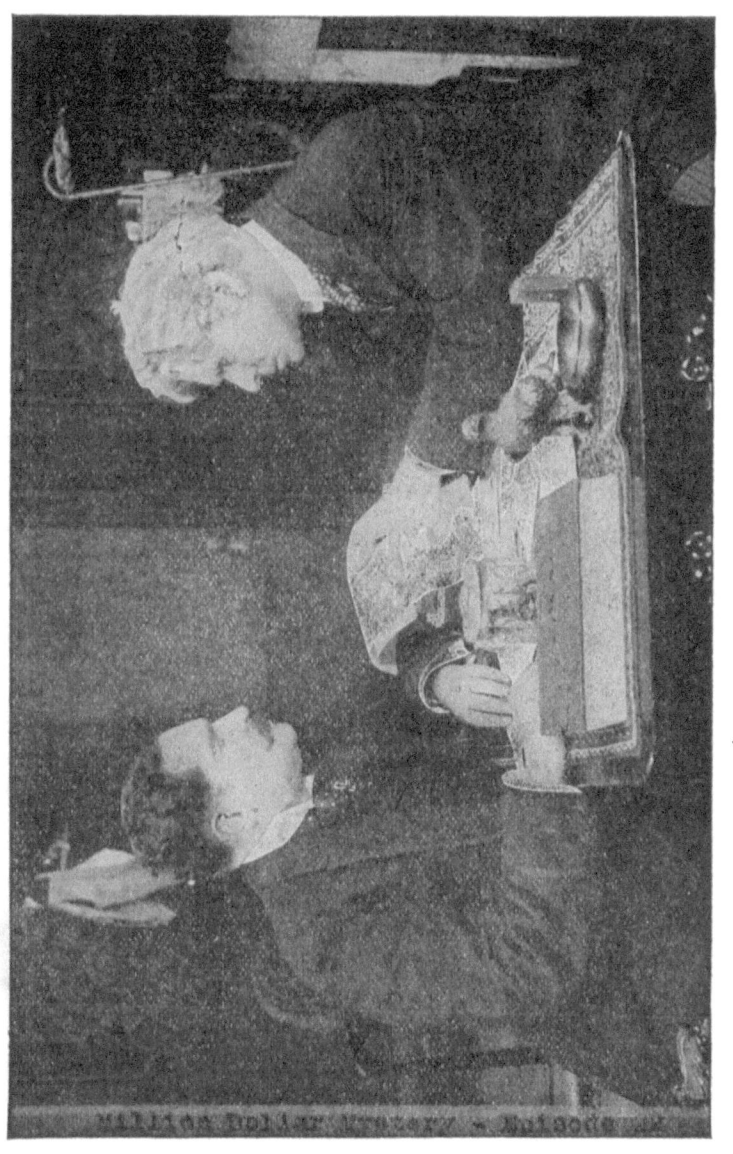

THEY HAVE ALL THREE TAKEN OUT NATURALIZATION PAPERS

"After dinner, then, since you know some of his haunts. There is a reward."

Jones laughed shortly. "Keep it yourself, sir. Mr. Hargreave would willingly double whatever this reward is to eliminate these despicable creatures from his affairs."

"Thanks."

While this conversation was taking place Norton idled about; and feeling the cravings for a cigarette, prepared to roll one, only to find that he hadn't the "makings." So fate urged him to step into the nearest tobacconist's. He asked for his favorite brand and passed over the silver.

Braine and his companions saw Norton enter the shop. It agreed with their plans perfectly. The tobacconist happened to be affiliated with the order. So they hurried into the shop. Jim instantly realized that he was in a trap.

"How can I get out of here?" he whispered to the tobacconist.

The latter smiled. "I have to obey these gentlemen. I don't know what they want you for; but if I made a move to help you I should find my own throat cut without saving yours."

"The devil!"

Jim made a dash for the rear door, to find it locked. Even as he fumbled with the key Braine and his companions flung themselves upon the reporter and overpowered him.

"Ah, my friend Braine!" he said.

"My friend Norton!" jeered the victor.

"And what do you want; some peaches?"

"A paper, my friend, a little secret of paper with invisible writing on it. We promise to give you something in exchange for it."

"What?" asked Jim with as much nonchalance as he could assume.

"Life."

"Search," said Jim. "You won't object to my smoking?" He began to roll a cigarette while they passed over him. He struck a match; the pleasant aroma of tobacco floated about his head.

"He's got it on him somewhere. I saw him take it. He's got his nerve with him."

The cigarette glowed. Jim smoked hurriedly.

Through every pocket they went. The contents of his wallet lay scattered at his feet; his watch dangled from the chain. The cigarette grew shorter and shorter. Suddenly one of the men stretched out a hand and whisked the cigarette from Jim's lips. He threw it to the floor and stamped out the coal.

"I thought so!" he exclaimed, holding out the scrap of burnt paper toward Braine.

The words "Dear Hargreave" were all that remained of the message. With a snarl of rage Braine whipped out his revolver.

"I will give you one minute to tell me what that paper contained."

"And after that minute is up?"

"A bullet in your stomach."

Quick as a flash Jim's hand shot out, caught the loosely held revolver, gave it a wrench, and brought it down savagely upon Braine's head. Then he reversed it and backed toward the front entrance.

"Au revoir, till we meet again, gentlemen!"

CHAPTER XXI

J IM said nothing at first about his adventure to Jones, whom he met half an hour later.

"Was it necessary to keep that invisible letter?" he asked.

"No," said Jones.

"Would it have given our affairs a serious turn if it had fallen into alien hands?"

"Decidedly," answered Jones. "It would mean flight for the Black Hundred or a long time under cover, if our friend Braine learned that Russia was now taking an active interest in the doings of the Black Hundred. And eventually all our work would have to be done over again."

"Ah!"

"You look a bit mussed up. Anything happened?" asked the keen-eyed butler.

"Nothing much. I made a cigarette out of the letter and smoked it."

Jones chuckled. "I see that you have had an adventure of some sort; but it can wait."

"It can."

"Because I want you to pack off to Washington."

"Washington?"

"Yes. I want you to interview those officials who are most familiar with the extradition laws."

"A new kink?"

"What I wish to learn is this: Can a man, formerly undesirable, take out naturalization papers and hold to the protection of the United States government? That is to say, a poisoner, menaced by Siberia, becomes an American citizen. He is abducted and carried back to Russia. Could he look to this government for protection? That is what I want you to find out?"

"That will be easy. When shall I start?"

"As soon as you can pack your grip."

"That's always packed," replied the reporter. "You see, I'm eternally shunted hither and yon, at a moment's notice, so I always have an extra grip packed for quick travel."

"The Russian agent wants Braine, Vroon, and the countess; and to-night I'm going to try to point them out to him. It would satisfy me more than anything I know to eliminate this precious trio in Russian fashion. It's thorough; and once accomplished, good day to the Black Hundred in America. The organization in Russia has still some political significance, but on this side of the water it is merely an aggregation of merciless thugs."

"I'll take the first train out. But you will tell Florence?"

"Surely."

"And take care of your own heels. You were watched at the hotel."

"I know it; but the watcher could learn nothing. Henri Servan as a name will suggest nothing to the fool who followed me. Besides we both knew that he was trying to peek through the keyhole. That hotel, you know, still retains the old-fashioned keyholes."

"To keep the maids in good humor, I suppose," laughed Jim. "Well, I must be on my way to make that flyer."

The two shook hands and Jim hurried off. The butler watched him till he disappeared down the subway.

"He's a good lad," he murmured, "and a brave lad; and money is only an incident in human affairs after all. I'll be a good angel and let the two be happy, since they love each other and have proved it in a thousand ways."

Meanwhile the Russian agent settled down before his writing portfolio; and once or twice as he wrote he thought he heard a sound outside the door. No doubt this butler of Hargreave's had been watched and followed. By and by he rose, drew his revolver, and tiptoed to the door obliquely so that the watcher outside might not become aware of his approach. Swiftly he swung back the door and the member of the Black Hundred stumbled into the room. Almost instantly the Russian caught him by the collar and held him up.

"What were you doing outside my door?"

The man, trying to collect his thoughts, did not answer.

"A spy of some sort, eh?"

"I'm a detective," said the man finally, thinking he saw his way clear.

"And what did you expect to learn by looking through the keyhole of my door?"

Servan laughed. "Show me your badge of authority."

The man fumbled in his upper pocket, hoping against hope that the muzzle of the revolver would waver.

"You're an ordinary thief," declared the Russian; "and as such I shall instantly hand you over to the hotel authorities unless you tell me exactly who and what you are."

The man remained dumb. He hung between the devil and the deep sea. If he told the truth the organization would soon learn the truth; if he kept still he would be lodged in jail, perhaps indefinitely, for he hadn't a savory police record. Presently his nerve gave way in face of the steady eye and hand, and he confessed the why and wherefore he had sought the keyhole of Servan's room.

"We are after this butler. Wherever he goes we follow."

"Well, you've wasted your time, my man. All I am here for is to take over some property Mr. Hargreave left in France for sale. I know nothing about your private feuds. Now, get out. But keep out of my way; I am not a peaceful man."

The spy tumbled out as he had tumbled in, by an act of gravity; and Servan was alone. He spent two days in comparative idleness. Then things began to wake up.

For a long time the leather box across which was inscribed "Stanley Hargreave" lay in peace undisturbed. A busy spider had woven a trap across the handle to the quaint lock. The box was still badly stained from its immersion in the salt water. At a certain time it was quietly withdrawn from its hiding place. It was stealthily opened. A hand reached in and when it withdrew a packet of papers was also withdrawn. The box was again locked and lowered; and presently the spider returned to find that his cunning trap had been totally destroyed. With the infinite patience of his kind he began the weaving of another trap. Perhaps this would be more successful than its predecessor.

Later Henri Servan received a telephone call. He was informed that his purpose in America would be realized by his presence at such and such a box that night at the opera. Further information could not be given over the telephone. Servan seemed well satisfied. He dressed carefully that evening, called up the office clerk and inquired if his box tickets for the opera had arrived. He was informed that they had. Instantly the spy, who had dared to linger about the hotel, overhearing this conversation, determined to notify Braine at once. And at the same time, Norton, in disguise, determined not to lose sight of this man whom he had set himself to watch.

The spy left by one entrance and Jim by another. Jim had learned what he desired; that the Russian agent would be followed to the opera and that it was going to be difficult to hand the documents to him. The spy entered a drug store and telephoned. Jim waited outside. When the man came out he strolled up the street and entered the nearest saloon. Jim's work was done.

It was Braine's lieutenant, however, who took the news to Braine.

"We have succeeded."

"Good!" said Braine.

"He will go to the opera. He will have a box. Doubtless they have arranged to deliver the papers there."

"And the next thing is to get the number of his box." This Braine had no difficulty in doing. "So that's all fixed. He calls himself Servan and registers from Paris. I'll show the fool that he has no moujik to deal with this time."

"And what are these documents?" asked Olga.

"Ah, that's what we are so anxious to find out. Some papers are going to be exchanged between this Russian spy and Jones or his agents. That these papers concern us vitally I am certain. That is why I am going to get them if there has to be a murder at the opera to-night. Norton has been to Washington. He was seen coming out of the Russian embassy, from the secretaries of state and war and a dozen other offices. I've got to find out just what all this means."

"It means that the time has come for us to fly," said Olga. "We have failed. I have warned you. We have still plenty of money left. It is time we folded our tents and stole away quietly. I tell you I feel it in my bones that there is a pit before us somewhere! and if you force issues we shall all fall into it."

"The white feather, my dear."

"There is altogether some difference between the white feather and common-sense caution."

"I shall never give up. You are free to pack up and go if you wish. As for me, I'm going to fight this out to the bitter end."

"And take my word for it, the end will be bitter."

"Well?"

"Oh, I shall stay. You know that my future is bound up in yours. In the old days my advice generally appealed to you as sound; and when you followed it you were successful. From the first I advised you not to pursue Hargreave. See what has happened!"

"Enough of this chatter. I've got to die some time; it will be with my face toward this man I hate with all my soul. You trust to me; I'll pull out of this all right. You just fix yourself up stunningly for the opera to-night and leave the rest to me."

Olga shrugged. She was something of a fatalist. This man of hers had suddenly gone mad; and one did not reason with mad people.

"What shall I wear?" she asked calmly.

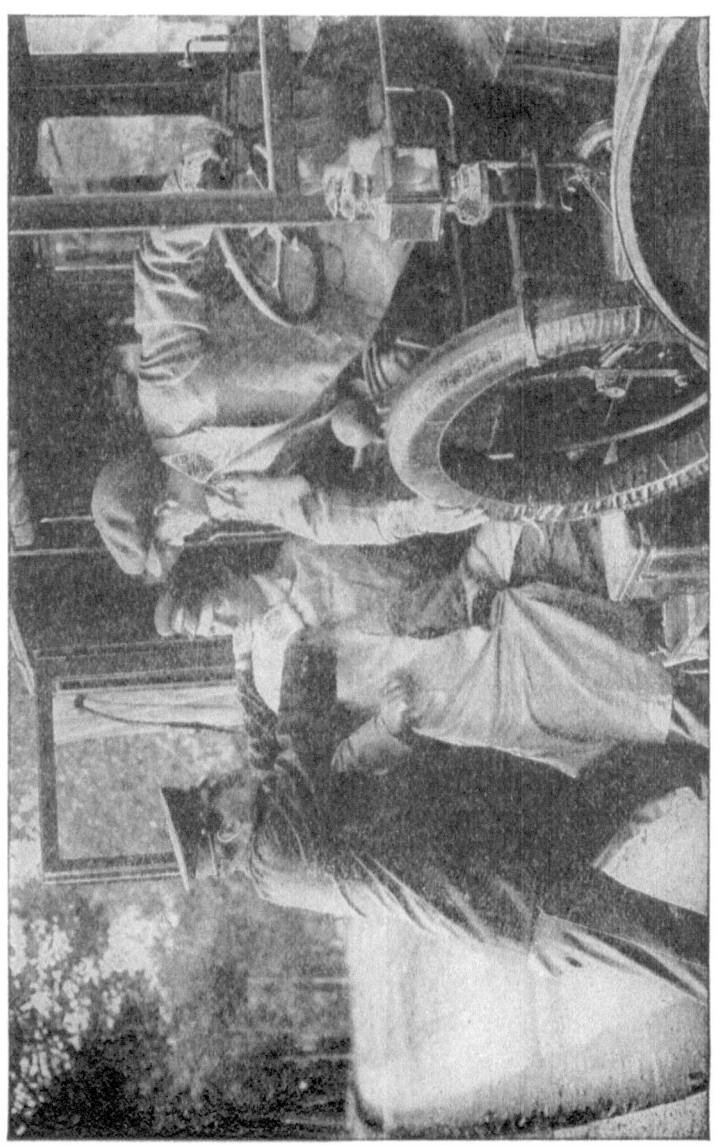

"JUST A MOMENT, GENTLEMEN"

"Emeralds; they're your good luck stones. You will go to the box before I do. I've got to spend some time at the curb to be sure that this Servan chap arrives. And it is quite possible that our friend Jones will come later. If not Jones, then Norton. I was a fool not to shoot him when I had the chance. We could have covered it up without the least difficulty. But I needed the information about that paper. With Norton going to Washington and Jones conferring with this Servan, I've got to strike quick. It concerns us, that I'm certain. Perk up; we've lots of cards in our sleeves yet. Be at the opera at eight-thirty. Pay no attention to any one; wait for me. Remember, I shan't write or send any phone messages. Be wary of any trap like that to get you outside. Now, I'm off."

Jones approached Florence immediately after dinner.

"I have important business in the city to-night. Under no circumstances leave the house. I shall probably be followed. And our enemies will have need of you far more to-night than at any previous time. I shall not send you phone or written message. You have your revolver. Shoot any strange man who enters. We'll make inquiries after."

"We are near the end?" whispered Florence.

"Very near the end."

"And I shall see my father?"

Jones bent his head. "If we succeed."

"There is danger?" thinking of her lover.

"There is always danger when I leave this house. So be good," the butler added with a smile.

"And Jim?"

"He has proved that he can take care of himself."

"Tell him to be very careful."

"I'll do so, but it will not be necessary;" and with this Jones set forth upon what he considered the culminating adventure.

The usual brilliant crowd began to pour into the opera. Braine took his stand by the entrance. He waited a long time, but his patience was rewarded. A limousine drove up and out of the door came his man, who looked about with casual interest. He dismissed the limousine, which wheeled slowly around the corner where it could be conveniently parked. Then Servan entered the opera.

Braine hurried around to the limousine. The lights, save those demanded by traffic regulations, were out. The chauffeur was huddled in his seat.

"My man," said Braine, "would you like to make some money?"

"How much?" listlessly. The voice was muffled.

"Twenty."

"Good night, sir."

"Fifty."

"Good night and good morning!"

"A hundred!"

"Now you've got me interested. What kind of a joy ride do you want?"

"No joy ride. Listen."

Briefly the conspirator outlined his needs, and finally the chauffeur nodded. Five twenties were pressed into his hand and he curled up in his seat again.

Servan entered his box. In the box next to his sat a handsomely gowned young woman. He threw her an idle glance, which was repaid in kind. Later, Braine came in and sat down beside Olga.

"Everything looks like plain sailing," he whispered.

Olga shrugged slightly.

During the intermission between the first and second acts, Servan took the rear chair of his box, near the curtains. Braine, watching with the eyes of a lynx, suddenly observed the curtains stirring. A hand was thrust through. In that hand was a packet of papers. With seeming indifference Servan reached back and took the papers, stowing them away in a pocket.

Braine rose at the beginning of the second act.

"Where are you going?" asked Olga nervously.

"To see Otto."

A bold attempt was made to rob Servan while in the box, but the timely arrival of Jim frustrated this plan. So Braine was forced to rely on the chauffeur of the limousine.

As Farrar's last thrilling note died away Braine and Olga rose.

"Be careful. And come to the apartments just as soon as you can."

"I'll be careful," Braine declared easily. "You can watch the play if you wish."

When Servan entered the limousine he was quietly but forcibly seized by two men who had been lying in wait for him, due to the apparent treachery of the chauffeur. Servan fought valiantly, for all that he knew what the end of this exploit was going to be. One of the men succeeded in getting the documents from Servan's pocket.

"Done, my boy!" cried the victor. "Give him a crack on the coco and we'll beat it."

"Just a minute, gentlemen!" said a voice from the seat at the side of the chauffeur. "I'll take those papers!" And the owner of the voice, backed by a cold, sinister-looking automatic, reached in and confiscated the spoils of war. "And I shouldn't make any attempt to slip out by the side door."

"Thanks, my friend," said Servan, shaking himself free from his captors.

"Don't mention it," said Norton amiably. "We thought something like this would happen. Keep perfectly quiet, you chaps. Drive on, chauffeur; drive on!"

"Yes, my lord! To what particular police station shall I head this omnibus?"

"The nearest, Jones; the very nearest you can think of! Some day, when I'm rich, I'll hire you for my chauffeur. But for the present I shall expect at least a box of Partagas out of that hundred."

Jones chuckled. "I'll buy you a box out of my own pocket. That hundred goes to charity."

"Here we are! Out with you," said Jim to his prisoners. He shouldered them into the police station, to the captain's desk.

"What's this?" demanded the captain.

"Holdup men," said Jim. "Entered this man's car and tried to rob him."

"Uh-huh! An' who're you?"

Jim showed his badge and card.

"Oho! Hey, there; I mean you!" said the captain, leveling a finger at Otto. "Lift up that hat; lift it up. Sure, it's Fountain Pen Otto! Well, well; an' we've been lookin' for you for ten months on the last forgery case. Mr. Norton, my thanks. Take 'em below, sergeant. You'll be here to make the complaint in th' mornin', sir," he added to Servan.

"If it is necessary."

"It may be against Otto's pal. I don't know him."

"Very well."

THE POLICE CAPTAIN'S DESK

And Jones and Norton and Servan trooped out of the station.

At last Jones and the reporter entered a cheap restaurant and ordered coffee and toast.

"You're a wonderful man, Jones, even if you are an Englishman," said Jim as he called for the check.

"English? What makes you think I am English?" asked Jones with a curious glitter in his eyes.

"I'll tell you on the night we put the rollers under Braine and company."

Jones stared long and intently at his young partner. What did he really know?

CHAPTER XXII

THE federal government agreed to say nothing, to put no obstacles in the way of the Russian agent, provided he could abduct his trio without seriously clashing with the New York police authorities. It was a recognized fact that the local police force wanted the newspaper glory which would attend the crushing of the Black Hundred. It would be an exploit. But their glory was nil; nor did Servan take his trio back with him to Russia.

Many strange things happened that night, the night of the final adventure.

Florence sat in her room reading. The book was *Oliver Twist,* not the pleasantest sort of book to read under the existing circumstances. Several times—she had reached the place where Fagin overheard Nancy's confession—she fancied she heard doors closing softly, but credited it to her imagination. Poor Nancy, who wanted to be good but did not find time to be! Florence possessed a habit familiar to most of us; the need of apples or candy when we are reading. So she rang the bell for her maid, intending to ask her to bring up some apples. She turned to her reading, presently to break off and strike the bell again. Where was that maid? She waited perhaps five minutes, then laid down the book and began to investigate.

There was not a servant to be found in the entire house! What in the world could that mean? Used as she was to heartrending suspense, she was none the less terrified. Something had taken the servants from the house. From whence was the danger to come this time? Where was Jones? Why did he not return as he had promised? It was long past the hour when he said he would be back.

She went into the library and picked up the telephone. She was told that Mr. Norton was out on an assignment, but that he would be notified the moment he returned. She opened the drawer in the desk. She touched the automatic, but did not take it up. She left the drawer open, however.

Earlier, at the newspaper office that night, Jim went into the managing editor's office and laid a bulky manuscript on that gentleman's desk.

"Is this it?"

"It is," said Jim.

"You have captured them?"

"No; but there is a net about them from which not one shall escape. There's the story of my adventures, of the adventures of Miss Hargreave and the butler, Jones. You'll find it exciting enough. You might just as well send it up to the composing room. At midnight I'll telephone the introduction. It's a scoop. Don't worry about that."

The editor riffled the pages.

"A hundred and twelve pages, three hundred words to the page; man, it's a novel!"

"It'll read like one."

"Sit down for a moment and let me skim through the first story."

At the end of ten minutes the editor laid down the copy. He opened a drawer and took out two envelopes. The blue one he tore up and dropped into the waste basket. Norton understood and smiled. They had meant to discharge him if he fell down. The other envelope was a fat one.

"Open it," said the editor, smiling a little to himself.

This envelope contained a check for two thousand five hundred dollars, two round-trip first-class tickets to Liverpool, together with innumerable continental tickets such as are issued to tourists.

"Why two?" asked Jim innocently.

"Forget it, my boy, forget it. You ought to know that in this office we don't employ blind men. The whole staff is on. There you are, a fat check and three months' vacation. Go and get married; and if you return before the three months are up I'll fire you myself on general principles."

Jim laughed happily and the two men shook hands. Then Jim went forth to complete the big assignment. Five minutes later Florence called him up to learn that he had gone.

What should she do? Jones had told her to stay in the house and not to leave it. But where was he? Why did he not come? What was the meaning of this desertion by the servants? She wandered about aimlessly, looking out of windows, imagining forms in the shadows. Her imagination had not deceived her; she had heard doors close softly.

"Susan, Susan!" she murmured, but Susan was in the hospital.

Oliver Twist! What had possessed her to start reading that old tale again? She should have read something of a light and joyous character. After half an hour's wandering about the lonely house she returned to the library, feeling that she would be safer where both telephone and revolver were.

And while she sat waiting for she knew not what, her swiftly beating heart sending the blood into her throat so that it almost suffocated her, a man turned into the street and walked noiselessly toward the Hargreave place. He passed a man leaning against a lamp-post, but he never turned to look at him.

This man, however, threw away his cigar and hot-footed it to the nearest pay station. He knew in his soul that he had just seen the man for whom they had been hunting all these weary but strenuous weeks—Stanley Hargreave in the flesh! Half an hour after his telephone message the chief of the Black Hundred and many lesser lights were on their way to the house of mystery. Had they but known!

Now, the man who had created this tremendous agitation went serenely on. He proceeded directly and fearlessly to the front door, produced a latchkey and entered. He passed through the hall and reception room to the library and paused on the threshold dramatically. Florence stepped back with a sharp cry of alarm. She had heard the hall door open and close and had taken it for granted that Jones had entered.

There was a tableau of short duration.

"Don't you know me?" asked the stranger in a singularly pleasant voice.

Florence had been imposed upon too many times. She shook her head defiantly, though her knees shook so that she was certain that the least touch would send her over.

"I am your father, child!"

Florence slipped unsteadily behind the desk and seized the revolver which lay in the drawer. The man by the curtains smiled sadly. It was a smile that caused Florence to waver a bit. Still she extended her arm.

"You do not believe me?" said the man, advancing slowly.

"No. I have been deceived too many times, sir. Stay where you are. You will wait here till my butler returns. Oh, if I were only sure!" she burst out suddenly and passionately. "What proof have you that you are what you say?"

He came toward her, holding out his hands. "This, that you can not shoot me. Ah, the damnable wretches! What have they done to you, my child, to make you suspicious of every one? How I have watched over you in the street! I will tell you what only Jones and the reporter know, that the aviator died, that I alone was rescued, that I gave Norton the five thousand; that I watched the windows of the Russian woman, and overheard nearly every plot that was hatched in the council chamber of the Black Hundred; that I was shot in the arm while crossing the lawn one night. And now we have the scoundrels just where we want them. They will be in this house for me within half an hour, and not one of them will leave it in freedom. I am your father, Florence. I am the lonely father who has spent the best years of his life away from you in order to secure your safety. Can't you feel the truth of all this?"

"No, no! Please do not approach any nearer; stay where you are!"

At that moment the telephone rang. With the revolver still leveled she picked up the receiver.

"Hello, hello! Who is it? . . . Oh, Jim, Jim, come

THEY WERE TUMBLING THROUGH THE LIBRARY AND READING-ROOM

at once! I am holding at bay a man who says he is my father. Hold him where he is, you say? All right, I will. Come quick!"

"Jim!" murmured the man, still advancing. He must have that revolver. The poor child might spoil the whole affair. "So what Jones tells me is true; that you are going to marry this reporter chap?"

She did not answer.

"With or without my consent?"

If only he would drop that fearless smile! she thought. "With or without anybody's consent," she said.

"What in the world can I say to you to convince you?" he cried. "The trap is set; but if Braine and his men come and find us like this, good heaven, child, we are both lost! Come, come!"

"Stay where you are!"

At that moment she heard a sound at the door. Her gaze roved; and it was enough for the man. He reached out and caught her arm. She tried to tear herself loose.

"My child, in God's name, listen to reason! They are entering the hall and they will have us both."

Suddenly Florence knew. She could not have told you why; but there was an appeal in the man's voice that went to her heart.

"You are my father!"

"Yes, yes! But you've found it out just a trifle too late, my dear. Quick; this side of the desk!"

Braine and his men dashed into the library. Olga entered leisurely.

"Both of them!" yelled Braine exultantly. "Both of them together; what luck!"

There was a sharp, fierce struggle; and when it came to an end Hargreave was trussed to a chair.

"Ah, so we meet again, Hargreave!" said Braine.

Hargreave shrugged. What he wanted was time.

"A million! We have you. Where is it, or I'll twist your heart before your eyes."

"Father, forgive me!"

"I understand, my child."

"Where is it?" Braine seized Florence by the wrist and swung her toward him.

"Don't tell him, father; don't mind me," said the girl bravely.

Braine, smiling his old evil smile, drew the girl close. It was the last time he ever touched her.

"Look!" screamed Olga.

Every one turned, to see Jones' face peering between the curtains. There was an ironic smile on the butler's lips. The face vanished.

"After him!" cried Braine, releasing Florence.

"After him!" mimicked a voice from the hall.

The curtains were thrown back suddenly. Jones appeared, and Jim and the Russian agent and a dozen policemen. Tableau!

Braine sprang at Florence savagely, and Norton tore him back, and they went tumbling through the library and the living room. It was a death struggle; make no mistake about that. The others dared not shoot for fear of hitting Norton. But the Countess Olga, in the hallway, dared the risk. As Norton's back came into view she fired. Almost at the same instant Norton had swung Braine about. A shudder ran through the arch-scoundrel, his hands slipped off Norton's shoulders, a surprised expression swept over his face, then he sank inertly to the floor, dead.

Olga ran up-stairs wildly, followed by a determined

BRAINE SANK INERTLY TO THE FLOOR, DEAD

policeman. She dashed into Florence's room and locked the door. Instantly she crossed over to the window, and paused.

Down-stairs the police were marching off the leaders of the Black Hundred.

"Well," said Norton, "I guess it's all over. And, my word for it, Mr. Jedson, you've played your end consummately."

"Jedson!" exclaimed Jones, starting back.

"Yes, Jedson, formerly of Scotland Yard," went on the reporter. "I recognized him long ago."

"It is true," said Hargreave, taking Jones' hand in his own. "Fifteen years ago I employed him to watch my affairs, and very well has he done so." .

Presently, Hargreave, Jones, Florence and Jim were alone. That smile which had revealed to Florence her father's identity stole over his face again. He put his hand on Jim's shoulder and beckoned to Florence.

"Are you really anxious to marry this young man?"

Florence nodded.

"Well, then, do so. And go to Europe with him on your honeymoon; and as a wedding present to you both, for every dollar that he has I will add a hundred; and when you get tired of travel you will both come back here to live. The Black Hundred has ceased to exist."

"And now," said Jones, shaking his shoulders.

"Well?" said Hargreave.

"My business is done. Still—" Jones paused.

"Go on," said Hargreave soberly.

"Well, the truth is, sir, I've grown used to you. And if you'll let me play the butler till the end I shall be most happy."

"I was going to suggest it."

Norton took Florence by the hand and drew her away.

"Where are you taking me?" she asked.

"I'm going to take this pretty hand of yours and put it flat upon one million dollars. And if you don't believe it, follow me."

She followed.

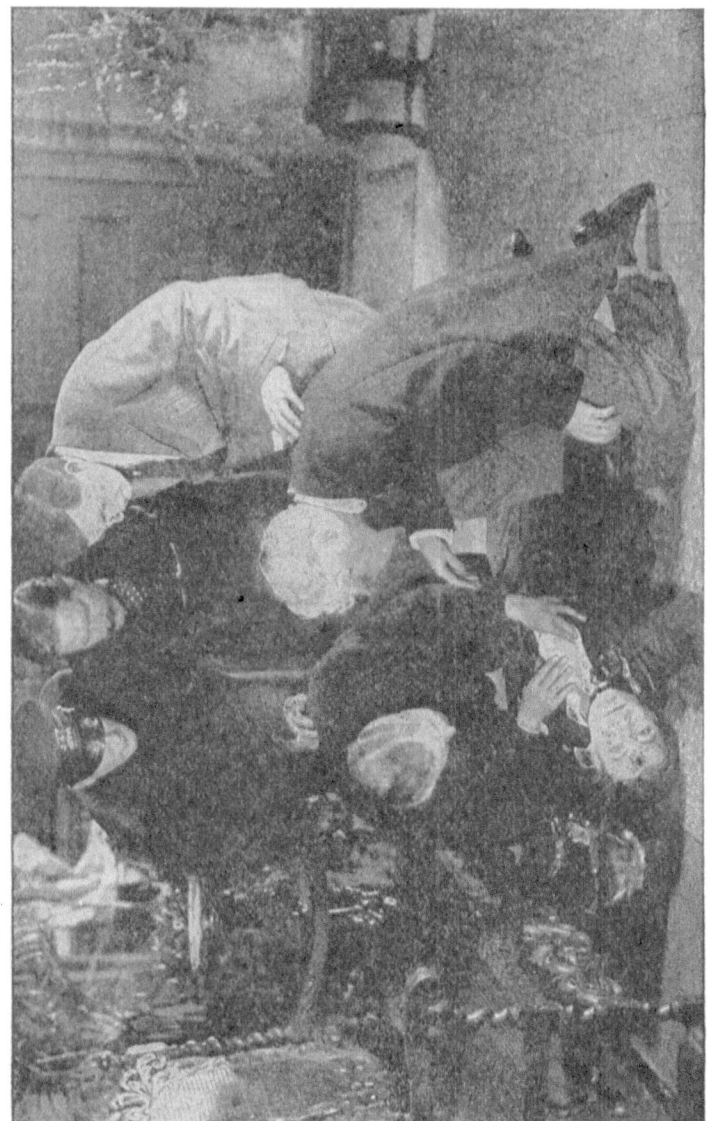

INSTANTLY THEY SOUGHT THE FALLEN MAN'S SIDE

CHAPTER XXIII

IT will be remembered that the Countess Olga had darted up the stairs during the struggle between Braine and his captors. The police who had followed her were recalled to pursue one of the lesser rogues. This left Olga free for a moment. She stole out and down as far as the landing.

Servan, the Russian agent, stood waiting for the taxi-cab to roll up to the porte-cochère for himself, Braine and Vroon. Norton had taken Florence by the hand, ostensibly to conduct her to the million. Suddenly Braine made a dash for liberty. Norton rushed after him. Just as he reached Braine, a shot rang out. Braine whirled upon his heels and crashed to the floor.

Olga, intent upon giving injury to Norton, who she regarded equally with Hargreave as having brought about the downfall, had hit her lover instead. With a cry of despair she dashed back into Florence's room, quite ready to end it all. She raised the revolver to her temple, shuddered, and lowered the weapon: so tenaciously do we cling to life!

Below, they were all quite stunned by the suddenness of the shot. Instantly they sought the fallen man's side, and a hasty examination gave them the opinion that the man was dead. Happily a doctor was on the way, Servan having given the call, as one of the Black Hundred had been wounded badly.

But what to do with that mad woman up-stairs? Hargreave advised them to wait. The house was surrounded; she could not possibly escape save by one method, and perhaps that would be the best for her. Hargreave looked gravely at Norton as he offered this suggestion. The reporter understood: the millionaire was willing to give the woman a chance.

"And you are my father?" said Florence, still bewildered by the amazing events. "But I don't understand yet!" her gaze roving from the real Jones to her father.

"I don't doubt it, child," said Hargreave. "I'll explain. When I hired Jones here, who is really Jedson of the Scotland Yard, I did so because we looked alike when shaven. It was Jedson here who escaped by the balloon; it was Jedson who returned the five thousand to Norton, who watched the countess' apartment; it was Jedson who was wounded in the arm. I myself guarded you, my child. Last night, unbeknown to you, I left and the real Jones—for it is easier to call him that!—took my place."

"And I never saw the difference!" exclaimed Florence.

"That is natural," smiled her father. "You were thinking of Norton here instead of me. Eh?"

Florence blushed.

"Well, why not? Here, Norton!" The millionaire took Florence's hand and placed it in the reporter's. "It seems that I've got to lose her after all. Kiss her, man; in heaven's name, kiss her!"

And Norton threw his arms around the girl and kissed her soundly, careless of the fact that he was observed by both enemies and friends.

A QUICK CLUTCH AND THE POLICEMAN HAD HER BY THE WRIST

Suddenly the policeman who had been standing by the side of Braine ran into the living-room.

"He's alive! Braine's alive; he just stirred."

"What?" exclaimed Norton and Hargreave in a single breath.

"Yes, sir! I saw his hands move. It's a good thing we sent for a doctor. He ought to be along about now."

Even as he spoke the bell rang: and they all surged out into the hall, forgetting for the moment all about the million. Olga hadn't killed the man, then? The doctor knelt beside the stricken man and examined him. He shrugged.

"Will he live?"

"Certainly. A scalp wound, that laid him out for a few moments. He'll be all right in a few days. He was lucky. A quarter of an inch lower, and he'd have passed in his checks."

"Good!" murmured Servan. "So our friend will accompany me back to good Russia? Oh, we'll be kind to him during the journey. Have him taken to the hospital ward at the Tombs. Now, for the little lady up-stairs."

A moment later Braine opened his eyes, and the policeman assisted him to his feet. Servan, with a nod, ordered the police to help the wounded man to the taxicab which had just arrived. Braine, now wholly conscious, flung back one look of supreme hatred toward Hargreave; and that was the last either Florence or her father ever saw of Braine of the Black Hundred—a fine specimen of a man gone wrong through greed and an inordinate lust for revenge.

The policeman returned to Hargreave.

"It's pretty quiet up-stairs," he suggested. "Don't you think, sir, that I'd better try that bedroom door again?"

"Well, if you must," assented Hargreave reluctantly. "But don't be rough with her if you can help it."

For Braine he had no sympathy. When he recalled all the misery that devil's emissary had caused him, the years of hiding and pursuit, the loss of the happiness that had rightfully been his, his heart became adamant. For eighteen years to have ridden and driven and sailed up and down the world, always confident that sooner or later that demon would find him! He had lost the childhood of his daughter; and now he was to lose her in her womanhood. And because of this implacable hatred the child's mother had died in the Petrograd prison-fortress. But what an enemy the man had been! He, Hargreave, had needed all his wits constantly; he had never dared to go to sleep except with one eye open. But in employing ordinary crooks, Braine had at length overreached himself; and now he must pay the penalty. The way of the transgressor is hard; and though this ancient saying looks dingy with the wear and tear of centuries, it still holds good.

But he felt sorry for the woman up above. She had loved not wisely but too well. Far better for her if she put an end to life. She would not live a year in the God-forsaken snows of Siberia.

"My kind father!" said Florence, as if she could read his thoughts.

"I had a hard time of it, child. It was difficult to play the butler with you about. The times that I fought down the desire to sweep you up in my arms! But I kept an iron grip on that impulse. It would have imperiled you. In some manner it would have leaked out; and your life and mine wouldn't have been worth a button."

THE MYSTIC MILLION

Florence threw her arms around him and held him tightly.

"That poor woman up-stairs!" she murmured. "Can't they let her go?"

"No, dear. She has lost, and losers pay the stakes. That's life. Norton, you knew who I was all the time, didn't you?"

"I did, Mr. Hargreave. There was a scar on the lobe of your ear; and secretly I often wondered at the likeness between you and the real Jones. When I caught a glimpse of that ear, then I knew what the game was. And I'll add that you played it amazingly well. The one flaw in Braine's campaign was his hurry. He started the ball rolling before getting all the phases clearly established in his mind. He was a brave man, anyhow; and more than once he had me where I believed that prayers only were necessary."

"And do you think that you can lead Florence to the million?" asked Hargreave, smiling.

"For one thing, it is in her room, and has always been there. It never was in the chest."

"Not bad, not bad," mused the father.

"But perhaps after all it will be better if you show it to her yourself."

"Just a little uncertain?" jibed the millionaire.

"Absolutely certain. I will whisper in your ear where it is hidden." Norton leaned forward as Hargreave bent attentively.

"You've hit it! But how in the world did you guess it?"

"Because it was the last place any one would look for it. I judged at the start that you'd hide it in just such a spot, in some place where you could always guard it, and lay your hands on it quickly if needs said must."

"I'm mighty glad you were on my side," said Hargreave. "In a few minutes we'll go up and take a look at those packets of bills. There's a very unhappy young woman there at present."

"It is in my room?" cried Florence.

Hargreave nodded.

Meantime the Countess Olga hovered between two courses: a brave attempt to escape by the window or to turn the revolver against her heart. In either case there was nothing left in life for her. The man she loved was dead below, killed by her hand. She felt as though she was treading air in some fantastical nightmare. She could not go forward or backward, and her heels were always within reach of her pursuers.

So this was the end of things? The dreams she had had of going away with Braine to other climes, the happiness she had pictured, all mere chimeras! A sudden rage swept over her. She would escape, she would continue to play the game to the end. She would show them that she had been the man's mate, not his pliant tool. She raised the window and stepped out onto the balcony . . . . into the hands of the policeman who had patiently been waiting for her to do so! Instantly she placed the revolver at her temple. A quick clutch, and the policeman had her by the wrist. She made one tigerish effort to free herself, shrugged, and signified that she surrendered.

"I don't want to hurt you, Miss," said the policeman; "but if you make any attempt to escape, I'll have to put the handcuffs on you."

"I'll go quietly. What are you going to do with me?"

"Turn you over to the Russian agent. He has extradition papers; and I guess it's Siberia."

"FLORENCE, THAT IS ALL YOURS"

"For me?" She laughed scornfully. "Do I look like a woman who would go to Siberia?"

"Be careful, Miss. As I said, I don't want to put the cuffs on unless I have to."

She laughed again. It did not have a pleasant sound in the officer's ears. He had heard women, suicidal bent, laugh like that.

"I'll ask you for that ring on your finger."

"Do you think there is poison in it?"

"I shouldn't be surprised," he admitted.

She slipped the ring from her finger and gave it to him.

"There *is* poison in it; so be careful how you handle it," she said.

The policeman accepted it gingerly and dropped it into his capacious pocket. It tinkled as it fell against the handcuffs.

At that moment the other policeman broke in the door.

"All right, Dolan; she's given up the game."

"She didn't kill the man after all," said Dolan.

'He's alive?" she screamed.

"Yes; and they've taken him off to the Tombs. Just a scalp wound. He'll be all right in a day or two."

"Alive!" murmured Olga. She had not killed the man she loved, then? And if they were indeed taken to Siberia, she would be with him until the end of things.

With her handsome head proudly erect, she walked toward the door. She paused for a moment to look at the portrait of Hargreave. Somehow it seemed to smile at her ironically. Then on, down the stairs, between the two officers, she went. Her glance traveled coolly from face to face, and stopped at Florence's. There she saw pity.

"You are sorry for me?" she asked skeptically.

"Oh, yes! I forgive you," said the generous Florence.

"Thanks! Officers, I am ready."

So the Countess Olga passed through that hall door forever. How many times had she entered it, with guile and treachery in her heart? It was the game. She had played it and lost, and she must pay her debts to Fate the fiddler. Siberia! The tin or lead mines, the ankle-chains, the knout, and many things that were far worse to a beautiful woman! Well, so long as Braine was at her side, she would suffer all these things without a murmur. And always there would be a chance, a chance!

When they heard the taxicab rumble down the drive-way to the street, Hargreave turned to Florence.

"Come along, now, and we'll have the bad taste taken off our tongues. To win out is the true principle of life. It takes off some of the tinsel and glamour, but the end is worth while."

They all trooped up-stairs to Florence's room. So wonderful is the power and attraction of money that they forgot the humiliation of their late enemies.

Hargreave approached the portrait of himself, took it from the wall, pressed a button on the back, which fell outward. Behold! There, in neat packages of a hundred thousand each, lay the mystic million! The spectators were awed into silence for a moment. Perhaps the thought of each was identical—the long struggle, the terrible hazards, the deaths, that had taken place because of this enormous sum of money.

A million, sometimes called cool; why, nobody knows. There it lay, without feeling, without emotion; yellow notes payable to bearer on demand. Presently Florence

AFTER THE STORM, THE SUNSHINE

gasped, Norton sighed, and Hargreave smiled. The face of Jones (or Jedson) alone remained impassive.

A million dollars is a marvelous sight. Very few people have ever seen it, not even millionaires themselves. I dare say you never saw it; and I'm tolerably certain I never have, or will! A million, ready for eager, careless fingers to spend, or thrifty fingers to multiply! What Correggio, what Rubens, what Titian, could stand beside it? None that I wot of.

"Florence, that is all yours, to do with as you please, to spend when and how you will. Share it with your husband-to-be. He is a brave and gallant young man, and is fortunate in finding a young woman equally brave and gallant. For the rest of my days I expect peace. Perhaps sometimes Jones here and I will talk over the strange things that have happened; but we'll do that only when we haven't you young folks to talk to. After your wedding journey you will return here. While I live this shall be your home. I demand that much. Free! No more looking over my shoulder when I walk the streets; no more testing windows and doors. I am myself again. I take up the thread I laid down eighteen years ago. Have no fear. Neither Braine nor Olga will ever return. Russia has a grip of steel."

Three weeks later Servan, the Russian agent, left for Russia with his three charges, Olga, Braine and Vroon. It was a long journey they went upon, something like ten weeks, always watched, always under the strictest guard, compelled to eat with wooden forks and knives and spoons. Waking or sleeping they knew no rest from espionage. From Paris to Berlin, from Berlin to St. Petersburg, as Petrograd was then called; and then began the cruel journey over the mighty steppes of that barbaric wilderness to the Siberian mines. The way of the transgressor is hard.

On the same day that Olga and Braine made their first descent into the deadly mines, Florence and Norton were married. After the storm, the sunshine: and who shall deny them happiness?

Immediately after the ceremony the two sailed for Europe, on their honeymoon; and it is needless to say that some of the million went with them, but there was no mystery about it!

THE END

IMMEDIATELY AFTER THE CEREMONY

Harold MacGrath

A Sketch of the Author at Work and at Play

HAROLD MACGRATH, author of more than a dozen best sellers, the book of an operetta, and short stories without number, is a native of Syracuse, N. Y., having been born in that city on September 4, 1871, and lived there ever since, except when he is out circling the globe or in Gotham looking things over.

Mr. MacGrath was a journalist before he essayed the higher form of literature that sells on a royalty basis instead of by the yard, and he claims that he owes his start in "romancing" to a physical defect. Mr. MacGrath is partially deaf and while serving as a newspaper reporter he heard only about half of what was said to him, and had to "make up" the other half himself. Thus, his imagination was given quite a course in physical culture before its owner's conscience began to prick him. "Why not do the thing right?" MacGrath asked himself. "I don't know," he replied. "Let's try it," he suggested. "All right," he answered. And he quit the newspaper game and started a novel, "Arms and the Woman," which appeared in 1890. This was followed by many good sellers, the speed limit of the author being three books some years.

Next to being a novelist MacGrath is a globe-trotter. He has been in every nook and corner on the face of the globe where white man dares to go and can get there without swimming or flying. As a result, he has obtained the inspirations for most of his novels while amid the fascinating surroundings in some Asiatic harbor town, while traveling down the Rhine, or while listening to strains of Viennese music in some little out-of-the-way café along the Danube. He is a genius in pen picturing and can impart the color, the life, the action of real life into his pages in a manner that is bound to attract.

He is fond of tennis and out-of-door sports. He likes boxing and is one of the best amateur pool and billiard players in the country. He has friends in almost every large city in the world and has met more "crowned heads" than any other author, perhaps, outside of Hallie Erminie Rives, wife of Post Wheeler, the versatile secretary of the American Embassy at Tokio.

As a collector and connoisseur, Mr. MacGrath has a wide reputation, his especial hobby being Turkish rugs and antique jewelry, of which he has a wonderful collection. Another of his hobbies is horses, and although he owns only one himself, he will never pass a good looking horse by without stopping to pat it. He even carries lump sugar in his pocket and takes great delight in feeding it to the horses of the mounted officers in New York, many of whom (the officers) know him.

His method of working up his stories is unique. According to his own statement, he first "thinks out" the start of his story, carrying his idea through what develops into the first few chapters of the book. Then he drops the thread of thought and starts again, but this time at the end, and figures out how he will dispose of his characters and how best the story should end. This accomplished, he sits down to his typewriter and "goes to work." While writing, he often strikes on good ideas to be incorporated in parts already considered. Immediately he jots down his idea on the back of an envelope or a scrap of paper and inserts the note among the pages of his manuscript just where it belongs. After completing his first draft, he goes back over the entire manuscript, making corrections here and there and additions. He then sits down to sum the whole story up in his mind and by this process is able to pick out the flaws. His second draft, therefore, is quite a finished product. He makes the final draft of his manuscript himself, as he has found that he often strikes upon improvements at the eleventh hour that go far to better his stories. If he turned the work of making the final draft over to a stenographer, this last chance would be lost.

He is one of the few modern writers who does not have to try to be funny. It is natural with him to amuse.

Those interested in the chronological order of his stories will find them as follows:

In 1901 he published his second book, "The Puppet Crown." "The Grey Cloak" followed in 1903, and by the time it appeared, most of the readers of fiction had acquired the MacGrath habit and were on the lookout for the next dose of his delightful literary stimulant that chased the "blues." Then came the story which established MacGrath's reputation, "The Man on the Box," which appeared in 1904 and is still one of the best sellers in popular editions. In 1905 MacGrath put on some extra speed. He worked a double shift in his brain mill and the result was that before the dawn of the next New Year's Day he had three more successful books to his credit. They were "The Princess Elopes," a novelette; •'Enchantment," a book of short stories, and "Hearts and Masks," a novel that dealt with entanglements developing at a mask ball. In the same year he wrote "Half a Rogue," another highly popular story. In 1906 he turned out "The Watteau Shepherdess," an operetta. These two productions were followed by "The Best Man" in 1907; "The Enchanted Hat" and "The Lure of the Mask" in 1908. "The Goose Girl" was MacGrath's next novel, and went far to uphold his reputation. "A Splendid Hazard" and "The Carpet of Bagdad" followed within the space of little more than a year. Next "The Place of Honeymoons" was published, then "Parrot & Co.," "Deuces Wild," "Pidgin Island," "The Adventures of Kathlyn," and "Voice in the Fog."

The "purpose novel," as that term is generally understood, finds but little sympathy at the hands of Harold MacGrath. Yet he has a definite purpose of his own. It is to amuse.

"The one definite idea I have in mind in writing stories," he says, "is to afford an agreeable, pleasant hour or two to my readers. I wish to amuse them, to make them wish that they, too, might have lived as this or that hero, in this or that land, probable or improbable. I prefer sunshine, mirth, buoyancy, and I believe most readers prefer the same. Grown-up people never wholly lose their love of fairy tales; and grown up fairy tales have been the scheme of most of my novels."

Could an author have a better purpose than this? Could he serve men to better advantage than by lightening the burden they are destined to carry through life by allowing their minds to dwell in pleasant places and to rejoice with the people of a make-believe world?

"I usually begin a story as a dramatist begins a play— with the end," says MacGrath. "The characters work out the plot themselves; I have very little to do with it after they have started."

"The structure of a plot must naturally be foremost; for, after all is said and done, the story's the thing. I never outline a plot; I carry the main thread in my head until I am ready to put it on paper, and after it assumes body on paper, it has many devious twists and turns of which I have no prior idea."

"I write whenever I feel like it, for when I am in the mood I do better work. I never force myself to do so much work each day. There are days when it is impossible to write one hundred words; again, I have written as many as seven thousand words a day. Obstacles? There are altogether too many to demonstrate. A character that doesn't "balk" never fails to be uninteresting. I have always tried to place human people in absurd or unique situations and to let them extricate themselves as you or I, if so placed.

"The anatomy of a motif for a story is a complex thing, but of a practical joke, 'The Man on the Box' was evolved. A young man disguised as a coachman drove his sister and her friend to a ball one night. This happened in my native town, Syracuse, and it amused me greatly when critics said that the exploit was highly improbable. Out of the Italian state and church marriage came the plot of 'The Lure of the Mask.' The most trivial thing sometimes will suggest a plot. I found the ten of hearts one night on the sidewalk. It became the motif of 'Hearts and Masks.' Once, in Indianapolis, I chanced to see an Italian selling plaster images. It gave me a starting point for 'A Splendid Hazard.' Walking down Broadway one day I stopped to look in a window where oriental rugs were being advertised. When I turned away the seed germ for my latest book, 'The Carpet from Bagdad,' was in my mind."

Mr. MacGrath is an enthusiastic fisherman. He goes to Cape Vincent, Lake Ontario, every summer, when he isn't ambling in China, or India, or Africa. He believes that the best bass grounds in the world are within a radius of twenty miles from Cape Vincent, which is really in the head of the St. Lawrence River. A friend undertook to convince him that there were other places, so MacGrath consented to accompany him to Canada. They arrived at sunset, and the host extemporized over the glories of the setting sun.

"Ever see anything to beat that, Mac?"

"Fine!"

On the following morning they went out for bass. At four o'clock in the afternoon they had caught exactly one.

The host again rhapsodized over the sunset.

The second day they caught no bass at all. On their way back to the hotel the host was silent. As they came up to the landing, MacGrath touched his host on the shoulder.

"There's your darned sunset, Jim!"